THE
TEMPLE
of
DOUBT

THE
TEMPLE
of
DOUBT

ANNE BOLES LEVY

Sky Pony Press
New York

This is a work of fiction. Names, characters, places, and incidents are either the products of the author's imagination or used fictitiously.

Sky Pony Press books may be purchased in bulk at special discounts for sales promotion, corporate gifts, fund-raising, or educational purposes. Special editions can also be created to specifications. For details, contact the Special Sales Department, Sky Pony Press, 307 West 36th Street, 11th Floor, New York, NY 10018 or info@ skyhorsepublishing.com.

Sky Pony is a registered trademark of Skyhorse Publishing, Inc. , a Delaware corporation.

Visit our website at www.skyponypress.com.

10 9 8 7 6 5 4 3 2 1

Library of Congress Cataloging-in-Publication Data

Levy, Anne Boles.
  The temple of doubt / Anne Boles Levy.
     pages cm
  Summary: Fifteen-year-old Hadara loves to go beyond the city limits gathering herbs and throwing off the yoke of her religious schooling, but when a falling star crashes into the marshes beyond Port Sapphire, two powerful high priests arrive from the god Nihil's home city to investigate, insisting it harbors an evil force, and choosing Hadara as a guide into the wilds, setting off a chain of events that will upend everything she has been taught about the sacred and the profane.
  ISBN 978-1-63220-427-1 (hardback)
  [1. Belief and doubt--Fiction. 2. Good and evil--Fiction. 3. Fantasy.] I. Title.
  PZ7.1.L489Te 2015
  [Fic]--dc23
                              2015012732

Cover design by Rain Saukus

Print ISBN: 978-1-63220-427-1
Ebook ISBN: 978-1-63450-005-0

Printed in the United States of America

In loving memory of my parents

The demons drove me from the stars and would hunt me to the far reaches of the unreachable end of the universe. They take different forms and different names but always pursue the same purpose: to erase my name from existence.

Yet I will be here to greet the end when it comes, the dying breath of Creation, the moment between order and chaos, the time when time stops.

I will stand on the edge of infinity and say my name.

My name is Nothing.

— from Verisimilitudes 9, The Book of Unease

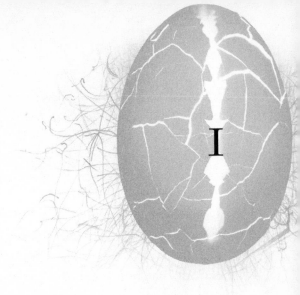

I

When we learn to tie knots, we call it knowledge. When we learn to untangle them, we call it wisdom.

—*Tengalian proverb*

The stick slapped my arm with a sharp crack. A red stripe raced across my skin, smarting and hot. I'd braced for it, fist closed, shoulders tense. The schoolmistress lifted her pointer as if to hit me again. She was hardly bigger than the item she'd struck me with, a slender reed of a woman with a cruel mouth that radiated fine lines when she frowned. It was something she did often, and the lines had begun to set that way.

"Tell us, Hadara, what's so important that it distracted you from your lessons."

I kept my voice level, unafraid. I hoped I sounded contrite.

"I apologize for my brief inattention, Mistress. I shall endeavor to do better."

Rubbish. I'd endeavor never to set foot in class again. I'd plead with Mami to bring me back out to the fens with her, once the priests allowed it again. *If* they allowed it again, I corrected myself. Who knew, with all the talk on the piers about what was going on out there.

In front of me, girls clad in the chaste gray uniforms of Ward Sapphire's school squeezed onto long rows of benches. Every pair of hands that wasn't waving a reed fan seemed to twitch and fidget. Several wrists bore telltale welts from that pointer, and all eyes were focused on me, standing useless at the front of the room. Humid air hung tight and heavy in the boxy classroom, though I'd have been sweating in any case. School did that to me.

Only the best families in Port Sapphire got to educate their children, and even then it was usually the sons. I should remember that. I tried to concentrate on feeling lucky and privileged and not sticky and uncomfortable.

"You've promised that before," the schoolmistress droned on. "Yet there you were, once again unable to name all Nihil's wives and their character flaws. Can you name even one?"

I struggled for the answer. Nihil. Wives. Nihil was our god, the god of the Temple of Doubt, source of all our magic and wisdom, and he took a new wife as soon as another died. There must be dozens of them. All their character flaws? Any of them? I glanced toward the middle row, where my sister Amaniel was sitting stock-still, a look of pure panic on her contorted face. I don't know why we never worked out a secret code or anything. She could be flashing me the right answer. She always knew them. She rolled her eyes and pretended to yawn. I fished around for something, anything, to say. If only I was ever asked a question I could answer, like which constellation appears on the southern horizon every vernal equinox, or what herb should never go in a burn poultice. Just one of Nihil's wives is all I had to pick.

"Bardusre? Aranel. Pulwe or Pulgre or something. She was stupid. I remember the first one was stupid." A few snickers flitted through the rows. This was all so unimportant when the fens were off-limits, maybe forever, and when there was so much more going on. When the talk on the piers . . .

"Amaniel, come up." The schoolmistress didn't even turn. "Maybe Hadara will pay better attention if you pay the price."

"It's my fault," I said. The pointer tip swung to a finger's length from my chest, over the Eternal Tree crest stitched in blue on my sun-bleached blouse. I struggled with my anger and to keep my voice from wavering. "You know it's my fault. Punish me."

The Ward was always pitting us against each other, Amaniel and me. I never wanted Amaniel in trouble because of me. Just like Mami tried hard not to make trouble for Babba. But it just seemed to follow us. I held out my wrist again.

"I'm beginning to think you like it too much," the schoolmistress said. "Alright, one last chance. To what fascinating and ungodly destination was your mind wandering today?"

I sucked in my breath and dove into whatever it was I'd started. May as well. I clearly wasn't going anywhere until I had.

"The falling star from a fortnight ago. I'm supposed to pretend I didn't see it, right? I'm sorry, I just can't. If it's going to bring Nihil to us, I just want to, well, to know. That's all."

There, it was done. Good luck to anyone trying to make sense of my little tirade.

"The falling star." The schoolmistress dragged out the vowels as if I'd spoken a foreign tongue. "Anyone else see a falling star?"

I shifted on my feet, aware the stillness in the classroom had become its own sound, of reed fans stopping mid-stroke, of clothing that no longer rustled, of breaths caught in throats.

"Anyone?" No one spoke. Her diction stuck on every consonant so each syllable pierced straight into my skull. "Well, I certainly saw something. Two six-nights ago, in fact."

Hands shot up. In a few moments, I'd be tongue-tied and looking like the dullest student again as the smart ones rattled off descriptions of the blazing thing. They'd have been indoors, most of them, and probably cowering beneath a stack of floor cushions. I'd been outdoors by our hearth, sand-scrubbing pots when the fireball started: tiny and far away at first, glowing and growing and aiming straight at us. I'd dropped a platter and it shattered on the tile at my feet. I must've yelled because soon neighbors had piled out of huts and houses and scrambled for a better view from the boardwalks.

I'd seen it first, I'm pretty sure of that, but Nihil blast me to smoldering bits if I can get a word in with all the girls impressing the schoolmistress with how observant they'd been. Now that she'd given her tacit blessing, they were droning on about how it was so bright this and it lit up the sky that. I'm not sure how one can tell if something's lighting up anything if you're having to peep through your fingers from behind shuttered doors. I raised my hand a few times, but the schoolmistress had her back to me. She called on a trio of girls who squealed about how it landed in the marshes beyond Port Sapphire, kicked up a wall of mud ten houses high, oh yes. I could've burst into flames myself at that point. That's word-for-word how *I'd* described it to *them* outside the Ward that first Sabbath afterward.

Amaniel saw me fuming and winked. I exhaled some of the tension and realized I'd been wiping sweaty palms on my uniform skirt. I tried to smooth the folds, but it was no use; I looked like I'd rolled on the floor in it. That, of course, was the exact moment the schoolmistress remembered I existed.

"So why does it take two full six-days to mention such a large event?" she asked me. I got one of those quick up-and-down gazes that said yes, she'd noticed my rumples and wrinkles. With any luck, this would be the last time I would wear a drab gray instead of the bright colors of the women. I would beg Mami if I had to.

"Hadara. Mind drifting again?"

"Um, two six-days. Yes. Sorry." I had no idea why it took everyone so long. I'd tried to ask anyone who didn't shush me. I reverted to my best humble-student voice. "Had I known of your interest, Mistress, I might have asked about it sooner."

Instead of an answer, the teacher turned to my classmates. "Anyone know why Hadara dares to speak of celestial events, alone of all of you? Why she would broach a subject even the priests have not chosen to discuss?"

A sea of blank faces gazed back. Doubtless they were thinking up reasons too rude to say aloud.

The schoolmistress didn't wait long. "Because she's a bold and curious girl. That might win you friends among barbarians, but pious girls maintain their propriety. You might be more like your sister, Hadara."

It had been a trap after all, one of her better ones. She'd let me bring up a taboo topic, openly airing it and then slapping me back down for mentioning it. Perfect. I looked up and caught Amaniel making a long face and shaking her head. She couldn't help being singled out; I bit back my jealousy. As long as I was bold and curious—and those were somehow bad traits—I decided to ask the second part of my question again.

"Mistress, is Nihil coming?"

Gasps. Stares. Well, I wanted to know if our god was coming to see for himself where the star had fallen. That was the speculation on the piers. That was truer than Scripture to me, especially if the priests were keeping mum.

The schoolmistress shook her head. "You don't know what kind of trouble that might bring, do you?"

"Then he's coming?"

"Hadara, would you know Nihil if he came?"

The only right answer was no. Yet I couldn't squeeze that one tiny word out of me. Several in the class snickered again. Most of them were younger than me and could use a firm switching. I pictured myself with that pointer in hand. I wouldn't need it long.

The lines deepened around her mouth again. The pointer tip waggled toward me, as if in reproach. "If he does come, I'll ask the high priest to offer you as a gift. If Nihil will take you, that is."

"Gift?" My mouth felt dry. The high priest happened to be her husband. "Wouldn't that kill me?"

"Be seated, Hadara."

"But you wouldn't really . . ."

"Be *seated*, Hadara."

I made my way to my bench, weaving through the rows of girls. A gift of a virgin would come from one of us. The high priest's wife, my schoolmistress, that rotted little twig, would insist that it be me. I tried to picture what it would be like to lie with Nihil, what a man's naked body might look like, how it might feel, and whether I would be awake afterward when he consumed my soul. My memories and daydreams and all my plans for earning my own way in this world would be dead. What was left of me would be fit only for the funeral pyre.

I slid in next to Amaniel, who clenched my hand until her nails bit into my skin. I winced and held on. There wasn't anything in that day's lessons that would hold me any longer. Nihil pity me if I wasn't happy for a loud interruption. The evening horn blared a single, sorry tone across the Ward courtyard. Horn signals could mean different things, but the lone note usually meant sunset prayers. It was only afternoon, when clouds usually jostled and crashed overhead, sending the summer rains that meant Mami and I would soon have more of our wild harvest to keep us busy.

But no rains had come since before last Sabbath, and now the evening horn sounded at the wrong time, in the clear light of a too-sunny day. The schoolmistress leaped toward the door, sliding it back on its track and shooing us out. "By the piers," she said. "You'll all want to go by the piers."

The horn must mean some special gathering, then. Maybe Nihil was coming after all.

Amaniel waited for me and grabbed my hand again.

"Sorry," she whispered. "She was worse than usual."

I shrugged. I didn't need Amaniel feeling sorry for her older sister. I was vexed enough for both of us. My sixteenth birthday couldn't come soon enough. Sixteen, and a place with the women.

The class marched out in double rows, right-step, left-step, toward the gates, my heartbeat matching the rhythm. Double rows of boys filed from an adjacent schoolroom, right-step, left-step, white tunics over gray short pants. They all looked so much younger than me. Yet another reminder of how out of place I felt. Right-step, left-step, out the high iron gates. Once outside, my classmates threw off the yoke of school discipline and the race was on for the piers. I picked up my pace, Amaniel beside me.

"Exciting, don't you think?" She gazed up at me, one eyebrow raised over her deep-set brown eyes.

"If it's really Nihil. You think I'm going to be sacrificed?"

She shook her head. "I don't know what the schoolmistress has against you. She doesn't try to frighten me like that."

"You're good at Scriptures."

"You're good at other things."

I gave Amaniel's hand a squeeze. That was just what I needed to hear. I was good at other things, lots of other things. I'd learned to name a thousand plants and animals, describe cloud formations and tell when it would rain, and perhaps how much. I wasn't sure how memorizing all Nihil's incarnations was going to earn me a single copper in the marketplace, and asking such a question would likely garner a few more stripes on my wrist. I let out a deep sigh for my beautiful marshlands, closed to me in recent days, and their wealth of herbs and medicines, all contraband, orders of the priests of Ward Sapphire, our local temple, which only made them more valuable to anyone who wasn't cured by their ministrations. Which was pretty much everyone.

As Amaniel and I walked, too anxious for small talk, Port Sapphire spread before us in a crescent on either side of the Grand Concourse, its barges and scows gliding beneath stuccoed footbridges toward the city's network of canals. I loved this, too, the bustle and hum of commerce, the size and sails of ships from across the trading lands, the jumble of foreign tongues and music on the piers, the tanned sailors in billowing, bright uniforms from a dozen countries I could name and more that I couldn't. The whole island was called New Meridian, a tiny dot at the center of the map, and Port Sapphire was its busy way station for people and cargo en route to all parts of Kuldor.

My sandals thunked across age-worn planks on a bridge that linked the two halves of the city, east and west, commerce and families. The bridge's arch gave me a flawless view of the flat rows of warehouses, the ships in their berths, the gleaming white of the Customs House at the mouth of the harbor. I could hear the singsong street vendors that gave Callers Wharf its name. It was already filling with crowds anticipating a spectacle. We hurried across the bridge and plunged into its teeming market. A brass trinket lured here, a whiff of savory spices pulled there. Amaniel tapped her foot impatiently while I took a peek into a few stalls before they closed.

"What if Nihil himself is coming? Honestly, Hadara, you'd make him wait while you tried on scarves."

"The kiosks are always closed by the time school lets out." I was sure I could face anything, even Nihil, in a pair of cloth slippers dyed a vivid pink, but they were about to vanish behind a reed shutter. "If Nihil's coming, the port might be closed for a long time. If he isn't, then maybe he won't be offended if I shop some."

Amaniel gripped my sleeve. "I'm dragging you if you don't come. I mean it. I'm not missing this."

"Alright, alright," I said. "I don't know what bitter root you've been eating today, but you're all pucker."

She pulled me along after that, threading around and between people, trying not to push but impatient to get closer. Near the harbor's edge, Callers Wharf widened into a pavilion in front of the Customs House, where scores of people crammed against a wooden railing. A balcony stretched the length of the Customs House facing the sea, and it was also packed with men in the green uniforms of the civil corps. One jade-green skullcap bobbed higher than the rest. I pointed him out to Amaniel and tugged her after me.

"We can't go up there," Amaniel said. "Can we?"

I rolled my eyes. "Let them try and stop us."

No one did. The clerks and tariff collectors parted for us as we crossed the Customs House's open floor and wound up the spiral iron stairs to the balcony. I took the lead, since Amaniel would be too caught up in what was proper and modest and formal, while I only wanted to get this over with and be by that tall fellow with whom no one would ever pick an argument. I felt safer just headed toward him, and he caught sight of us the moment we set foot through wide doors onto the sun-soaked balcony. That tall, imposing man was the city's Chief Port Inspector and my father, and he gave us the stiff, formal nod appropriate for public greetings. We partly bowed in return, careful to place a hand over the loose fronts of our blouses.

"By all three moons, you'd think Nihil himself was arriving, with all the fuss." Babba scowled at the crowd and squinted into the distance. "There's sails on the horizon, don't you know."

Amaniel brightened at that, seeming entirely too chipper. "Red sails?"

Babba guided us to a spot along the balcony edge, where I had a perfect view of Ward Sapphire across the wide half-moon of Sapphire Bay. It was the only building taller and grander than the one we were in, the two buildings gleaming like bleached pillars of a giant gateway; one sacred, one secular. I felt more at home here on the commercial side of the city, surrounded by clerks jostling one another in handsome uniforms of flowing frock coats over gauzy shirts and ballooning trousers.

Babba wore four different shades of green, all clashing, but I thought the hues looked stunning against his bronze skin, and Mami had embroidered vermillion vines around the collars and hems. I could be proud of the figure my Babba cut. Crowds would part as if he were some visiting potentate or a powerful priest and not an ordinary, if high-ranking, bureaucrat.

A few men stared at me, but I averted my eyes. That was the proper thing to do, even if what I really wanted was to stare back and soak in their features, figure out what made one handsome and another hideous. I wanted to look. I wanted to revel in whatever it was that kept them looking at me. I followed Amaniel's example and kept my eyes on Babba.

He kept his own eyes on the horizon, and we quickly figured out why. There, in the distance, two sets of crimson sails soared above the waves, billowing like a baby's cheeks in the coastal breeze.

It was as if lightning had swept the crowd, both below and around us on the balcony.

The Temple of Doubt was here! Nihil himself, perhaps!

How our lives would change, someone said. What a blessing, said others. A blessing, yes!

A blessing.

I felt cursed. My whole world was about to change, I knew it even then, peering across the harbor at the pretty ships, not knowing what to expect, except the worst. The mighty Temple of Doubt had arrived, at least the part that wasn't built from rocks on a faraway cliff. It could still flatten us all. I had my own doubts, even if I couldn't quite figure out how to say so.

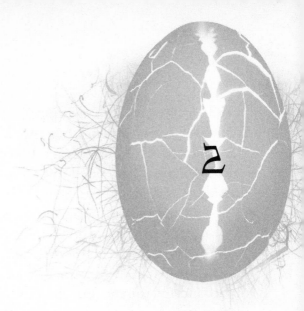

Keep my enemies from me, stand between me and them; stamp them out like quick tender, else we would burn together, a bonfire of souls, razing a civilization as a field in drought.
—*from Oblations 14,* The Book of Unease

The days leading up to this official visit had made everyone fretful and stupid. The adults had scurried around fixing things that looked just fine to me, until I wondered if I'd also get a coat of whitewashing if I stood in one spot too long. All eyes were on the harbor, even mine, as if those crimson sails would appear between one footstep and the next. The worries were a contagion that nothing in Mami's bag of physics would cure.

At last, the day had come, and two fine schooners closed in on our deep blue bay. I couldn't see what difference the preparations had made. The pier was a jumble of bodies as people pressed and jostled for a better view. It was all as delightfully messy and chaotic as ever, maybe more so. The god we worshipped might be coming here. We were no longer beneath his notice. Even so, I struggled to feel excited. If Nihil was anything like the priests or the schoolmistress, it promised to be a long visit, full of things I couldn't and shouldn't do or say or even think.

The lookouts began signaling the rest of the city, and Babba translated for Amaniel and me. Neither ship sailed Nihil's flag. Instead, the vessels flew the banners of two mighty magi, called Azwans, a word meaning "navigator" in an ancient tongue. People around us argued whether that meant good news or bad, whether we were too far or too barbaric or too bothersome for a godly visit.

But why should that be bad? I tried to recall what I could of the day's painful lessons. Perhaps there'd be no human sacrifice after all, if Nihil wasn't coming. My sigh was a crisp, loud burst of air that instantly unraveled entire knots of emotion. I caught myself and glanced around. The milling of the crowds below had swallowed up the sound, and I wouldn't have to explain why I felt so relieved.

Others, Amaniel among them, whispered that the Azwans came to spare us a terrible war between Nihil and his enemy.

I didn't understand, and said so. A falling star wasn't a living thing, was it? How could it be Nihil's enemy? Besides, two of the Temple of Doubt's greatest magic users were coming, people who could wipe out evil before it gained a foothold on our world. If, in fact, evil had landed in our midst. "Isn't that honor enough?" I asked.

"It's not our honor that's at stake, Hadara." Babba didn't take his eyes from those crimson sails. "Nihil is god, he can make anything happen . . . except one thing."

"Oh, I know this," I mumbled before Amaniel could cut in, pleased I knew a little something, at least. "Kuldor is his prison and our planet. He can't leave here. Am I right?"

The men closest to us chuckled. One said, "It's medicines she knows, I suppose."

That drew more chuckles, of a knowing, winking kind. He may as well have praised my knowledge of picking locks or tipping scales. In a world where magic could supposedly cure anything, or at least anything the priests said we deserved to have cured, medicine was regarded with suspicion. The man hadn't paid me a compliment at all. My ears burned. Worse, I'd embarrassed Babba, who had his mouth set in a firm line. "Oblations 14, Hadara. You'll memorize it tonight."

Scriptures. I made a face. It was Nihil this and Kuldor that, begetting fruits of the trees and crops of the fields and who did wrong to whom and was smited for it, unless they conquered someone else without Nihil's permission so he smited them, too. And then there were his women. Many, many, many women. Of which I wouldn't be one, which made me happy, no matter how awful it would be to have to memorize Oblations 14.

Amaniel nudged me and whispered, "A conflagration erupts when one of his foes attacks him face-to-face. The last one nearly destroyed the whole planet."

Babba's eyes looked beyond us to the bulging sails. "Nihil stays away from our island, so there'll be no conflagration if his enemy is here. His Azwans will wage any battle instead."

The men around us murmured their agreement, though Babba had spoken softly. I got a glimpse between two sets of shoulders. The ships floated high above the water. Powerful spells must have lifted those massive vessels from the sea, under full sail, with their double-masts perfectly perpendicular. Nothing but empty air coursed beneath the keels, sunlight glinting off waves disturbed only by the ships' rippling shadows, which left no wake. Now I knew why there'd been no rain in days: that, too, must've been the work of magic designed to speed the ships here.

The schooners slowed as they approached the bay, and each unfurled a banner atop the main mast: one white, one purple. Each bore a constellation embroidered in glittering thread. I remembered them instantly, but then I've always had a knack for the stars. The white one was closer, with three silver crescent moons. The purple one bore the twisted, double strands of a wisdom knot. That ought to make that one more important, I reasoned.

Amaniel elbowed me again and whispered, "No, the white one is. It's the Azwan of Ambiguity."

I'd thought aloud, but only Amaniel had heard. "Ambiguity, what does he do?"

She rolled her eyes. "He's in charge of all five Azwans. The other one is Uncertainty."

"Let me guess, he's number two."

"No, he's number four, but in some ways he's number one because he's Nihil's ear. Nihil's confidante, in other words."

"But you said the other one is in charge."

"I know. But it's Nihil, so it's supposed to be enigmatic."

More like confusing, I muttered to myself.

The white banner's ship bore the name *Sea Skimmer* on its hull. It pulled in first while the other waited out in the harbor and glided along a length of pier before halting just beyond our balcony perch; then it eased itself into the water with the gentlest splash. Once in the water, *Sea Skimmer* groaned and heaved with the currents, as any other ship.

The second was the *Nomad's Grief*, an unsettling name for a ship. Perhaps it was some Scriptural reference, but I wasn't about to set Amaniel on one of her windy jags by asking. The ship came to rest with the bow below us. On deck, an ebony-skinned man in a flowing kaftan to match the banner stood praying. The Azwan. He looked no different from any of the Tengalian merchants who roamed the docks haggling down shipping prices or giving Babba and his inspectors an earful. This Azwan had that same haughty air, his shoulders back, master of everything he saw. He was no older than Babba, I was sure, but better fed, judging by the way his kaftan swelled around his barrel chest.

Babba turned to Amaniel. "You recognize the Azwan of Uncertainty, of course."

Someone from the back piped up, a light note in his voice. "Let's hear it then, Amaniel. The full honors. Just for our little crew up here."

"Full honors, yes," chimed a few others crammed in beside us.

Amaniel's grin was matched only by Babba's. I sighed. It did sound pretty impressive when she recited the whole pious honors bit. She took a deep breath and began, only loud enough for those immediately around us to hear, since it wasn't polite for a girl to shout:

"The Azwan of Uncertainty, Nihil's Ear, Son of the Second Moon, Curator of the Limitless Repository, consort of the Princess Pelia of Tengal, the scholar S'ami, son of the astrologer Shmulai."

A trickle of applause greeted the end of the honors. I felt a surge of pride in my sister, who smiled and bowed her head, as custom dictated. One of us should be able to show off a formal education, at least. I had another, younger sister at home, too small for school yet. I found myself hoping she wouldn't take after me, the wild sister, the bold and curious girl, off to the swamps on adventures that yielded strange items no one could mention in public.

"Oh," Amaniel said, holding a finger up. "And he just gifted his daughter to Nihil. She was only twelve."

Babba clapped her on the back with a nod on his serious face. "Praise Nihil's whims and wishes, child."

"Nihil's whims and wishes," several of the men muttered in reply.

Had no one heard what I heard? A twelve-year-old girl, sacrificed to our god? I remembered my teacher's warning. The girl was dead. The proud man on the deck below us had served up his flesh and blood to the god who stayed far away and found us wanting. The Azwan's fine clothes rustled in the breeze, but his upright bearing didn't look like it would budge for anything. I dwelled on the one thing I knew for certain about him: he had been someone's father. And now he wasn't.

I shuddered and shifted my focus to the Feroxi crew, anything but the proud Azwan. I almost hadn't noticed those big men. Not that anyone could fail to see them for very long.

They weren't proper giants, exactly, since monsters who stood twice the size of a man existed only in myth.

These sailors stood two and three head-lengths taller than Babba, the tallest man in our city. That alone would make them gargantuan enough, even without shoulders as wide as some folks are tall. This was the part I liked best. I wasn't usually allowed to stare at men—it's not a modest thing to do, but who was going to stop me now?

I let my eyes roam over those oversized, muscular bodies as they scrambled about the deck to anchor and secure the ship and furl its sails. The Feroxi were from a chilly northern clime and had the fair hair and pale complexion I'd expected. Their skulls grew a peculiar browridge that jutted over their eyes and formed a chevron over the bridge of the nose, giving them a dark, brooding look, as if permanently annoyed.

They sang, and it sounded cheerful enough, though I don't understand a word of Fernai. The sailors dwarfed the Azwan, who ignored them, and they thudded about barefoot, sweat dampening their coarse, crimson uniforms and gleaming from bare arms. As they lowered the gangplank, their song switched to the common tongue for a verse:

Thorn and thistle and brave men bristle
Lest flesh be torn to shred
Thistle and thorn the roses adorn
Be careful where you tread

"They're singing about their women," Babba said. "They are also fierce warriors."

The crowds began to draw back, prodded by port watches with their long pikes and shrill cries. Only the city's welcoming committee remained, and I recognized the

Lord Portreeve, my father's boss, with the high priest in the sapphire-studded breastplate he wore on holy days. They bowed at first sight of the Azwans and held outstretched palms beneath their chins so that any word that left their mouths might be found acceptable. Really, it looked like they were vomiting, but I kept that interpretation to myself.

Our perch allowed us a clear view of the Azwans: the one in white robes was an old man with a leathery face, stooped and gray. He raised one hand in greeting to the crowds.

Polite genuflections disintegrated into wild applause, even cheers. Calls of "Reyhim! Welcome home!" rippled across the pavilion. Women held up babies for a better view, men threw copper coins at his feet. He took it all in with studied calm, his eyes scanning the many faces as though trying to spot someone he knew.

"Reyhim's aged since his promotion," someone whispered behind me.

"There's always a price for doing Nihil's bidding," said another.

"How long since he left, anyway?"

"Thirty years, maybe? A little less?"

My father shushed them both, as the younger Azwan's baritone soared across the pier, sounding annoyed, like honey mixed with acid, the way you'd swat at stingflies with your voice, if you could. We all leaned forward to catch every sharp word from him. S'ami, if I remembered correctly. He didn't sound uncertain.

"I'll take some adjusting, is all," S'ami said. "You must remember my more civilized sensibilities."

The high priest answered him, and while I could detect an apologetic tone in his voice, the words didn't carry back to us. S'ami continued.

"All these teeter-totter huts and crooked boardwalks," he said. "It's like someone squatted and shat this place into existence."

The words "That awful man" echoed from the balcony, all too audible and entirely too distinct. The crowd hushed. Everyone around me froze. The words hung in the air, drawing the Azwan's gaze. With creeping horror, I realized once again my tongue had wandered free from my brain. Babba moved in front of me, blocking my view again. I couldn't see his face, but I could see color flush the back of his neck.

I didn't know who down below had heard, but I imagined Nihil himself, all the way across the ocean in his rocky, hilltop home, had caught every insolent syllable. The stripe on my wrist throbbed. I tried to swallow back the sudden wave of nausea and wondered if I could cover my entire body with my scrap of a kerchief. Hiding sounded like the best option.

Amaniel ducked behind me, which forced me forward again. Wonderful. No one could miss me. Maybe one of the giant Feroxis would carry me off like they do in legends, and no one would ever hear from me again, except to talk of the brassy girl who insulted an Azwan on his one and only visit.

"You, up there," a voice boomed. That meant me.

My father hissed. "Haaadaara, don't you. . ."

"Woman!" It was a soldier's voice.

Well, it was nice to be called a woman, if nothing else. The men parted so I could make my way to the front. A crowd gawked up at me. The soldier who'd shouted was another hulking Feroxi in black leather armor. A bronze helmet covered most of his features, except for a scarred chin and two piercing dark eyes glittering from slits. That didn't stop me from imagining his gaze to be utterly contemptuous, hateful, even. He wasn't someone I'd ever want to get to know.

"The Azwan orders an explanation for your words." His clipped tone held no trace of a foreign accent, an odd thing for me to notice when I should be looking for a way to vanish from the face of Kuldor.

My father grabbed my arm and clenched. Hard. I'd have a bruise later. He answered the soldier for me. "The girl means no disrespect, she answered . . ."

"The Azwan orders her to speak." The soldier's eyes never left my face, as much as I tried to look away, look down, look anywhere else.

I made the chin-cupping motion with my hands, closing my eyes as I did so. Both Azwans peered up at me, the one in purple and the one in stark white. The older man, Reyhim, appeared to be grinning, or maybe jeering. Sheer terror clouded my powers of observation at the moment.

"My apologies," I said. I opened my eyes to meet the soldier's unfeeling glare. My throat felt dry, as if any words would get stuck there.

A stage whisper came from over my shoulder. Amaniel. "Great Guardian of Nihil's Person."

"Great Guardian of Nihil's Person!" I practically shouted. The soldier nodded. "I, uh . . ."

Amaniel pressed closer. "Am solicitous of the worthy priestly one's forgiveness."

I froze. The crowd below was so immense. And everyone I ever knew was in it.

I stared down again at the soldier, judging me. I swallowed.

Amaniel nudged me again. "Am solicitous . . ."

"Am silliousness, solicationous, solicitous. Of the priesty one's forgiveness." I'd taken twenty years off my father's lifespan, I thought, and probably thirty years off Amaniel's. I couldn't help it. My tongue was completely knotted. My stomach was, too.

The old Azwan chuckled harder, his chest shaking. The purple one, S'ami, narrowed his eyes at me. He shoved a hand in a leather pouch by his side and withdrew something that flashed gold. He cocked his head toward me, our eyes locking as if trying to read my thoughts. The men around me noticed and followed the Azwan's stare. I felt a thousand crawling insects burrowing into my flesh and tried to scratch them away. I was wriggling, not obviously at first, but more uncomfortably as the moment wore on. I pulled at my clothes and rubbed my arms and thighs, suddenly frantic. I couldn't make the sensation stop or break away from it. He held me by some unseen force, rooted to the spot, angry prickles burning my flesh that didn't spare any part of me, and burned most fiercely between my thighs. I panicked, clenched my legs tighter, and grabbed at Babba's sleeve, furious this Azwan could see what no man should without my permission. He could sense and explore and violate the most sacred and secret part of me, even with my father standing there.

Then S'ami turned, breaking our unseen connection, and I collapsed in a heap, Amaniel beside me, trying to right me so I could sit up. I felt dizzy and ached in places I shouldn't mention. I dreaded Babba's reaction; I didn't think I could filter his heated disapproval through my reeling brain and body. But he only held me, making shushing noises and stroking my back. I dared myself to meet Babba's gaze and found a thoughtful and sad expression, his voice low and comforting. "I believe you've been rejected as a sacrifice, if it's any consolation."

I hoped he was right. Babba was pious; he would know. I struggled to my feet, leaning on Babba in a weak attempt to get my bearings.

Below me, the soldier kept his eyes on me. I adjusted my dress, my kerchief, a loop of hair, an earring. I turned my entire head toward Babba.

A clerk whispered to him: "She held her ground, though. Didn't faint. I'd heard that's good."

For whom? Me or Nihil? I wanted to storm out, or loop a headscarf around the Azwan's throat and pull. Hard. He'd turned back toward Reyhim and pointedly ignored me. Maybe the moment had passed. Maybe, please, oh, blessed, protecting Kuldor, our sacred planet, let the moment have passed. I hovered closer to Amaniel. Below me, S'ami scanned the pier with a scornful grimace and addressed the crowd. I kept my eyes on him, until the soldier was a blur in the corner of my eye.

"The demon's here," the younger Azwan said. "I sensed it from far offshore. But it's weak and afraid. It won't take long to find it and crush it."

I instantly hated the emphasis he placed on the word *crush* and how he squinted at me when he said it. I wondered if he was talking about the supposed star-demon creature at all.

He held up the glittering object from his pouch: it was a wisdom knot cast in gold, and it gave off iridescent rays of light in every hue. The crowds below us gasped as streams of color lifted and swirled in a tight gyre and then exploded in showers of sparks above our heads. A soft, low music thrummed in our ears, like a continuous chime, pleasant and soothing. It was a magic I hadn't deserved to see, with my twisty tongue and foggy brain.

"This is my music," S'ami said in his lyrical voice. "My magic, my lore that protects us."

The older man harrumphed and muttered. If I weren't standing over them, I might not have heard his rasping voice. "It's Nihil's magic, Nihil's lore, in case you've forgotten. Put that away. You'll draw the dybbuk."

S'ami continued at full volume. "It's a demon, to use the proper term. Let it come. I will vanquish it."

"We." Reyhim's expression was flat. "We will vanquish it."

I recalled the piece Amaniel had said about one being in charge but the other being number one. I was willing to bet two coppers those two holy men didn't understand it any better than I did.

But both men were gone, headed down the wharf past genuflecting crowds. Our high priest followed after a single backward glance toward the balcony, a pained and disbelieving look on his face. I'd likely never be allowed back in school again, a thought I found oddly deflating. I'd never set out to be the class laughingstock; it was just so hard to reconcile all that book learning with what I envisioned for my future at Mami's side.

I had no time to dwell on it.

With a sudden boom of drums and the stomp of over-sized boots, hundreds of soldiers poured down the gang-planks. The balcony shook from the pounding cadence of Feroxi feet on the wooden pier below. These men were soldiers, not sailors, and as different from their barefoot brethren as fish and sharks. Nihil had sent a contingent of his elite guards, the likes of which had never been seen here. I spied the glint of bronze helmets, black plumes arching back, oval shields taller than my entire body and painted to resemble swooping night raptors, their beaks and talons bloodied.

Babba gave my shoulder a squeeze in a feeble attempt to cheer me up. "How many do you count? I say about four hundred."

I squeezed my legs tighter, if that were possible, though what threat the soldiers presented, I didn't know. Just the same, I clenched my whole body, every muscle. The bal-cony began to close in on me, though I had only cloudless sky above me.

Everyone seemed ready to forget the Azwans, so I nod-ded along with the chatter. I hadn't bothered to count the individuals in the long columns. I'd been too busy imagin-ing a flock of night raptors descending upon Port Sapphire, black and crimson, fierce and unforgiving as they stormed the wharf.

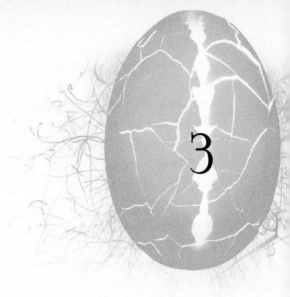

3

The careful astrologer must distinguish between a shooting star that flames out in the sky and portends fleeting good fortune, from a falling star, whose plummet to Kuldor must, by its force, carve for itself a terrible niche.
  —*from* Anatomy of the Heavens: Common Interpretations of the Stars and Planets, *by Shmulai, Astrologer to the Court of King B'rakh of Tengal*

Maybe there was a demon, and maybe it would crawl out of the marsh and creep into someone's head. That was the talk—of a possession of some sort by a creature who would war on Nihil. I wanted so much to believe the star was a different kind of magic, a lovely flame-out from the night sky, a tiny spark from the great infernos that twinkled beyond our reach.

Not that I dared open my mouth again. I did what I do best and kept busy. I hustled about the outdoor hearth we shared with several other families. I rinsed tea glasses and refilled them, set out plates of cut fruit, bussed old aunties and hoary uncles, waved greetings at cousins and friends and cousins' friends. I adored every loud, gossipy moment.

The Ward had declared a holiday in honor of the Azwans' visit. They'd set out for the fens at first light, leaving the town to its wagging tongues. It's easier to stop the rain than a rumor, the saying goes. So I listened in on the gloomy murmurs and scare-mongering whispers and tried to keep from laughing. Of all the hazards in the fens, a fallen bit of meteorite likely wasn't one of them.

Folks took up every seat by the outdoor hearth. They came for company and gossip and for Mami, smiling even now with all the worries, welcoming people and sitting the older ones down with a fuss and a hug. People sipped Mami's teas from coarse, jewel-colored glasses as they traded rumors. The drinks were more properly called tisanes, or infusions of carefully selected herbs. Mami was serving one of her more soothing brews today, probably to calm her own nerves as much as anyone's. A few people asked in hoarse whispers if this or that tisane was medicinal. I shook my head and held a finger to my lips. No one wanted trouble with religious men out and about.

The talk was of Reyhim, especially.

"Handsome, he was," recalled an old auntie.

"Not so much anymore," said her husband. She elbowed him.

"His sermons, those were something to hear," she continued. "So full of fire."

Others nodded. The sermons, the Sabbath prayers, how he looked in his vestments, all dignified and solemn, they remembered it all.

"So he got promoted?" I asked. "From high priest of our little island? All the way to Azwan?"

I was impressed.

Oddly, though, my questions quieted down everyone. I received no answer, just strange looks and awkward silence. Mami handed me a platter to refill.

"That's your cue to mind your mouth," she said. "Go."

"But I didn't say anything!"

"Go anyway."

Talk turned back to aches and pains and the sudden absence of medicine. The old folks looked troubled. For them, it was a battle between their aching bodies and their battered souls. A widowed neighbor complained of boils the healers had only made worse. That was typical, as was a newly married cousin who'd already miscarried after a spell misfired and rid her of more than her morning sickness. My cousin's pained look added another mark to my mental tally of reasons to hate the whole Temple, or at least avoid anyone religious.

With the Azwans here, there'd be no poultice from Mami's store of tart citrine and pungent hydrocanth for a while, or the cooling effects of witch's wort and pain balm for the other aches and ills people pointed out to me. In the best of times, it was a risky business trading in herbs and tinctures and such. I shooed the curious away from jars and potted plants, tucked some in hideaways, and sent my youngest sister, Rishiel, inside with armloads of clay vials.

An uncle grabbed my sleeve. He was my father's great-uncle, the oldest of the old, but his grip was firm. "Your father's gone with the search party?"

"No, just to the city's edge."

"Along with the usual dignitaries and such, I suppose. Official entourage and all?"

I nodded.

The uncle regarded me with a gleam in his eye. His voice carried an unstated request when he spoke. "I'm sure it's insufferably hot out there by the fens. Probably could use some refreshment by now."

"You mean like tea?" Then his meaning hit me. He wanted me to bring the entourage some tea—and return with news. The sly lift in his smile told me I'd jumped to exactly the right conclusion.

"Mind you don't give them any of your sass," the uncle said. "Just show them the gracious Hadara we all know."

I dropped my chin, my chest caving in. He spoke the truth, of course, and tempered it with a compliment, but it stung anyway. My sass—only the elderly could get away with being so blunt, I suppose. Pious girls were supposed to be quiet and deferential and wide-eyed, like Amaniel. A flush crept across my chest as I thought again of how the teacher kept trying to punish Amaniel to get me to listen. I did listen. I just didn't think all that tree-sappy sweet behavior worth my time.

But my uncle had given me a mission, and I was off before I could keep second-guessing myself. Amaniel loaded some fresh brew into the largest jug I could carry while I nestled tea glasses in a soft towel. Only once did she hint at any jealousy.

"Wonder why great-uncle asked you to go," she said.

"He didn't ask; he roundabout suggested it in that way of his."

"Still."

"I suppose it's safer for me to go."

Amaniel looked offended. "I know the way as well as you. It's not like I'd get lost or drop anything."

"No, I meant I seem to have some invisible tattoo marked REJECTED BY NIHIL. You've forgotten?"

She thought it over. "I hope they reconsider after you bring them refreshments."

That wasn't quite the reassurance I wanted, since my goal was to never, ever be at risk of getting anywhere near a sacrifice altar, but I didn't want to sit and argue. I balanced the jug on my head, where it wedged against the knot of a floral hair wrap I'd made myself. I hoped I looked modest enough; fashionable, but modest. It was an almost impossible trick to pull off, but the more stylish women could do it. I glanced over at Mami in her best dress, with its riot of colors and patterns, her long neck glittering with beads, her raven hair tucked beneath an embroidered scarf that tufted above her high forehead, making her seem even taller and more elegant, if that were even possible. Everyone told me I had a high standard set for me. It chafed to be constantly reminded, even as I acknowledged the truth of it: Mami was beautiful.

With no more time to dawdle, I tucked the tea glasses gingerly under an arm. The search party was out in the fens, which meant a long hike through the city, out along the winding boardwalks if I wanted to skirt the waterfront and a whole new set of gossips and worriers.

31

I arrived overheated and winded to where the board-walks gave way to wild marsh grasses. A crowd of women apparently had had the same idea, and we all were carrying jugs. Some had wine in theirs. I wish I'd thought of that. Those women were at the front of the group, where men in the jade green of the Customs House and the rich blues of Ward Sapphire sipped from sturdy cups, their heads bent toward one another, their voices a studied hush that signaled some Very Important Business.

I didn't see Babba among them. I tried to push my way forward and got an elbow to my ribs, then another to my shoulder. I couldn't see how the other women could manage to attack me with their hands on the jugs on their heads, elbows at right angles. Both of the women who'd jabbed me kept their eyes forward, faces blank. Yet another useful life skill that school didn't teach. At least I had one advantage. Being a tall man's daughter isn't always a curse. I swung my own elbow straight at the jug atop one woman's head. It lurched enough to send the woman reeling in a panic to right it. By then, I was one body closer to the front of the crowd.

I used the same move to slip past one, then another, then another woman who gave me a squinty glare as she wiped droplets of wine from her sleeve. Then there I was, in front of a short, sturdy man in a constable's cheery yellow long-coat, a pike by his side. He gave me an appreciative up-and-down look, even though he barely cleared my shoulder.

"That pringle mint I smell?" he asked.

"A mix of stuff," I said, brightening. I tapped the jug. "Want some?"

"You have the prettiest eyes."

Blood rushed to my cheeks. My eyes were an odd shade of hazel, almost golden, not the usual luscious brown. I thanked him and dropped my gaze.

"Aw, don't be like that, golden girl. You can give me a glass of tea, and I'll give you a kiss and a secret."

"What kind of secret?" I pretended not to hear the kiss part. The constable wasn't going to play along, though.

"No objection to the kiss? Your father not around?"

"He's the Chief Port Inspector," I said, leveling my coolest glare at him.

"Ah. You're House Rimonil. Not my lucky day after all. But no kiss, no secret."

"And no tea."

"You're haggling? With a thirsty constable, out here doing his duty, guarding your lovely golden-eyed self on the hottest day of the year? With some sort of horrible something out in the swamps?"

His tone suggested he didn't believe anything was out there. I smiled. "I think that sums it up."

I figured his secret was something to the effect of you-have-a-tea-leaf-in-your-teeth. I ran my tongue along the inside of my mouth to be sure. I lost interest in the flirty constable and looked around for someone who might know what was going on. A commotion drew everyone's attention to the marsh. I could only make out shouting and splashing and more shouting. Deep voices and angry ones, making the throng of us women pull closer in our shared worry. The constable was once again all business, holding his pike horizontal with both hands to push us gently away from the edge of the boardwalk.

"They didn't find anything." The constable's voice had dropped to a low growl.

I tried to focus on him. "What?"

"That's the secret. I heard it earlier from a lookout."

"Then why all that hollering?"

"They didn't come here for our fine beverages, yes?"

I didn't answer. A flotilla of punts and canoes pulled up to a boat launch at the end of the walkway. Guards perched awkwardly in some, while others waded ashore lugging sacks. They were soaked head-to-toe, and what wasn't muddy was sunburned an angry red. Pale complexions don't do well here, and I felt a brief instance of sympathy, quickly shattered by the first scream.

The women around me shrieked and covered their mouths with their free hands. I was in front but didn't see what they had seen.

Then I did. A pit opened wide inside me.

The guards weren't carrying sacks, but bodies.

They dumped three men—human men—on the boardwalk with a few grunts.

"Their guides," said a woman. "Those were their guides."

Lamentations rose around me, adding to the confusion and noise. The men were known—I spotted one who sometimes rowed out to the fens with Mami and me for some light fishing. Why had he died? I struggled for air. The heat closed in around me, the other women pressing against me, the wails insufferably loud in my ears. I don't shed tears easily, and I fought them off with a few determined blinks. My stomach was another story. I had to look away finally to wrestle down its contents. The nausea left a bitter taste behind.

The side of the constable's pike pressed against us. "Back. Back now."

We listened and crept backward, the mound of bodies already giving off a sickening smell. The shouting grew louder and came from the boats. The two Azwans sat in the front punts, S'ami shaking a fist at the older one, Reyhim, who waved his arms in an exaggerated way, mocking his younger colleague. His voice was unnaturally raspy and grating, as if it had been hollowed out with a pitted knife, all jagged edges and danger.

"Oh, Nihil's Ear, are you? I'd love to hear what he whispers in it when you tell him you brought us all the way here for a muddy hole in the ground."

S'ami seemed too busy with his own bluster to have heard. "It's your pernicious, money-grubbing, barbaric little tribe out here that's to blame."

"This 'tribe' was taming this jungle when your people were still crapping in the sand."

They swapped even more shocking insults this way, words I'd never be allowed to repeat, while their sweaty guards came ashore. Several helped the Azwans out of their punts, but the men didn't pause in their verbal duel even as they stepped ashore—and around the bodies. It was as if the dead men were a pile of rags in their way or an uneven plank in the road. The Azwans switched languages a few times to tongues I didn't speak, but anyone who lives in a busy port long enough learns a foreign phrase or two. I recognized Tengali and some references to the stars and a man. A star man? Could that be? Oh, an astrologer. They were talking astrology.

Reyhim was comparing something to dysentery. No, that couldn't be right. A woman behind me gasped and translated. I was right. He'd likened the astrologer in question to a disease. Other women nodded and filled in the rest, with one adding. "S'ami's father is the astrologer in question, I think."

A guard positioned himself between the two quarreling Azwans and thumped his fist across his chest.

"A salute," a woman whispered.

"Don't seem as if they deserve it, the way they're behaving," said another. That was met with hisses and shushing and more muffled weeping. I silently agreed, but I'd missed whatever the chest-thumping guard had said. S'ami had turned to him to speak.

"It's here. I know it's here; I sense it's here."

Reyhim interjected. "Then it's back in the town. In someone's head. One of the men who went out to find it after it fell came back with an unwanted visitor within him." He waved toward the dead men.

"Well, now, whose fault would that be?" S'ami's voice dripped venom. "Perhaps their former high priest's? The one who was supposed to instill in them a respect for doctrine, perhaps. Teach them not to meddle in, oh, I don't know, celestial events, say, without consulting the Temple."

"It's been years since I presided at the Ward here," Reyhim said. "Plenty of time to unlearn what I'd taught them."

"Ah, then, we'll just dispatch with the current high priest along with all the other incompetents and greedy fools in this Nihil-ignored, pestilence-plagued mudpit."

His voice dripped with sarcasm, but I don't know if anyone could doubt he'd do exactly that: randomly kill anyone he found unworthy. The one thing I had learned in my lessons is that Nihil considers us all unworthy, no matter what. This didn't leave me with a good feeling.

A shadow fell across my cheek, and I looked up to see the guard that had saluted S'ami. I gasped at the familiar brown-eyed glare, the scarred chin. It was the guard from the pier who'd shouted up at me. Now he was the one gazing down, with a solid frown. I didn't need Babba there to remind me not to stare impolitely. I cast my eyes downward before trying to peer around that hulking torso with no success. The jug flew from my head, plucked by an oversized hand.

"Tea or spirits?" The guard waved the jug at me.

"Tea," I said. "Would you like a glass?"

"Not needed." He unplugged the top of the jug and took a long pull, wiping his lips on his sweaty forearm. His eyes never left my face.

"Those men." Did I dare ask? My stomach leaped again. "The guides."

"Useless." The guard shrugged and walked off with my jug, handing it to other guards. Other women passed their jugs to the thirsty men, and there was a brief, incongruous moment where we were all being quite civilized while the Temple debated the merits of all our deaths. No one spoke, not even the guards, except for the Azwans, who seemed to have calmed their voices from irate to merely irritable. I couldn't catch all of it, since being the tall one in the crowd meant I had a load of jugs to pass back and forth between petite females and towering giants.

The one guard—I'd begun to call him S'ami's guard in my head—wouldn't budge from blocking my view. He didn't bother to stoop or lean for anyone or anything as he passed jugs, which meant I got in a week's worth of stretching in a short time. I tried peering around him again.

"You want a better view of your friends?" he asked. He angled one shoulder so I could glimpse the gory pile of corpses. "Help yourself."

I shuddered and looked away, only to exchange worried glances and jugs with the women around me. I finally had to listen in as best I could for whatever sound could pass through the body of that thickly armored soldier. The gist of the Azwans' discussion, as best I could tell, was that something might be out there yet, but not at the impact crater the starfall had left. That only held muck and dead fish. Reyhim wanted to check the town. S'ami wanted to search the swamps. Both ideas lifted the contents of my stomach again, but S'ami couldn't know what was in those swamps, as I did.

He seemed more interested in the mud spatters on his elaborate robes, rubbing at them in short, forceful bursts. He muttered curses in Tengali while Reyhim sneered: "You might've worn a more practical frock."

S'ami ignored him and turned to one of the many dignitaries standing around looking emotionally constipated. I'd have to visit a sick ward to find a more stopped-up bunch. I recognized the Lord Portreeve, our highest official outside the Ward. He ran the port and everything in the town connected to the trading world. His lordship bowed and cupped his hands beneath his chin as S'ami addressed him.

"What do you know of the Gek here?" S'ami said, turning his back on the other Azwan. I sucked in a breath. So he did know about the city inside the swamp.

Reyhim spoke louder to compensate: "A peace accord was signed years before I became high priest here."

S'ami tensed at the news. "Peace accord? Who makes peace with Gek?"

"It's the Nihil-blasted frontier, S'ami. The Gek were here first."

"Then we should go there first."

The man must be an idiot. The Gek hated anything magic. They called it unnatural. Mention Nihil's name, and they'd be all over S'ami and his gold knots, with not enough leftover for a proper cremation.

S'ami kept his gaze on the swamp. "The trees look passable enough."

"It gets worse." That was Reyhim, sounding wiser than I'd given him credit for.

The Lord Portreeve interrupted them. "Please, trust us doubtful souls, who know these waters. What the Azwan of Ambiguity says is true. At least give us a day or so to round up proper guides for you." He glanced at the dead men. "I hope the new ones prove more sufficient."

S'ami sniffed. "They'd better. You have dealings with those creatures?"

The Portreeve continued, "Even the Gek have things to trade. I might know the area very well, actually."

No, he didn't. His portly lordship couldn't find anything beyond the bottom of a spirit flask. Any foray he led to the Gek city would end in another heap of bodies—if anyone made it out alive to deliver that heap. A human needed gifts, and there were rules and protocol and favors to exchange . . . the thought made me frantic. The Gek might never have seen giants. What then?

I changed my mind about Reyhim, too. He started agreeing with his lordship, all cozy and friendly. "That's what I miss about this place: pure mercantile greed. You'd sell the muck out from under us if you could."

"Thank you, kind Azwan," said his lordship. "May you want for nothing, in this life or the next."

"If I do, I'll call on you to obtain it for me."

I'd reached my breaking point. Even with a jug on my head in the maddening heat, I was pretty sure I had more sense than the three of them. I had no reason to like the Temple, but I had no reason to wish them a mass slaughter. Their deaths would be so needless. So I blurted—well, of course, it came out in a blurt:

"You need me!"

No one heard, or no one noticed. Even the guard in front of me didn't acknowledge a thing.

"You need me. I know the way, and I know what they're like."

Not a word. The Lord Portreeve cast me a sideways glance and kept up his bargaining with the Azwans. I tried again.

"Sirs!"

A hand on my shoulder broke my concentration. I turned, expecting to see a thirsty guard. Instead, I met Babba's stern gaze. I could've collapsed with relief. Until then, I hadn't realized how much his absence weighed on me. He could've been in that pile of bodies.

"Let's go," he said.

I followed with one last turn of my head. I could see over the crowd to where S'ami's guard was staring after me, expressionless. I wondered if anything ever moved someone like that, if they ever loved anyone.

"Now, Hadara." Babba used his don't-argue-with-me voice, so I followed him back along the wooden streets toward home. When he didn't reprimand me or pepper me with questions about my behavior, I worked up the courage to ask what he thought the Azwans would do next.

"Whatever they wish."

"Do you think they'll search the swamps or the town?"

"If you heard what I heard, then it comes down to whichever of those men backs down first."

"Then maybe nothing will happen because they'll be arguing so long."

Babba frowned. "There's nothing funny about it. This isn't the face the Temple should be showing us. Already this creature, this star-demon, must be working its evil."

"How could that be?"

"I don't know, nor do I want to."

And that was that. I knew better than to try and pry anything else out of Babba when he got all tight-lipped. I let him be, lost in my own thoughts as our feet followed the familiar path home. Whatever I imagined coming from an evil spirit, however, it could not match in ferocity and terror what the Temple itself had planned.

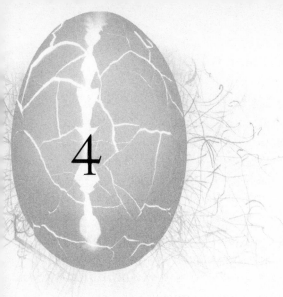

4

When he saw the widow of the man he'd killed, Ludsor paused. The dawn light shone in her hair, her lip trembled with fear and sorrow. Ludsor had no wife, and Ulwe pleased him. With none to stand in his way, Ludsor swept her up and made her his wife, though she wept for what she had lost.

— *"The Fall of Ulwe," from Verisimilitudes 3,*
The Book of Unease

The rain began late that night—Babba said the Azwans must've lifted their sailing-weather spells. It came in thick, blinding torrents that leaked through thatching and made the boardwalks too slippery to tread. The canals refilled, and our cistern soon overflowed. I rose early with my sisters to move our pots and kettles beneath an awning at the hearth and bring inside several urns of dried beans and herbs and other food we'd forgotten.

We toweled ourselves dry and began peeling fresh citrines for breakfast. Without warning, the door crashed open, torn from its track with a single firm kick from a Feroxi boot. Three soldiers barreled in, shouting in Fernai.

I snatched my sisters out of harm's way, and we huddled in a corner, the guards looming over us, shouting instructions we couldn't understand. One headed up the angled ladder to the loft, where Babba and Mami slept. The noise had already brought them halfway down. Babba opened his mouth to speak, but the soldier yanked him off the short ladder and threw him to the floor.

Rishiel screamed. Amaniel clamped a hand over Rishiel's mouth, and I pulled them both closer, feeling their shivers against my skin. I pretended I was in the wild, hiding from a mash cat or another predator. It'll soon pass, I told myself. Just don't move. Mami clung to the wide, flat rungs as the same soldier grabbed her around the waist and ripped her from her perch. He carried her, kicking and thrashing, to the broken doorway and heaved her outside. She landed on the rainy boardwalk and rolled, immediately soaked. She raised herself up and beckoned to us, but my sisters and I were stuck, frozen, petrified. Babba leapt to his feet, but two soldiers grabbed him by either arm and held him. A third shouted. He spoke in the common tongue, his voice harsh and clipped:

"Surrender the house. By order of the Temple of Doubt."

I hugged my sisters firmly enough to feel their ribs beneath their clothes. I tried to keep either of them from screaming, but they clawed at the hands over their mouths. I'd clamped too hard, too focused on my own pounding heart to notice I'd nearly smothered them. Rishiel sobbed into my shoulder. None of us could budge for all our panic.

"What have we done?" Babba asked. "Just tell me what we've done."

The soldier drew a dagger to Babba's chin. "Surrender it. Now."

"Go, girls. Go." Babba nodded toward me, the eldest, the responsible one. I willed myself to move, pulled my sisters to their feet, and herded them to the door. Amaniel grabbed Rishiel's hand, and they raced to Mami. I paused, as I always do on the swamp's edge, and made a quick study of the hostile terrain. That meant surveying the soldiers, from plume to bootstrap, dwelling on the menacing way they hunched over Babba. Whatever they were up to, they were enjoying this.

"You, too." One soldier crossed toward me and hovered, his face a finger's width from mine. For the third time in as many days, I stared into zigzag scars on his chin and narrow, brown eyes. He was S'ami's guard, the one who'd barked at me from the pier, the same guard who'd sneered about the pile of bodies. I clenched up again, remembering, and tried to keep from glaring.

Up close, he was young, maybe only a little older than me. He was shorter than the other two, perhaps just a little taller than Babba, and nowhere near their pale, anemic look. Again, those dark eyes—not blue—glinted fiercely at me beneath a helmet hammered just a shade shallower than the others with their wide browridges. Something seemed off about him, like he didn't quite fit with his taller, snowy-skinned, heavy-headed comrades.

Without thinking, I spoke. "You're a half-brow."

A mistake. The man's face contorted in rage, his body stiffened, and he wrapped a hand around my throat.

"*What?*"

"I'm sorry. Y-You look half-human, that's all." I tried, but I couldn't take the comment back for all my wishing. I hadn't known it was a slur.

"You ignorant island girl."

Babba struggled to break free of the two other men. "She's a child—let her go."

The half-brow whipped around. "Get him out of here. We'll make the girl do it."

Girl. At the pier, he'd called me "woman." I tried not to let myself get distracted, I had bigger worries.

The soldiers dragged Babba, still struggling, and tossed him out to where Mami and my sisters cowered in the rain. Beyond them, I could make out other families fleeing and shivering and hear the booming cries and stomping feet of soldiers. The invasion must've hit suddenly. We'd heard nothing, or maybe the rain had covered the sound.

The half-human soldier hadn't forgotten my loose tongue. No sooner was Babba outside than he towered over me, using his height to try to intimidate me. It worked. I shrunk from his glare. "Half-brow, eh? I'm more man than you've ever seen in this Nihil-forgotten backwater."

I hugged my arms to my chest, unable to meet his gaze, and swallowed again and again, as if I could take back my hateful words. Ignorant island girl, indeed. Me, who loved listening to the chatter on the piers but knew not to repeat the coarse language I heard there. My neck and ears felt impossibly hot.

The soldier backed away, still redfaced, and muttered something in Fernai that the other men found funny. They gave low, grunting chuckles and kept looking me up and down in a way I didn't like at all. The half-brow motioned toward our cupboard and said something to the guards, one of whom grabbed me by the arm and pushed me forward. The new guard was taller, blonder, and had a wicked leer I found even less appealing than the half-brow's frown.

This new man backed me into the cupboard door and pressed his body against mine. I cowered as the waterlogged, clammy leather of his armor dampened my clothes, metal rivets pressed into my chest where my heart suddenly battered my ribcage as if trying to break free. I glanced up into bemused blue eyes and felt tears form in my own. This man meant to harm me.

The blond jerked back, yanked by the half-brow, who barked something unpleasant and then said in the common tongue, "Leave her be."

"Then why keep her here?" asked the blond one in a thick, rolling accent.

The half-brow barely glanced my way. "She needs a lesson."

The blond shrugged. "Then we can all teach her."

I didn't break eye contact with the half-brow. If I had any shot at mercy, it had to be him, but you don't beg a mash cat not to eat you, and neither would I plead for my life or honor. I stayed as steady as my shot nerves would let me.

The half-brow merely snarled. "Don't sink to the level of these barbarians."

He said that last bit with a long, mean look down at me.

Who was he calling a barbarian? His overgrown, blond comrade had just insinuated the most boorish, obscene thing possible. I scrunched up my face, willing my mouth to stay firmly shut. I knew I should feel relief that the half-brow had pulled the other man away. But I couldn't stop trembling. Then the half-brow grabbed my shoulder and spun me toward the cupboard door. "What's in there?"

I instinctively reached for it when I felt him lean forward, not quite touching me. He took a long breath. My shoulder tingled beneath his hand. I had to keep myself calm. I had to think. I had to somehow plot and plan my way past this moment with this big, hairy, rain-soaked boy-man. I drew my arms back and wrapped them around myself again. He could open the cupboard himself.

"You've nothing to fear if you've nothing to hide," he said.

"This is obscene," I said. My voice came out in a hoarse whisper. "My father should be here."

He gave my shoulder a squeeze and leaned in close. "Don't worry. I don't take what's not freely given."

I glanced over my shoulder at him and flashed him my worst not-impressed look, my brows furrowed and my lips pressed firm.

"Then get out of our house," I said.

"Ah, there's fight in you yet. Good to know. Now open the cupboard."

Furious, I reached for the cupboard, but only to brace myself. It fooled him just long enough for me to draw up my left leg. It came slamming down again, the hard heel of my sandal against the soft leather of his boot. He lurched back, cursing. Let him open *that*.

One of the other soldiers barked something in Fernai. The half-brow didn't answer and whipped me around, locking his eyes on mine. "You're very lucky I'm so forgiving. But your luck is running out."

I turned, hiding my own thin, mean smile at my tiny victory, however fleeting. I'd survived how many forays into the wild? I could survive this overgrown bully. But I fumbled with the cupboard latch, aware of how close his body was to mine, as if the short space between us had become charged, like static, crackling with unspoken threats. The latch broke in my hand, and he reached over me and tugged it free from the cupboard door, which swung open with a squeak.

The soldier yanked jars and urns from the shelves, shoving them into my chest and ordering me to open them. My fingers trembled as I tried to undo seals and pry off lids. This was nearly a year's worth of work for Mami and me. The soldier snatched them back and tossed them against a wall, shattering them one by one.

"Nothing in there," he said as the first burst open, its liquid contents splattering. He did the same with several others. "Nothing in that one. Or that one."

"Why are you doing this?" I stared in disbelief at the destruction. "None of that was illegal."

Almost none, I corrected silently. Maybe a little more than almost none.

"Your word against ours." He was still punishing me for opening my mouth. Anything I said would make it worse. So I stood there, flailing my hands or tugging, tugging at loose threads in my dress, as if I could unravel the whole morning and reweave it, while the soldiers made a sport of destroying our home. I ducked as they overturned the divan I shared with my sisters, and I dodged a hand-loomed rug that sailed across the room. They shoved me aside as they dumped the contents of bureaus and shelves on the floor and barked a sharp *no* at me when I tried to scoop up an armful of clothes.

They fished out a couple items: an embroidered rendering Amaniel had made of Nihil's last incarnation as a woman and Rishiel's favorite doll, the one with white hair just like Nihil's.

Another soldier waved these artifacts in my face and said something harsh in his tongue. I guessed he was looking for explanations, so I told him, my voice faltering. Most of my fear hadn't subsided. I'd only been spared for the moment, but my heartbeat was steadying even if my stomach kept up a fitful churning. There were two other surly soldiers who could easily change their minds about keeping me unharmed so far. The one facing me grunted, as if comprehending my stammered explanation as he waved the two items.

He tucked them into a bag, which in turn went into a larger sack I hadn't noticed before. It bulged with bags of loot they must've taken from other families. I had no idea when, unless they'd started on the opposite side of town. None of it made any sense. One of the soldiers heaved the sack over his shoulder, which I hoped was a sign they were all leaving. It wasn't.

The half-brow pointed up the ladder and said something that struck them as funny. They stared at me, guffawing, their gaze roaming from the top of my uncovered head to my toes, lingering on my chest. Armored or not, they were a pimply, gangly, adolescent bunch. Then again, that might make them more dangerous. They were far from the Feroxi's frostbitten realm along the shores of the Warmless Sea. Here they could do whatever they wanted and then never have to live with the results. Port Sapphire could be left in ruins, and it wouldn't matter one copper to them as they sailed back over the horizon.

If I could wish them back to Ferokor, I would have. The two items they'd seized were nothing, less than trifles. Every herb Mami and I had gathered wouldn't garner an arrest, but a doll could get me hurt?

"Up," said the half-brow, pointing.

He wanted me to go to my parents' sleeping loft with him. I began to shake again, my breathing coming in fits, bile rising in my throat. My stomach again. I had imagined myself a gift to Nihil, not understanding it wasn't the worst fate I could meet.

"I won't go. I'm pious." I wasn't going to beg. Never mind that I was the worst excuse for a pious girl in recent history, and they were from the Temple itself. In some version of Scriptures, there must be a passage about carrying out official important duties without violence and leering. At least, there should be. I tried to cover my blouse with my arms in a futile show of modesty, which brought more laughter. A meaty hand clamped on my shoulder and spun me around.

"I told you I won't take what's not freely given. Just show us what you're hiding up there."

Relieved, I giggled; a hysterical, jittery, utterly inappropriate squawk that made my throat sore. They were resuming their search; that was all. I wanted to puke.

"What's so funny?" The half-brow's frown told me he didn't find anything amusing at all.

I struggled to catch my breath. "You're not going to hurt me, right?"

"Don't give me a reason to." The half-brow reached for the hilt of his sword. I took the hint and scuttled up the ladder, nearly tripping on my long skirt. Once upstairs, it was much the same as downstairs: he ordered me to pull apart bedding and empty my parents' wardrobe. At last, he stopped in the middle of the room by the heap we'd made. I wasn't sure why he needed me there when he could've managed to be reckless and destructive all by himself.

I edged closer to the ladder and found myself hoping that by some powerful luck he'd forgotten me. He hadn't. He beckoned me over, and I took short, halting steps forward. I hadn't given him any reason to harm me, had I? Would I know if I had, or was he the sort to invent a reason?

"What's your name?" he asked. Before I could answer, his voice became husky and low. "You shouldn't insult a Feroxi. We're not a forgiving race."

"I didn't mean anything by it, I . . . I've just never seen a, ah." I clamped my mouth shut again. No use making matters worse.

"A half-brow, right?" He folded beefy arms high on his chest and glowered. "Did you not hear me when I said that was an insult?"

"No, please. I'm so sorry. I'm an ignorant island girl. Can't we leave it at that?"

"Or what? You'll crush another of my toes?"

My mouth fell open. He was joking. Amid the wreckage, he was wisecracking. I stared back without blinking. He'd opened a door of sorts, and I intended to walk through it. "I'm truly sorry I crushed one of your toes. I was aiming for all of them."

"You're forgetting where you are."

"In my own home?"

"You are in the presence of a Guardian of Nihil's Person with a full complement of arms."

"If not the full complement of toes."

A bewildered look spread across the half of his face that poked beneath his bronze helmet. He opened his mouth and shut it, lifted his chin, opened his mouth again . . . and nothing came out. I'd stumped him. Maybe he lacked a full complement between his ears, too.

A black plume popped up from the floor below and a Feroxi face peered up, unsmiling. The two soldiers exchanged words I was glad I didn't understand because I'd decided I despised them. Judging by their mocking tone, the feeling was mutual. My opinion of them obviously mattered little, and my shaky bravery seeped away. The half-brow flung me into the other soldier's arms, and I found myself dumped to the floor. The landing hit hard, but it wasn't a long way to fall, and I picked myself up without pausing and straightened my skirt. I smoothed my hair, sorry it wasn't under wraps in a proper show of modesty around men. Not that they deserved it.

"A tough girl, aren't you," the half-human one said, clambering down behind me. "I think you might even like us. And if you want something else to call me, it's First Guardsman Valeo."

I pursed my lips and glared at him in what I intended to be my most menacing expression, but he only chuckled and motioned toward the door. My ordeal was ending, just when I was thinking up a few more opinions he needed to hear.

He reached for me, and I jerked away, hitting my head on the open cupboard. The men laughed again. I seethed. I wanted to grab shards of urns and shove them in all their faces, but what could I do? I turned and followed the first two soldiers out, simmering, not even caring about the torrents that soaked me to the skin in an instant. I didn't notice Babba running up to me until he'd clutched me to him.

"What did they do to you?"

"They tore up the house. Everything, they ruined everything." I melted against Babba's shoulder, but the sobs wouldn't come. I simply stood there, letting the clammy wetness of his longshirt paste itself to my cheek, my arms limp by my side. Babba led me under the awning, where several families were huddling. Smashed earthenware littered the patio; all Mami's carefully tended herbs were destroyed, along with her stores of medicines. She shook her head at Babba.

"This is Reyhim's doing," she said.

"Because of what he'd said yesterday?" Babba asked. "About searching town first?"

"No, the way it's being done."

53

He nodded. "You'd have special reason for believing that, I suppose."

"It's not a belief. Look around you. Tell me this isn't . . ."

"Stop."

". . . like with my mother."

"I mean it."

Amaniel and I both stared at Mami, at each other, at Mami again. We weren't allowed to mention our grandmother. I knew only scant details of her story, except that she was long gone and little remembered.

Beyond our ruined home, the soldiers moved on, banged down more doors, startled more families, and upbraided those who gawked from the boardwalks. The rain covered us all, the pious and the unworthy alike, gray and cold and without mercy or end.

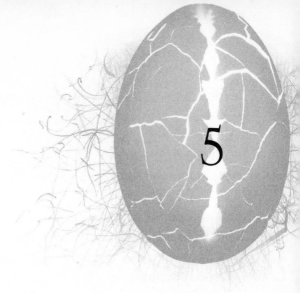

5

Make no graven images of me or of my enemies.
Nor shall you abide those whose faith wavers; I
am god, you shall follow only me.
—*from* Oblations 10, The Book of Unease

The downpour gave no sign of letting up. We huddled against one another under an awning at the outdoor hearth, listening in terrified silence to the city being upended and people's lives overturned. The huddling didn't offer much warmth in the rain and wouldn't protect us from whatever was happening to us, but it was all we had.

In the distance, women's screams tore at the air, and sounds of things smashing, of entire homes crashing as wooden stilts gave out, then panicked shouts and more screams.

Babba and the neighbor men led us all in prayers, which we got down on our knees for in the rain, since we were already soaked through. We prayed for forgiveness for the sin of assumption, for wandering from the certain path, for being caught cutting corners and transgressing in ways we could only guess, for everything and anything that might make it all stop.

It went on so long, all of us murmuring or wailing or weeping or standing up and shouting, pleading into the air that shed only rain and no redemption. At long last, all the way into the late afternoon, a dull silence overtook the city. The storm slowed to a steady rhythm, the chaos and confusion becoming more distant and then fading away. A horn sounded several long blasts that ended in uplifting notes.

Babba told us that was the all-clear signal, the one they used after a battle. I hadn't known we were at war. We headed inside, and Babba propped the broken door closed behind us as Mami set us girls to work with a few nods at the mess. We dried ourselves off with blankets we dug out from the bottom of several heaps of belongings.

Nothing at the outdoor hearth would be salvageable in the rain, but inside Mami and I sifted through the shards for anything usable. I did most of the work, as Rishi sobbed in Mami's lap, her skinny little-girl arms locked solid around Mami's neck. The dried beans and lentils were still good— we'd have some food, at least, if nothing to flavor it with. Picking them up one by one wasn't my idea of sport, but it kept my fingers busy, which was better for them than flying nervously through the curls that had been uncovered and exposed. I felt embarrassed about that. The half-brow had been so close to my hair, I wondered if he could smell it.

I wondered if it's something he'd have noticed. I smelled like spice flowers, I suppose, which we put in our soaps, or like a hundred kinds of herbs I either picked or worked with day after day. If only he'd known what those smells represented, I might've been in bigger trouble. I smelled like the things he should've been searching for. I smelled like evidence. I was lucky he didn't know that.

I worked hunched beneath the cupboard with its broken latch, where the other soldier had pressed into me, almost crushing me. A hand flew protectively to my chest at the memory of that spiky armor. The half-brow had stepped in and pulled him away. *I won't take what's not freely given.*

I'd stolen looks at him like I do with sailors on the piers. Every rotten word of his leaked out of my memory, so I could dwell instead on the broad sweep of those shoulders, and there was that majestic inverted triangle his torso made, with the way his leather corselet seemed perfectly wrapped to him like a second skin, muscular and tough.

Oh no, this wouldn't do at all. What was wrong with me? How could I have so many thoughts that bordered on unchaste, even as I cleaned up the mess the man had made? Not man—soldier. If I thought of him as a man, I'd keep thinking about that deep voice or his build, and soon enough, I'd be thinking he was attractive instead of monstrous. If I remembered he was a soldier, then I could keep in mind he'd come here to do a job and had gone about it rather efficiently.

Thanks to him, I had two messes to clean: one on the floor, and one inside my head.

Mami peered deep into my face, as if trying to decode something cryptic in my irises. "Amaniel's been talking to you."

Sure enough, a hiccupy, red-eyed Amaniel was sobbing up stuttered words.

"Didn't you tell them I was pious?"

"Tell who?"

"The Great Guardians of Nihil's Person!"

Was she serious? Did she think I gave those vicious boy-men a house tour, boasting of my sister's academic accomplishments?

My mouth pressed into a firm line before I uttered the word "No" and nothing else.

"But how could you!" Amaniel sobbed and hiccuped again. "You shifted the blame onto me because you're jealous, and now I'm the one in trouble."

I glanced around at the swept up pile of debris. "I'm absolutely certain I've no idea what you're talking about."

"You've no idea? Mami, she has no idea. My needlework! They took it." Amaniel's face resembled a bloated anemone, hands flying like tentacles over her flushed face.

Mami was the sort who talked with her eyes more than her lips, and her expressions were more sad than stern. She shook her head. "Amaniel, you're forgetting your sister was put on the spot here."

"And look what an awful job she made of it, too." Amaniel waved her tentacles around the room. "How many insults does it take to ruin our entire stores? A few dozen? Just one really disrespectful one? Why not just spit in the man's face?"

Both Mami and I sat in stunned silence. Babba came downstairs from the sleeping loft. Even Rishi turned around and stared.

I let Amaniel's words eat deep into me, like acid. Like molten rock. I melted. Flash. Gone. A pile of ashes where my soul had been. I didn't even know if I could be angry.

I had a sudden vertigo.

Every family. Every single one. They all had this happen. And she—my sister—was blaming me. I was spiraling downward, and there was no bottom. I just kept falling into the deep, wide hole she'd dug for me. I'd been worried I was some sort of traitor for thinking about Valeo. She'd been thinking about him, too. And if there was anything at all at the bottom of this abyss she'd just pushed me into, it was likely to be spikes.

"Amaniel." Babba's voice was low and controlled. "This isn't acceptable. Not at all."

Mami joined in. "Take back every word. This moment."

"I may have spoken in haste." Amaniel balled up her fists and planted them on her hips. "But what I said is true."

That brought Babba down from the last rung and across the room. The smack that landed across Amaniel's face was something I'd see and hear the rest of my life. I had never, ever seen Babba strike any of us, not ever. Mami switched us once or twice when we were little, but it was nothing like this. Not ever.

Babba towered over Amaniel, who'd begun weeping again, only this time with a nasal whine to it, eyes scrunched closed, snot streaming down her face. Welts in the shape of Babba's hand were already flaring from her left cheek.

"This family," Babba said, "stays together. Together. And if Nihil himself were to bang down our door, we face him together. As one. And you will remember that. Yes?"

Amaniel gave a curt nod and then fled for a far corner of the room, where she balled up on the floor and sobbed into the wall. Babba and Mami exchanged long, unhappy glances. An entire conversation happened in that moment, all unspoken. I pulled Rishi off Mami's lap and hugged her to me so Mami could rise to her feet. Without either asking the other, both my parents headed outside, as they always did when they wanted to talk without us overhearing.

I distracted Rishi by softly pointing out some of what I'd salvaged and making her identify the different types of beans. I set her to the task of separating them all and finding a mostly unbroken container for them. This stopped her snuffling while she squatted on the floor and gave all the beans pet names and scolded the naughty ones.

Babba poked his head through the doorway and motioned for me to join him outside. There was a small overhang created where the eaves of our A-frame hut met, so I squeezed between my parents to stay dry. Babba pointed across the canal. A single sentry stood at attention on the boardwalk, a vertical stroke of a man between two houses directly opposite.

"Is that the same one?" he asked.

I nodded. It was. I didn't need to see his chin or his skin color or the angry glare to recognize his broad outline, even through the downpour. We stared at the soldier staring back. For a moment, no one moved or said anything.

"It's probably just a normal patrol," Mami said. "He's just stationed there, I suppose."

Babba shook her head. "He's watching our house."

Mami sucked in her breath. "If it were something Hadara and I had gathered in the swamp, they'd have collected that, too."

"But what if they're watching us for signs of illegal activity?" I said, my voice low.

THE TEMPLE OF DOUBT

The guard remained rigid, his eyes on the three of us, one hand hidden beneath his shield, the other loosely gripping a pike. The rain streamed along his form and cascaded from the end of his shield. If it bothered him, he didn't show it. Mami backed toward the door. "Time to go in, I think."

"Wait." I grabbed both my parents' arms. "I'm going to apologize."

"I forbid it," Babba said.

"Amaniel might be right," I said. "I mean, I didn't know that word was a slur, but what if using it did make things worse for us? And what if our impiety wasn't enough any one single time to draw Nihil's wrath, but it all added up over time?"

Mami shook her head. "Then it's my fault, not yours, Hadara."

I barreled on. "Amaniel's in trouble for the first time in her life. She has no idea how to feel, I suppose."

Babba smiled grimly at that. "True enough."

"And she's not thinking straight. I owe her a chance at fixing this. It won't get her stitching back or Rishi's doll, but can it hurt?"

Mami looked over at Babba. "Do you want to tell her no?"

Babba looked down his nose at me. "I would defend you with my life, if I had to, daughter mine. But no, you're not going out in this storm to say so much as a word to a fully armed guard with orders to kill."

I gazed across the canal again. The soldier was gone and then reappeared between the next two sets of houses. He was making his way to the main boardwalk again.

"Maybe he's going away," I said. "Maybe his shift is over."

The three of us stood there watching, sharing the single hope that our personal sentry was off-duty for the afternoon. Instead, he tramped toward our row of houses, making the turn onto our stretch of boardwalk. Babba positioned himself ahead of us, and I was relieved to hide behind his shoulder, peering out only just enough to see the soldier pause and turn to face Babba.

"First Guardsman Valeo," I whispered to Babba. "That's his name."

Babba nodded and repeated the man's name and rank.

Valeo nodded back. "You have some concern, Rimonil of Mansoril?"

He knew Babba's name, and my late grandfather's, too. A shudder rippled down my back, and I hugged my arms to my chest. There'd only be one reason this soldier would use my father's family name instead of his title as Chief Port Inspector, which the whole city would know. He wanted Babba to realize he knew who we all were and didn't give Nihil's tiniest toenail for Babba's position.

Even at my angle over Babba's shoulder, I could see the long, considering gaze Babba gave Valeo, the faintest squinting of Babba's eyes as he weighed his next words. "I have only those concerns that our household may have offended our Great Numen in some manner, for which we would convey to the Azwans our deepest remorse."

Valeo drew himself up to his full height. His face was still turned toward Babba, but his eyes were on me. They'd always been on me, since the moment I'd stepped outside. I shrunk even as he rose, as if Babba's shoulder would ever be wide enough to hide me completely. Mami's reaction was exactly the opposite of mine. She swept past Babba and bowed effortlessly, one hand on her billowing blouse front, the other arcing outward in a graceful display of humility. I did my best to curtsy without bumping into Babba.

"First Guardsman Valeo," she said.

"Lia of Rimonil," he said.

She straightened at that, and so did I. How did he know her name, too? Maybe he'd indeed been told to watch our house specifically.

Mami donned her most appealing grin, the one that charmed every man on the isle. "I see you already know all of us."

"I know of you," he said. "But I only know one."

Heat swept up the back of my neck as his gaze met mine again and held it.

"My husband and I hope your sojourn to our isle will be a comfortable one for you."

"And brief," he said with a grunt.

"I beg your pardon, First Guardsman?" Mami cocked her head, still smiling, but it was tighter, more forced. Babba leaned toward Mami, as if ready to grab her out of harm's way.

"If your family is truthful, as I believe you to be, then you should also hope our sojourn here will be brief," he said. "And I join you in that wish."

Without Amaniel there, I would've figured such rudeness was a part of being a soldier, having never met any. But Babba's shocked look told me this wasn't standard Temple conversation, and that should've worried me.

Except that I thought the remark was the kind of thing I'd probably say if anyone ever let me, and that made me hotly jealous.

Yes, indeed, we wished his visit here to be extremely brief. Yesterday would've been a great time to have left.

"I assure you, First Guardsman . . ."

Valeo cut her off with a single tap of his pike against the wooden street. "You're to remain indoors until the morning, when your civil authorities will collect your rubbish."

And that would've been that, had Amaniel not shoved past me into the rain. "Oh Pious Keeper of the Unsleeping Vigil over our Great Numen's Borrowed Personage, I wish to know what has become of my . . ."

She didn't finish, because Babba had already yanked her back.

Valeo gave no indication he'd heard. I could feel his eyes on mine, though I looked away. I suppose soldiers could stare at whomever they wished. He could insist until the next rains that he'd accepted my apology, but I wouldn't believe him. And my resolve to apologize again had pretty much vanished with that tap of the pike.

Mami cleared her throat. "There is the matter of two small items you and your men found? My middle daughter wishes to know if . . ."

Another tap of the pike.

"Your high priest will summon you when he is ready," Valeo said. "Now you may go."

Babba crooked his head at Mami, who herded us inside, which I managed to do though my spine was rigid as Amaniel slid indoors without looking at me. I'd thought about apologizing to Valeo again, sure, but there was nothing I wanted to say to him after all the pike tapping and order barking, no apology or excuse-making or exchange of polite whimsies.

If I had to remind myself a few more times, then I would: he was here to do his job, and he did it well. And I both hated and envied him for it.

Babba followed us back inside but stood just inside the doorway, peering out. When I'd go over to see out past him, there would be Valeo's silhouette again on the opposite shore.

"He kept looking at me," I said. "And not at you or Mami."

"I noticed that."

"Why do think that is?"

"For reasons I don't wish for you to dwell on."

I wasn't satisfied with that answer, but I knew better than to push Babba when he didn't feel like talking. So I went back to sweeping, and he stayed by the doorway. Amaniel stayed out of my way and kept herself busy stifling more sobs and folding blankets and clothes. I tried to ignore it, tried to focus on how Babba had defended me, on what he'd said about us as a family staying together. But all I could think was that Amaniel had ripped a limb from me, and I didn't know how to sew myself back together. And then I knew that the limb was Amaniel herself, and she'd ripped us in two, and I needed us to be whole. She had always stood by me in school, when I was frankly an embarrassment even to myself.

We had to be whole. Only it wasn't going to happen just because Babba said so. I sighed and decided to turn in for the night. I needed today to end. I needed to rest and rethink this whole day.

But it wasn't until long after the moons had risen that Babba gave up his vigil by the door.

"Still there," was all he said.

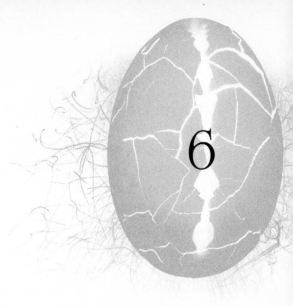

6

The pious may seek refuge within the Temple walls, but there is no shelter for those without merit. Seek no forgiveness from me until I have found you worthy.
        —*from* Oblations 2, The Book of Unease

The rain had finally cleared, but my sandaled feet landed with wet splats as Amaniel marched Rishi and myself to the Ward. Morning had indeed brought another all-clear horn, and constables had made the rounds to tell people to put out their debris. That brought everyone outdoors to sweep and mop and scrub, with workmen hired to haul off barges loaded with trash.

Stuck in Amaniel's head, however, like the refrain of a bad song, was some notion about her being hanged for a scrap of needlework the size of a dinner bowl. She'd paced the floor snuffling and sniffling and hiccuping unhappily. She didn't dare utter a word, but every now and then, she'd gaze around at the piles of sweepings and then over to me, and then her eyes would tear up again, and she'd flop down into the corner.

I finally gave in and decided to take her to the Ward, since the streets seemed busy enough, and there were few soldiers about. Babba had already gone to the Customs House, and Mami wanted to check in on several elderly aunties. She had given her nod to our plan, provided that Rishi—and not me or Amaniel—would be the one to decide if she was scared. And if Rishi was scared, we all turned around for home. Instantly. So be it . . . or else.

The only reason Amaniel gave into Mami's orders was because Rishi herself pointed out that her doll had been taken, and it was only fair she be allowed to go, too.

So Rishi led the way, skipping around knotholes in the planks and playing rhyming games, while Amaniel began muttering under her breath the moment our house was out of view. I was right to realize there'd be no end to her misery short of going with her to Ward Sapphire and watching her throw herself at the high priest's knees, or whatever she'd planned. I don't think she knew, even for all the fuming she did on the long walk there.

I did my big-sisterly duty, escorting them with what I hoped looked like stoic maturity rather than barely concealed mortification. All along our route, people swept up the filth and debris, much as we had. Entire houses leaned where guards had taken an ax to one of the stilts—more than one of the smaller huts had toppled completely and lay half-submerged in the canal. We weaved around piles of salvaged furniture and bigger piles of scavenged wood.

Amaniel plowed on, oblivious to the wreckage, intent on her mission, while I had to tug Rishi away from gawking.

We reached the cobblestone plaza before the wide gates of Ward Sapphire, only to find them firmly barred and manned with Temple guards. That was enough for me. I turned to go, with Rishi asking why we were leaving and Amaniel insisting we weren't.

Well, pluck all the leaves on the Eternal Tree if she didn't decide to get us through those gates anyway. She turned to one side and then another, this way and that, as if searching for someone in particular. Then, apparently finding him, made a diagonal toward one of the soldiers off to one side.

And it was *him*. Again. And staring at us, as if he'd just been lifted and dropped down again in a new spot, with the same hard stance and harder stare. He'd dried off, at least.

I hissed at Amaniel through gritted teeth.

"Why, by Nihil's thumbs, are you headed toward First Guardsman Valeo?" I said.

"He knows us."

"Oh right, he's practically family by now."

Rishi pulled on my sleeve. "He's the only one all by himself."

She was right, of course. She was only five, but an observant little creature. And it wasn't just that Valeo wasn't patrolling in twos or fours, like the others, but stood off as if his isolation was itself a job, like there was some purpose to remaining aloof and alone. He never took his eyes off us as Amaniel strode up to him. I took my time, indulging Rishi in the bugs she needed to stomp or the cracks in the stones that begged for skipping over. Whenever I glanced up, however, his eyes had followed me to my new position, until Amaniel was in front of his helmeted nose. It was as if he didn't even see her. He saw me, though, with a look that made every long, tucked-away strand of my hair stand on end. It was getting harder to remember to look away.

Amaniel cleared her throat. "Great Guardian of Nihil's Person, First Guardsman Valeo."

He didn't even glance at her. "I already know who I am."

"I do, in all piety, gently request entrance to Ward Sapphire for the purpose of . . ."

"No."

". . .pleading my case . . ."

Tap went the pike. On went my sister.

"If I could, with your gentle assistance, great warrior, but gain entrance . . ."

Every muscle went tense on his body, from the vein in his neck that bulged, to the biceps that flexed imperceptibly, the jawline that set like rock—I caught up to my sister and nudged her. I may say the wrong thing, again and again, but I can read people the way Amaniel pores over her scrolls and hand-sewn folios. She'd ignored him, and that was an unwise thing to do.

She brushed me off and smiled up at Valeo, while addressing me in a singsong, patronizing tone. "Hadara, dear sister, perhaps you can wait at a short distance?"

"Hadara," Valeo repeated. "Your name is Hadara."

And then I knew why he stared at me, and I knew why Babba didn't want me to dwell on it.

"I already know who I am," I said, smiling tightly.

Amaniel wheeled toward me and then whipped back again to Valeo, whose eyes were glinting with amusement that didn't register on my nearly overwrought sister. His stance had relaxed almost imperceptibly. "Please, good guardian, forgive my sister, for . . ."

"Follow me," he said with a grunt. Valeo spun on his heels and headed toward the gate, which guards opened for us without so much as a nod from him, as if they'd anticipated him escorting us through. Amaniel held her head high as she whispered a little too loudly, "You see, all it takes is some formality. I wish you'd at least try sometimes."

I congratulated myself for not elbowing her in the head and followed Valeo and his giant strides into the main courtyard. He pointed his pike toward a breezeway to the row of classrooms where I'd sweated out nearly a decade of formal education.

"Your high priest is in one of those classrooms," he said.

Amaniel gushed and thanked him about four different ways, while I simply whispered my own thanks, and I'm the one who got his curt nod by way of reply. As Amaniel began flattering his great guardian worthy self and all that, two more soldiers strode up to Valeo and thumped their right fists, thumb first, against their chests.

"Azwan to see you," said one.

And then the three men were gone, stomping off toward the sanctuary without a backward glance. Amaniel sputtered about how important Valeo must be and how worthy, and brave, and other things that sounded like she had a mountainous crush on the man who'd slashed open our shared mattress and threw its straw stuffing all over our floor. Of course, Amaniel would admire someone with such authority and obvious standing. He was off to see an

Azwan at the Azwan's request, while we were hoping the high priest would grant us a brief moment of begging.

My irritation swelled up in me, so I shrugged it off. "Maybe whichever Azwan just needs a good backscratching with that pike," I began wriggling. "Oh, here, no, a little lower, ooh, that's it!"

Rishi squealed. Amaniel scowled. "You're impossible."

She went into the first classroom in a row of them and came out not too long after, beaming. Rishi hadn't even finished twirling around the breezeway's columns.

But Amaniel wouldn't say a word, not even drop a hint, until we were well on our way back, past the gates, past the guards patrolling the pavilion, nearly halfway to our stretch of boardwalk.

"I suppose you want to know what a mite of courtesy and modesty gets you," Amaniel said. "And don't tell me you're not curious."

"I just want you to be safe," I said. "And if you had to say something extra mightily religious, well, then, I'm proud of you."

She shot a glance at me. "You mean that?"

I nodded. "With all my soul."

I wanted us to be whole, if I could manage to do so without making myself feel worse or making Amaniel believe she'd had no part in ripping us in half.

She took another few steps in silence. "The high priest said he would personally put in a word for me with the Azwans, should they question my devotion."

"So you're out of trouble?"

Amaniel's mouth twitched. "Not exactly. He did say I'd created a graven image."

"So there will be trouble? What kind of punishment did he say you'd face? You can still go to school, right? It wouldn't be worse than that, I hope." I could picture many things worse than being barred from school, but Amaniel would likely disagree. She knew every mark on every bench, every stain on the walls, as well as I knew every footpath out of town.

I had more questions for her, dozens more, but she cut me off.

"Of course, I'm still going to school. The high priest will talk to the Azwans." But her voice didn't sound very assured.

I didn't know what to make of the situation. "Did he say what they wanted with all that stuff?"

"Well, obviously, people have been perfidious."

"Maybe they all just made mistakes, like you."

"I did not make a mistake!" Amaniel picked up her pace. "It's so useless explaining it to you, anyway."

On that, she was right. It would never make sense to me why a patch of cloth and a doll could be worth all this trouble. I gripped Rishi's hand a little harder, as if I could ward off the Temple's might with a few reassuring squeezes of her tiny hand.

Babba came home early that day, looking as if he'd aged a decade overnight. He brought home a basket of fruit and flatbreads from the market so we could have dinner. But once it was over, he ordered Amaniel to take Rishi inside.

She did as she was told. Babba wanted a word with me and Mami. My sagging spirits rallied at the idea that I'd be with the adults and share their secrets, though I didn't savor the idea of any scolding along with it. Babba held a finger to his lips and looked straight at me, a signal to listen in and speak only when he allowed it. Mami hugged a handful of nesting baskets to her chest like they were another child. We used them to gather herbs, and they'd survived in all their simple, woven glory. It was almost worth risking a smile, if Babba hadn't sounded so grim.

"We're being punished," he said. "That's what this whole raid was about. Punishment."

Mami nodded. "But no more so than others."

"Our neighbors will likely blame it on us or people like us. The go-our-own-way sort."

"I was afraid you'd say that."

"Am I wrong? Will our neighbors just shrug this off? This collective warning, this, this big, ugly reminder of the Temple's reach?"

Mami hugged the baskets tighter. They'd been my grandmother's, she once told me. The only thing she had of her dead mother, except her name, which was now mine. Mami paused and stole a few moments to think—I'd seen her do this when she had no clear answer for him. When she spoke, it was with a rueful look at the broken, empty cupboard.

"I thought I was helping. There wouldn't be a market for medicines if not."

Babba edged in closer. "There'd be a market for murder if the Temple looked the other way."

"Oh, please. I'm your wife, not a murderer."

Babba relented, pulling us both into his arms. "This has gone on too long, this odd duet of ours. All the times you go gather your crazy plants, and I drop hints to the Ward that it's all about business, something commercial, a few coppers for your marketing days, that's all."

Mami scowled. "You think the high priest won't be back to take more herbs? I don't know about that. They always want something."

Babba pulled back, his jawline set and his eyes narrowing. "It's Nihil's own men stomping around now, not the Ward. And let's stay away from the Ward until the Sabbath. The girls have no reason to go there with school canceled."

Mami sighed. "It's Amaniel, and she's taking this very hard."

I nodded and made sad eyes at Babba. It was true—the girl's brain had gone all swamp-addled in the last day. How could I have let her storm off there all alone in that state?

But Babba wasn't open to interpreting anyone's mood but his own. "The women of this household have had a little too much independence for their own good. I've been far too indulgent. I am not letting anyone out of shouting range as long as the city's within bowshot of a Temple Guard. They're Nihil's very, very best, I'm told, personally picked by each Azwan. Stay. Home."

I remembered the crude bunch that had taunted me and briefly wondered what the very worst would look like. How much training did it take to rough up a teenage girl? I was always imagining the world of adults would open up to me like a vast, many-petaled moonbloom, radiant and fragrant with its promise of forbidden splendor. What if, in only a few six-days' time, I found myself among the adults battling simply for survival or to keep my hide intact from soldiers or a hundred other hazards? The thought of braving a world full of such violence, a world ruled by the fickle, unpredictable Temple, was beginning to unnerve me. How would I know when I was ready to take my place in that world?

"And you," Babba had turned that hot look at me. "You won't be going back out to those fens with your mother. You're to find a suitable trade for a pious girl until it's time to marry."

He held out his hands to Mami, waiting for the baskets. She turned them over with an irritated huff. He shoved them back into a bin by the hearth with a finality that said we weren't to fish them out for a while, maybe ever.

If my soul were glass, it would be on the floor needing to be swept up with any remaining shards. I had a whole new reason to be miserable. No more fens. A suitable trade. There were only a handful of jobs a woman was allowed to do outside the home. Nihil's navel, I'd be looking after other people's poopy toddlers or hawking secondhand cooking pots from a market stall.

Mami stared at her sandals, her face rumpled and her chin quivery. No more fens together, giggling and gossiping the whole way, hair tucked under reed sun hats like it was a Sabbath every day. Sun hats and work gloves, our idea of uniforms.

Seeing her cry made my own throat seize up again.

The Azwans had to get out of our lives. Their few days here had been enough. If Mami wasn't going to seethe, I could muster enough disgust for the whole family, and then some. I'd been a failure long enough. If I could get them to go, my constant humiliation wouldn't have to keep spreading to my entire family. Amaniel was right. Babba was right. Even Valeo was right. My ignorance and indifference was the pox that infected them all.

Babba noticed Mami's unhappiness and wrapped her in a tight embrace, rocking her, his lips to her forehead. I could see him mouth "love you," and I turned away, embarrassed my parents were getting all tree-sappy sweet on each other, but also relieved. They would make it work. They always did. He did love her, even if it took a day of horrors to pry the words out of him.

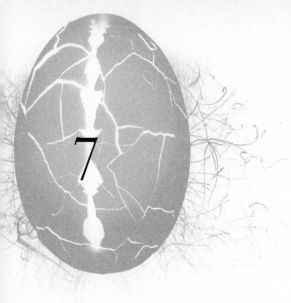

7

The past is not a woolass. It cannot be yoked
And made to pull the plow of our days backward
Nor return our hard harvest of tears to the soil.
We cannot thrash the past into bearing the weight
Of bundled memories to some distant market.

Our pasts are the churning tide, ebbing before us.
We steer ourselves onto the sharp shoals of regret
Again and again, unable to free ourselves
From the unyielding grip of its undertow
Until the mercy we would claim as our future
Has drowned in our wake.
                    —*by Markden of Ilyadell,*
                    translated from the Fernai

By the next morning, our house was as tidied as we could make it, the rugs smoothed against the tile floor, the furniture righted and pottery shards buried out back. Just in time, as the neighbors were dropping by our hearth again. Mami had no tea to make or glasses to serve it in, so they sat with their hands folded and lips sealed and watched the swollen canals carry away odd bits of clothing, wooden bowls, and other flotsam from people's lives.

"Nihil sows doubt among us," someone would say.

"His way is uncertain, his path marked by discord," another would add. That would bring a "so be it" or two before everyone lapsed into silence again, not wanting to talk but not wanting to go home. An uncle from several streets over insisted I should praise Nihil to have escaped my brush with the soldiers without harm. He'd heard other girls hadn't been so lucky. They'd have to cut their hair as a mark of their shame. Only the chaste—virgin girls and married women—could keep their hair long, if modestly hidden.

Mami overheard us talking and waggled a finger. "Why is it always the woman's fault? The soldiers have prostitutes in town they could've used. It's their shame for what they've done."

A few people shook their heads at Mami. I could hear murmurs, but only a neighbor, a healer friend of Mami's, spoke. "When we've mastered our doubts, Lia, our faith will be strong."

Mami rolled her eyes at the platitude. "Small comfort."

I sidled up next to her. "Well, why is it always our fault? Why is it that way in Scriptures, too? It's always *us* tempting *them*."

But it was already too late for an answer. Babba put a hand on Mami's sleeve, and changed Mami's whole demeanor. I could see the defiance slip away as her shoulders sagged. She was remembering Babba's warning.

"Yes, of course," Mami said. "When I've mastered my doubts, my faith will be strong."

One of my old aunties beamed up at her. "Ah, Lia dear, and Hadara, you know we all love you, but the Azwans won't care what you mean to us. We're just looking out for you."

Mami sighed. "I know, I know. And the girls, too. They should learn from a better example than their nearly heretical mother."

The auntie chuckled. "And that's why you send them to school. Though Hadara, you're out in the wilds at least once a six-day, no? That'll have to stop."

I didn't need the reminder that my beautiful fens were a world away until the Azswans were gone.

The healer friend of Mami's stood and stretched. "I likely have some healing to do. You should come with me."

"I have no more herbs. And I wouldn't dare use them if I did."

"Nihil's ambiguities are the best salves. It is for us to trust the mystery of his intent, darling Lia."

The two women strolled off arm in arm with a fluttering of skirts, and I caught a glimpse of Mami smiling as they turned the corner. I had no idea why Mami thought school would be a better example than hers, when her kindness did more for people than lashes with a stick. Why didn't that bring honor to families, instead of how fervently one prayed?

For myself, my uncle's warning reminded me yet again of the hated half-human soldier. My thoughts wound around like a skiff caught in a whirlpool to the moment

Valeo had pulled the other guard away from me. Many other Feroxi didn't seem to have any sense of restraint at all, if what my uncle said was true. I wanted to believe Valeo had some sense of honor the others didn't. I wanted to believe the impossible.

Why was that so important to me, to believe in one man's goodness? I'd grown up surrounded by good people. Sure, they gossiped all the time, and not all of it was very pleasant, and much of it was about Mami and myself. But they were good, at least by my definition. They shared hearths and cookpots and often food and passed along hand-me-downs to strangers and looked out for each other's kids and old folks. I could count on anyone at our hearth to look after me if I were sick.

Surely, such people existed on the mainland, too, and had birthed and raised these soldiers like my aunties and uncles had raised their sons. Yet the soldiers believed they had a right to do what they had done, and that Nihil himself approved. I couldn't reconcile cheerful Feroxi mothers sending their big boy-men off to school with the idea they'd approve of their actions here.

I sighed and stared down the walkway where the healer and Mami had gone, only to see them hustling back again, waving and shouting to everyone to come quick and pointing toward the canal. Like most of the houses in Port Sapphire, ours was a rickety triangle on stilts on a shady peninsula. These stuck out like scores of jagged fingers, each sporting several clusters of homes and hearths. Canals wove between and around us, with boardwalks built on either side, forming a crazy maze of both watery and wooden thoroughfares that threaded through the city.

We raced to where the healer pointed. A man on the opposite bank was trying to lift something out of the water with a long pole.

It was a body. A man, it looked like, naked except for a tangle of weeds and brambles. He'd been strapped to a barrel to keep him afloat, but the barrel kept rolling and bobbing, the man's body submerging and resurfacing in the swollen canal. The rushing waters kept tugging the lip of the barrel away from the pole's tip, and the man holding it was getting frustrated. He was leaning as far as he could without falling in. Two men on our side clambered into one of the many small boats moored to the boardwalk.

"Hurry!" people shouted.

The canal swept the body free of the pole. The rowers pulled with the tide, and a few swift oar strokes brought them downstream of the body. It didn't take long to free it from the barrel, pull it out of the water, and turn it over as the women and girls shied away so we wouldn't see the parts a man keeps hidden. All I could see were flashes of blue-gray skin and knots of hair and seaweed. The men rowed back, and, with the waters high enough to lap the boardwalk, the other men heaved the body out of the boat. The man was portly, and his body required the help of nearly every man there to lift so much deadweight and ease it onto the ground.

Babba let out a cry. "The Lord Portreeve."

The words echoed across the crowd. The Lord Portreeve had drowned. Mami shook her head and sighed. Other women dabbed their eyes with the corners of their head scarves. He had a reputation for drinking; I hoped it hadn't killed him. My stomach had rolled along with the sight of the barrel bobbing in the water, and it wasn't settling down any. Drowned. But how did he end up on a barrel?

"Not drowned," a male voice said. Then Babba again: "He's been murdered."

Cries went through the women. Mami grabbed Rishi, and I grabbed Amaniel, who clung back, as if whoever had killed his lordship might be among us. Forget modesty, though; I wanted to know what had happened. So did Amaniel, and the two of us tried to push closer. Through the mass of arms and shoulders, however, all I could see was the bloated outline of the man and that horrid, mottled skin. Someone moved aside, and I got a single glimpse of a wide gash at his throat, emptied of blood to a bluish white. His death mask bore all the signs of a violent death, his head thrown back at a garish angle, the mouth agape, tongue swollen, a face forever locked in silent screaming.

I clung to Amaniel, my breath coming in pained wheezes while I fought to control the upheaval in my stomach. I shut my eyes, breathed deeply, and slowly opened them.

The healer squeezed in next to his lordship's body and knelt over him. "Slit his throat."

More murmurs and gasps around me. But curiosity is a hard taskmaster, as they say. It drives people on even when they should know better. The two of us girls peered between elbows and shoulders as the healer kept talking.

"And burned a mark on his chest. Someone meant to send us a message."

"What mark?" several asked at once. Others elbowed us girls aside for their own peek. "Looks like an Eternal Tree," someone said. "Not a Feroxi rose?" "No, definitely not." The Eternal Tree, where pious souls congregated after death. So it was the Temple. The burn mark would be the same symbol as on my school uniform, Nihil's promise to the virtuous—and his implicit threat to the wicked. I guess I hadn't thought about who decided who went to the Eternal Tree, or who got dumped in a canal. What had the man done to deserve damnation? He was a drunk and a fool, but there were worse sins, weren't there?

Everyone had an opinion on the man's death. The verdict: obviously he'd angered the Temple.

"No, no, the Azwan of Ambiguity had flattered him," Babba said.

A woman's voice came from the rear: "You don't think the portreeve was the one, do you? The dybbuk?"

Everyone turned to Babba. We may share hearths with other families, but it's as if my Babba owns every place he sets foot in. I grew up believing if he didn't have the answer to a question, then you shouldn't have asked it. But the Temple was making me doubt even that. There were things Babba didn't know and couldn't understand. The fens, for example. Why let Mami and me go out there all these years just to take it away?

The commotion sent me to the edge of the crowd, and then I backed away even farther to put distance between myself and the grim spectacle. First, the heap of men at the boat launch. Now this. It was too many bodies for me in such a short time. An argument developed over whether to carry the dead man back to his family or spare him this last humiliation through the streets. Someone suggested rowing him back, and that was quickly rejected as again too public. Finally, a neighbor retrieved a rug and wrapped the man like a giant sausage roll. It'd be funny, but it wasn't.

Babba led the men who carried off the portreeve, hoisted with grunts and groans onto half a dozen shoulders, and the rest of the crowd thinned and headed for their homes as if that offered some semblance of safety. I looked my house up and down, the creaky boards and flaked paint, the frayed thatching, the broken-down door propped clumsily up again, and knew I didn't want to be there at the moment. Babba was wrong—our home was no safer than the streets. I could've died or lost my honor right there on the floor of our house. I hugged my sides and dug my nails into my arms, but it didn't help.

No, I couldn't face it. The canals weren't safe. Nor were the boardwalks or my own home. It all reminded me too much of how I wasn't up to the Temple's standards. None of us were, but me most of all. No one else in this city should have to feel this way. No one should be tainted with the scourge of my stupidity and awkwardness around all things religious. Even Amaniel was balking at me these days. It didn't matter if I read better than any of the girls in school, or as much, or could do numbers and plot star charts or doodle plants that looked lifelike. I didn't belong, and Babba said the city was going to blame any new misfortune or unwanted attention on people like us—like me.

Before I was really conscious of having made the decision, I had slipped onto the main boardwalk and was following it north, away from the Ward, away from home, toward a stretch of beach usually crowded with couples holding hands or children tossing pebbles into the roaring surf. The beach faced toward the open sea, and I wanted to drown my worries in its steady thunder.

As the houses thinned, I passed the low-lying croplands and became aware that I wasn't alone. The sound of distant bootsteps reverberated forward. I glanced over my shoulder.

I don't know why I was surprised to see Valeo stomping along after me. This put to rest the idea he'd been assigned to routine patrol by our house earlier. I slowed my pace and then stopped, wondering if I should run, and where. Ahead of me lay the beach, which I could see was deserted. Why hadn't I listened to Babba? I didn't even care about the trouble I'd be in. I'd rather have him hollering loud enough for half the city to hear than be in this spot at this moment with that terrible man coming up behind me.

My first instinct was to bolt through the rows of crops, but I fought that back. Something was wrong. Something that didn't have anything to do with Valeo. The air was unnaturally still. No birds, no people, no movement. No birds. At all. Not one cry or chirp or flutter of wings.

I glanced around at row crops to either side and spotted a flash of glowing eyes, low to the ground, and far too close. A mash cat swished its tail and crept forward on its haunches. Adult, and big, and no doubt hungry. It was near sunset, its usual hunting time. As bony as I was, I was still an easier catch than a crane. After all, I couldn't fly away. I spread both legs as wide as I could and slowly, cautiously raised both arms over my head, making my body as large as possible. I kept my eyes locked on the cat's and waited.

I spread one hand out to stop Valeo, and I shushed him, without breaking my lock on the glowing eyes. I could deal with only one predator at a time.

"No sudden moves," I whispered.

From the corner of my eye, I could see Valeo raise his pike as he eased toward my side. He must've spotted the danger, as he placed his shield in front of both of us, the pike raised over my shoulder. I was close enough to feel his breath on my neck and the coarse friction of leather armor against the back of my dress.

We didn't move.

The cat's eyes shifted from one of us to the other, taking in our larger size and making its own mental calculations of how to take one down while avoiding the other. Finally, it backed away with a few frustrated snarls before bounding toward a stand of trees. I'd have to tell lookouts later to flush it out of its hiding place so close to the city. I lowered my arms and relaxed my stance, but Valeo didn't budge. It felt invasive, to have him so close with the danger past.

"What was that thing?"

I angled my head to see him staring down his helmet edge to me. "You don't have mash cats on the mainland?"

"Can't say I'm sorry for it. Looks like it would eat all the livestock."

"And people, too."

He humphed. "So why create a bigger target for it?"

I answered with a puzzled look and slid out from under his arm. A little distance felt more right than not.

He slung the shield over his back as we edged away, and I walked backward for a few paces, peering around the shield, making sure the mash cat didn't change its mind. When we'd gone far enough for me to feel fairly safe, I turned back around, and we instinctively headed for the city and safety.

He shook his head at me. "You stretched for it. You have a death wish? Or just practicing your morning prayers?"

Morning prayers involved a dance-like series of stretches while we chanted, called the Dance of Life. I managed to let a piece of smile escape as I turned to him.

"You have to make yourself as big as possible to trick it," I said. "It has to decide I'm not worth all the effort it would take to bring me down."

"I think you'd be worth every effort to bring down. I missed my chance back at your house."

A trembling ran through me, starting from my shoulders and fanning outward, until all of me shivered. My breathing grew ragged, and all I could think was that it— that terrible, unthinkable thing—was going to happen here, now. My body recoiled, turning halfway around, my eyelids squeezed shut. I managed only a hoarse whisper. "Please don't. You said you wouldn't."

He spoke after a quick intake of air. "I didn't . . . this isn't . . . ah, Nihil's nuts. It was a joke. A bad one, apparently."

I couldn't bring myself to look at him. My fear was giving way to rage. How dare he. A joke? It wasn't a joke that any woman in Port Sapphire would laugh about. It was disgusting. Disrespectful.

"Maybe you joke about such things, where you come from."

He held up one hand, the pike balanced in the crook of his elbow. "If you're about to insult my native lands, stop there."

"I need to go."

"Wait, what did you come here for, then?"

"To be alone. To think. To get away from you and people like you." I'd hoped to sound angry, but it came out as defeated, an admission there was no way to win with him around. And it was true; I just wanted one precious moment to collect all the shambled pieces of the last few days and piece them back together.

Valeo was stuck in those same moments as I was and wasn't letting go. "Why, have you run out of vulgar names to call me? Or does everyone on this sting-fly-riddled isle think like you do, that I'm some bastard mongrel . . ."

"I don't think that," I said. This was escalating too fast for my liking, from a few sparks to the threat of a flash fire, and I was going to have to quench it fast. "I was hoping you'd forget it."

"I have a long memory." His head angled down toward me, until I could see the flash of his pupils from behind the bronze plating that apparently kept his head from falling off. His feelings were still all bruised and rubbed raw from the other day.

There was only one thing to do, which meant taking a big bite of my pride and swallowing it whole.

"If it helps, I'll apologize again, now that I've thought about it," I said. "Now that I've seen the word's effect on you."

"Why should you care about your effect on me?"

I drew a huge breath and slowed my pace, lowered my tone, and held eye contact until it almost hurt. "First Guardsman Valeo, I know that you're anxious to be done with your mission and be gone from here. But if what I said—anything I've said—has contributed to your feeling unwelcome, then I apologize."

I dropped my gaze to the ground, as Mami had taught me to do, like some helpless, cuddly she-cub. It's a simple trick to work on a man when you've overstepped your bounds, Mami had said, and it works every time. I glanced back up briefly.

Mami definitely knows her man-lore.

Even from within his helmet, it was hard to miss the raised eyebrows. His jaw dropped, and his own tone grew suddenly lighter.

"You mean that." It was a statement. "Thank you."

Well, why did I care about my effect on him? For one thing, it did seem like I'd increased my chances of getting home safely. "You're a guest here, and I've been an ungracious host."

I let drop the thought that most guests didn't upend their hosts' homes.

"Nihil break my bones, but I'm also sorry for frightening you just now," he said. "I came to see if you were out gathering contraband. Your family has a . . . reputation."

I almost laughed. He only meant the usual sort of harm the Ward was always threatening. "I came for a walk on the beach. I promise by all Nihil's incarnations."

"May they be infinite."

"May they be infinite." I nodded agreement.

"And if you'd stooped to pluck so much as a flower," he said, "I would've killed you."

I gasped. Killed? It was a flower—a hypothetical one. Would he really have . . . but wait, a flash of insight flared into my thick head. "You pounded along this boardwalk like it insulted you. If I had been out picking flowers, you weren't exactly sneaking up on me. It's as if you wanted me to notice you. To warn me, perhaps?"

Was that a grin, lopsided and toothy, or a smirk or a leer? A smirk, I decided.

"Looks like I came along in time," he said. "Before you danced that mash cat creature into submission."

I took my time forming an answer. I'd tried to imagine that he had some basic goodness or a sense of honor about him, more than the other guards. But I didn't want to make an idiot of myself for believing too much of him too soon.

"You've been outside my house. Guarding it? Why?"

I didn't like the way he shook his head and grimaced. "We've all taken up posts around your city."

"And you chose my house? Or were ordered?"

His eyes darted around, everywhere but at my own, avoiding me. "Doesn't matter. Not your place to question what we're here to do."

I sucked in my breath. He was veering back toward sparks and flames again. "I . . . I think what you're doing, what you're all doing . . . I know you have orders. I know the Azwans think there is a demon. It's just too much to take in, to understand. So frightening."

"You don't seem like much frightens you. Or does everyone here do the Dance of Life for savage beasts?"

"No, just me. Most people would run. And the cat would run after." What did an ordinary mash cat have to do with the Temple? It seemed a stretch to compare the two.

"Ah. So Hadara doesn't run." He stroked his chin as if contemplating this. "She stands her ground, and when she gets knocked around, she gets back up, ties up a man's tongue, and flips her head of curls at him. That mash cat was lucky to get away while it could."

"Why are you saying such things to me?"

"It's called flirting. I'm better at it over a flask of wine. You should join me."

Mami's advice had worked too well.

"No, I'm going home, please." I hoped I sounded firm. "If you'd escort me."

"And I'm going to pretend you were really out for a casual stroll during a citywide curfew."

"Curfew?" I glanced back at the empty beach. "I feel very stupid. What is the punishment for this curfew?"

"Just to get arrested and questioned."

I didn't like the sound of that. "And why haven't you arrested me?"

"Would you like me to?"

"No, of course not. What I mean is, you keep saying all these scary things to me but never do them, which is good for me, but are you always like this?" He didn't strike me as soft, and he'd said at the house that he wasn't the forgiving kind. He was a puzzle, this armored hulk who was easily bruised. And he'd stomped around noisily so I wouldn't pick flowers, and the other day he'd ordered his comrades not to harm me, when they easily could've.

He sighed. "Do you think I should notch my pike for everyone I harm? It's not like I'm out looking for reasons."

"And should I find that reassuring?" We'd begun walking back, more like strolling, passing the first outcrop of houses. I no longer felt in any danger, and unnerving conversations about killing and violence were starting to seem fairly normal with him.

"I take no pleasure in killing, if that's what you mean. In your case, I might have to think hard on it."

"You like me." As soon as I'd blurted that out, I wished I hadn't. What could I have meant by that?

He stiffened and looked ahead, not at me. "Nothing can come of any friendship between us."

"I know. You don't want to like me. You want to leave here and go home." His denial stung. He liked me. I didn't know how I knew, but by Nihil's navel, I knew. "Where is home?"

"Wherever Nihil sends me."

"Have you no family?"

The helmet hid too much of his face for me to read his expression, but the change to a more guarded voice, one of caution and unspoken meanings, was easy enough to understand. "The guards are my family."

"I have a very large family," I said, lightening things before he started stamping that pike again. "You can borrow them, if you like. They're very good at ordering people around. Just try to return them unharmed, yes?"

He chuckled at that. "I'd like that. I came from a small family, but . . . but that was long ago. I'm alone, pretty much."

"You miss them?"

He started to nod and then stopped. "The past is not a woolass. It cannot be yoked."

I recognized the poem. "Our pasts are the churning tide, ebbing before us."

"Markden. I didn't know your island would have the translations."

"We're not *that* remote. The Customs House has a few of his scrolls, and many others. The merchants bring them from their travels. They swap them around, what with ships always coming and going."

He grinned. "Like the way Feroxi trade weapons and tools. I like it."

"You ought not to like anything about us. It'd make it harder to leave."

"Nothing would make it hard to leave this place."

"Sorry." I sighed. This conversation was getting nowhere, but at least our feet had gotten me home. My house was around the next bend in the boardwalk. Maybe Valeo wasn't a good man like the men I'd grown up around, always volunteering at the Ward or fixing old ladies' roofs or making elaborate toys for orphans or going about some important business something. But I knew he was trying.

The question was why. I didn't believe for a moment it was because he imagined I'd flirt with him over a flask of wine, either.

I wheeled on my toes and stared up at him. He stared back and waited for me to speak.

"The mercy we would claim as our future has drowned in our wake," I said, reciting the last line of the Markden poem. "Don't drown yourself, First Guardsman Valeo."

He exhaled a long, ragged breath. "What am I to make of you, Hadara of Rimonil?"

"You said nothing could come of any friendship between us. Yet any two people who can chase off a mash cat together aren't enemies, either. So: friends."

He nodded. "Friends."

I wheeled with a last flounce of my skirts and gathered them up enough to stride smoothly the rest of the way home without a backward glance, giving Valeo a last glimpse of my calves. That wasn't exactly unchaste, but it felt like the closest I could get to flirting. Babba had already come out onto the boardwalk to watch for me. As I reached him, I gave only a backward glance at Valeo, who was nodding to Babba in that way men have of communicating just with looks and grimaces and grunts and such. How they manage to say so much with so little, I don't suppose even Mami knows. Man-lore. It's a mystery.

Only the creases in Babba's face gave away his anxiety for me. I'd obviously worried him and ought to have felt more ashamed of that, I suppose. If I'd come back alone, I'd likely have faced a tongue-lashing, but instead, I was simply told to go help Mami at the hearth for all our guests.

It was Mami who satisfied everyone's curiosity on what that soldier had wanted with me, giving me a chance to natter on about curfews and the mash cat to oohs and ohs before I was loading a platter of charred redroot, lentils, and summer greens for supper. I pretended to be too busy to hear any other conversation, and this was true—I knew I would revisit my encounter with Valeo in my head a dozen or more times before the evening was through.

Our exchange, from the threats to the jokes and back again, crowded out any other thought, with his words and mine pooling like a school of fish darting beneath the surface of my waking moments, bright flashes of silver to distract my gaze and keep me guessing.

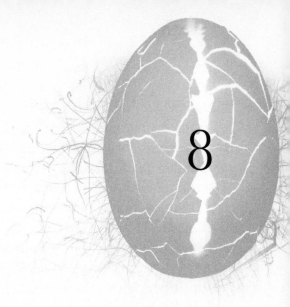

8

I shall bless those appointed by me for special ser-
vice. Among these shall be the high priests of my
Temple, and higher than that are those who in
the vulgate tongue are called Azwans, meaning
Navigators. They shall steer you toward me, that
you may never waiver from the true course.
—*from Oblations 11,* The Book of Unease

Although I'd joked there were at least a hundred reasons
Valeo shouldn't think twice about an ignorant island girl,
there must be a thousand reasons—without exaggerat-
ing—why I shouldn't be wasting so much thought on him.
I needed a distraction, something besides platters of piping
hot food, or I'd end up cleaning them by eating everything
on them.

I hadn't forgotten the reason for Valeo's being here in
the first place, or what the Temple Guards' presence meant
to our normally busy port. It's just that it was hard to feel
any danger any longer, what with Valeo making threats

he didn't keep and even agreeing to friendship. I couldn't grasp the reality of trouble of any sort, as if the Azwans and their new curfew had settled into being merely inconvenient rather than ominous.

Fortunately, I had an Azwan to set me straight and re-instill the proper sense of terror the Temple seemed to prefer. Before anyone could get too comfortable over supper, our chatter was drowned out by a commotion farther south, toward the Ward pavilion. Babba and the other men got up to see what was the matter, and Rishi ran up and hugged Babba's legs. He hugged back, looking thoughtful.

As if by some unheard call, the pounding of giant boots resounded on our boardwalk. No one moved. More soldiers came. With them strode S'ami. Even if I hadn't recognized him, his clothes gave him away. Not many people could afford that much spider silk. Flowering vines seemed to sprout along his chest and toward his shoulders, even curling on his shaved head.

As he drew close, I could see the flowers were an illusion created by beadwork, painstaking and minute, on a breastplate and skullcap that blossomed with thousands of seed beads shaped into a shining tropical garden. He was wearing his wealth, and it suited what little I knew of his character. Impressive, though. Maybe I was simply predisposed to hating him. I shrunk back to the safety of the crowd to watch the spectacle S'ami proudly made of himself, and my thighs clenched together of their own accord, remembering his power over me at the pier.

He headed straight for our cluster and held up a hand to stop everyone from scurrying off. Soldiers took up positions at rigid attention, pikes at their sides. I searched for

Valeo and didn't see him; then I hated myself for feeling disappointed.

"Good people, have you some celebration here?" S'ami asked. "An odd day for one, wouldn't you say?"

Babba was standing in front of the others, as this was his house and his patio, and everyone looked to him, even the neighbors who lived right beside us. He made the cupping motions with his hands before his chin as he bowed. Then he straightened, and became again the tall, imposing man whom everyone liked to surround. "My neighbors come only seeking news, Most Cryptic of Nihil's Servants."

"And what news is there?"

"I do not know, sir. It is from you that news would come."

"So you anticipated my visit?"

"No, Most Worthy. We are nonetheless grateful for it."

The Azwan gave Babba such an ominous stare that the distance in heights appeared to vanish. "So, you desire news from me yet didn't know I would be here. Wouldn't you seek me at your Ward?"

Babba bowed again. "I don't believe any of us would presume to bother a mighty Azwan at the Ward."

"What good then would it do to gather here and wait for news? Or do you simply invent it?"

"I don't believe I understand, Most Worthy."

"I'm told your people are good at determining the value of nearly anything. A pity the truth isn't one of them."

Ah, see, another trap, just like in school. Only the schoolmistress could use a few lessons of her own. S'ami was a master. Nihil must really love tripping people with their own words, since it seemed something the most pious people were good at. I hoped Amaniel flunked that particular lesson. My father chafed. We all did. We were all bowing, some nearly to their knees. "Have we offended you, sir?" Babba said.

"Your Lord Portreeve dared lie to the Temple of Doubt." S'ami tapped his foot impatiently.

"Your Worthiness?"

"He could not lead me to the Gek. He didn't in fact trade with them, despite his boasting. I had to learn through much difficulty it's actually a woman who comes and goes among them. She knows their hand gestures and has walked in their trees. You know this woman."

It wasn't a question. Babba straightened as Mami took slow steps forward. She'd been right again, and the Temple had something to ask of her. Babba reached an arm around and held her tightly. "My honored wife, Lia."

Mami rested a hand on Babba's side and met the Azwan's gaze straight on. His broad mouth cracked into a grin, but there was no warmth to it. "You are Lia, wife of Rimonil, then."

Her voice was soft, almost imperceptible. "Most Worthy."

"Your family has a history of defying the Temple. Am I right?"

"We serve the Temple as do others, each according to our gifts, great Azwan."

"A good answer. It'll suffice. I'd be reluctant to see you meet your mother's fate when I'm apparently in some need of you."

Mami blanched at that and bowed her head. She, too, made the cupping motion under her chin. Again, a mention of my grandmother. That made twice in two days. I had never heard the full story of her death. What I did know made me fear for Mami. My grandmother had been hanged and her body dumped in a canal and ordered left there for the wild animals.

S'ami accepted Mami's hand-cupping with a curt nod. "I'm sure it isn't easy to earn the Gek's trust. A pity you'll have to betray it."

"Please, what is this about?"

"We leave before daybreak for their swamp. They won't willingly give up what we seek, if they have it, so there'll be soldiers. I can't guarantee your safety, but I assume you're smart enough not to protest."

Mami's voice betrayed no emotion. "I can talk with them, perhaps . . ."

"Perhaps. And perhaps they'll kill us while you're chatting." The Azwan took a step toward Amaniel, who'd crept in behind Mami. He pinched her cheek. "You're the daughter she's training?"

At least this time, leaping forward didn't seem rash but the sensible thing to do. I lunged in front of Amaniel and registered the look of recognition that flashed on S'ami's face. His expression remained neutral as I spoke, and I squelched the urge to flee screaming. It wasn't fear for my sister that made me do it. I had no doubt Mami would straighten matters out, given a chance, but it'd be just like Amaniel to want to trail along into the swamps in some twisted sense of reverence.

Indeed, she was smiling, both hands over her heart, the very portrait of adoration, with her eyes wide and lips parted. I elbowed past her. The good sister had to stay home, where she belonged.

"You'll want me along, Azwan. I'm the natural one. Hadara."

A quick glance around at all the stern faces told me I'd said something unseemly. I added a quick "Your Worthiness" and did my best hand-cupping beneath my chin, inwardly shrinking for this display of subservience. I was always bowing and scraping to a priest or a teacher and yet always somehow getting it wrong. I swore I'd figure out all this protocol and tradition someday, but obviously not this day. I wrapped my arm around Amaniel in what I'd hoped a sisterly fashion, more for boosting my own bravery than hers.

The Azwan waved dismissively. "Hadara, the natural one. Not a title I'd be proud of, if I were you. It seems you're going to keep shouting at me until I find some use for you. Alright, you come. You'll learn some piety if you make it back tomorrow. Not to mention manners."

He strode off a moment later with a last flutter of amethyst silk, his soldiers falling in behind him. I exhaled crisply and tried not to look around at all the mortified faces. I didn't think they were mad at me, but once again I'd made myself an easy target for other people's blame. The natural one. Why did I say that? How stupid could I be? To love anything natural was to hate all that Nihil could do for us through magic. I may as well have stood on Ward Sapphire's rooftop and shouted that I'm an unrepentant doubter. At least I'd gotten my wish—that I'd be going along on their mission, whatever it was.

I wanted to be rid of the Azwans already. Either one or both. Both. I didn't have many skills the Temple of Doubt considered useful, and the ones I did have were likely going to be the death of me. S'ami had already said we were unlikely to return the next day, so I was going to need every copper-weight of smarts and strength I'd ever possessed.

Maybe I knew less than I should about the Temple and much more about things the Temple didn't want to know. There had to be an advantage in there somewhere. If there was anything in Mami's lore that could keep religious men at bay, Mami could make them go, but I knew in my soul she'd never risk seeing us harmed—any of us, even down to the most distant cousin. That left me—and the Gek. If those creatures had found something the Temple wanted, then I wanted it first. Maybe it had some power, or maybe it was something to trade, and maybe I could manage to do so without getting myself killed.

I exhaled crisply and watched S'ami disappear the way he'd come, my resolve wavering. Take on the Temple? Of course, and make Kuldor rotate backwards, too.

But one glance at Babba changed my mind back again. He was staring past where the Azwan had gone, his mouth open, stock-still, his hand poised above Mami's shoulder, frozen.

He looked like a man who'd just been told his wife and oldest daughter would die the next day.

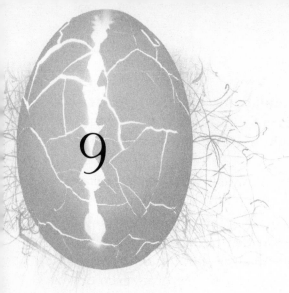

9

Gold at dusk, then silv'ry bright,
Mighty Lunyo rules the night;
Qamra flaunts a changing mien,
While Keth's bright orb is seldom seen.
— *"The Three Moons," a children's rhyme*

I couldn't sleep on what promised to be my last night alive.
I drifted off in fits of almost-dreaming but then lurched
back into a sad, tossy-turny wakefulness. My mind darted
between thoughts of the haughty Azwan and remembering how it felt to be behind Valeo's shield, his chest to my
back, the heat of his breath on my neck. I'd try to recall
what I could see of Valeo's face beneath his helmet and
then squeeze my eyelids shut as if they could scrub away
the image like a stain.

Then my imagination would dive into the next day's
mission. I was calling it that in my head, as if I, too, were a
Temple Guard. A mission. My mission. I tried to go over
how I might escape or fight back. I couldn't outrun Gek,

and I had no skill with weapons. I'd be among soldiers and the Azwans, who would insist I help them get whatever it was they thought the Gek might have.

What could they have? Some sort of rock from the night sky that S'ami wasn't calling a meteorite? I'd noticed that. He and other clerics, priests, and Azwans alike, had been referring to it as a star or a demon, or both. Amaniel wasn't much help. She'd repeated what she'd told me on the pier the day the Temple's ships came—Nihil couldn't battle a demon from the stars in person or we'd all die in some terrible fire. She'd shown me the passage in Scriptures, but it didn't tell me what could possibly be alive in a fallen piece of moon or however such things came to be.

All I knew was that come morning I would die, and Mami too, and probably some soldiers, unless I was badly overestimating the Gek.

All for this star-demon. What was it? I watched Lunyo wax full and cast chalky moonbeams through the slats in the window onto the wide divan, where my sisters slept beside me. As the moon rose, its stripes of pale light broadened to a series of horizontal bands that worked their way across the room. As a tot, I'd memorized that Lunyo is the Feroxi moon, the biggest and brightest. Humans get rotating Qamra, who can't sit still or make up her mind. And tiny Keth, like the Gek, darts out of reach in its elliptical orbit. Myths, all of them, but with rational and natural workings beneath them. So what would be rational about the star-demon? What laws of nature did it obey?

I had always loved astrology. I wished I could sneak over to my chest of drawers and pull out my star maps with all my scribbled notes. I wondered what moons Valeo would've been born under. Perhaps both Lunyo and Qamra, the Feroxi and human moons, with traits of both. Steadfast and fiercely loyal on the one hand, adventurous but fickle on the other. What destiny was wrapped up in the mooncast of this soldier who kept threatening me and then changing his mind?

Twice in my lifetime, I'd seen Lunyo and Qamra full together, making evening as bright as twilight. It made for a fierce spring tide, when we could walk near halfway out the harbor, and flocks of cranes had dived and darted for stranded crayfish. The last time had been when Mami was pregnant with Rishi, watching us lazily, feet dangling off the boardwalk, and rubbing her tummy while Babba twirled his two daughters in crazy dances through the suddenly shallow canal. We'd splashed and kicked, swirling wetly to made-up songs, peals of giggles splitting the eerie half-light.

I wanted to believe in double moonlights and impossibilities.

Alone in the shimmering rays, I thought and over-thought scenarios that could work against the Gek, things I could say or explain or ask. Mami and I had only been out that far a few times this year, but it was a few times more than anyone else. I stood a chance if the Gek had no more idea about a star-demon than I did. We could all beat an apologetic retreat and be home for supper.

But S'ami had waved that gold totem of his and insisted he'd felt something. That was another mystery to me. Amaniel had shrugged when I asked, saying he'd have told us what he was feeling if he'd wanted us to know. The girl could be a mountain of not-helpfulness.

I bunched my blanket around me, and Amaniel woke with a start. I hadn't meant to do that and whispered my apology; then I told her why I wasn't sleeping.

"When we've mastered our doubts," she said, "our faith will be strong."

"I know," I said. But I didn't.

"The Azwan stared at you at the Customs House. It's right you should go."

"He remembered me today."

"Of course." She propped herself up on one elbow. "He is certain. We are uncertain. That's why he's here to minister to us."

"Then why isn't he the Azwan of Certainty?"

She groaned. "You're the worst student, Hadara. We learned why back in first year."

There was no denying my ignorance. "Well, if I had a temple, worshippers would be certain."

We both muffled our giggles into our sleeves, and Amaniel tucked in closer to me. "I'll miss you. I know I said horrible things. I'm sorry. I really will miss you."

"I'm not dead yet."

"I hope they bring your body back. You can't wait for us beneath the Eternal Tree if we can't cremate you."

"Amaniel!" More not-helping. I wasn't ready for the Eternal Tree and greeting all my dead relatives. I didn't even know those people. "Don't you want me to come back alive?

"Oh, Nihil's earlobes, yes. I'll cry a lot if you really do die. But at least you'd be martyred in the fight against the dybbuk. Nihil would remove all doubts from your name."

"I suppose."

"He would, Scripture promises. You'll see."

I won't, I wanted to say. Not if I'm dead. I squeezed Amaniel's hand instead. A pair of skinny legs thrashed on the other side of me. Rishi was stirring. Amaniel and I shushed her, tucked her blanket close around her, and settled back down to rest. I closed my eyes and tried to focus on a memory of Qamra and Lunyo full together, outshining the stars.

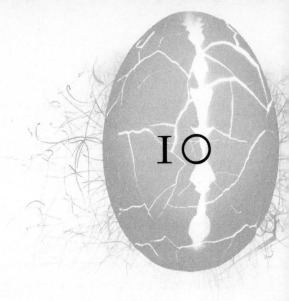

10

From winds and from water, from stardust and sand, Kuldor sculpted men and women from the gifts I had given him. Two peoples I saw first: one towering and proud, the other shorter, with handsome, even features. Then Kuldor pointed overhead to the treetops, where I saw the mud-and-stick huts of another people.

Who are they? I asked.

Lizards, he replied, with skin like jewels.

I like them best, I said, as they are small and live simply.

But the lizard people ran from me and hid.

> *— from "The Creation of the Races,"*
> *Verisimilitudes 2,* The Book of Unease

Brown snakes as thick as a man's arm slid from branches on either side of our punt and into the water, where they writhed across the murky surface. The boat paused to avoid them and then skirted the narrow, spiked waterwood roots that poked above the water line. A pole wedged between several roots the puntsman couldn't see, and he twisted it free.

I shared the narrow craft with Mami and S'ami and two guards to pole us along. It was a tight fit, and knees would knock at any unexpected turn of the craft. I wasn't going to make good on my days-ago wish of throttling S'ami with my head scarf, but it did take effort not to wince whenever he looked my way. He was the only Azwan with us. The other Azwan and half the guards had remained behind in the expectation that S'ami would die.

I'd forced myself to keep my head straight and not glance around, feverishly looking for Valeo. I hadn't made up my mind whether I wanted him here or not. I didn't want anyone I knew, even slightly, to be out in the wilds with us. But I also didn't want to die alone here without a single ally among the hulking Temple Guards. Who else besides Valeo would care even a little whether Mami and I made it back?

Around me, soldiers waded through black water up to their thighs, making passage slow through the muck. Boots stuck with every step as the men fanned out, wordless and grim. They enjoyed the swamp far less than I did, and I wanted to tell them they'd feel the breezes better without their armor. The wind stirred under the dark spread of leaves, and insects chirred unseen all around. Flocks of gray cranes rose like sudden smoke from the tall grasses, while solitary raptors circled above their high nests. Steam rose from the water in pale wisps that dissolved into a fine, silvery mist.

The men passed all this without speaking, holding their pikes aloft to avoid dragging them through the water. More than once a guard would stab the blunt end into the mire to regain his balance. Their shields would throw them off again, sliding across their backs or catching on low-slung branches. I imagine in soldiering school they didn't teach proper swamp wading, but they'd clearly mastered the official sharp-eyed lookout glower. They kept their focus straight ahead, never wavering, as they tramped through dense brush and silent water that hid a hundred hazards and gave off a musky aroma of decaying leaves and ripening fruit.

Stingflies buzzed in the men's ears and found all the places they couldn't reach to swat or scratch. I'd have offered them hydrocanth oil mixed with citrine extract to smear on their skin if it wasn't considered immoral, so Mami and I alone were spared the welts and itching. More than once, we'd exchanged looks that said if only we weren't too intimidated to even offer the help. She'd reach over and pat my hand a few times, as if making sure I was still there. I couldn't seem to muster up a smile for her, so we simply sat and watched the murky water slip beneath the small craft.

The whole day had been odd and unsettling, not what I'd expected even after imagining a solid day of terror. The first leg of our trip went through the salt marsh with all the soldiers in rowboats or punts, and it had all been disturbingly cheerful. You couldn't shut S'ami up. We'd expected haughty silence. Instead, he gave us a tour of the blackened spot in the fens where the meteorite had hit.

He described measuring it with spools of rope, how all the world's astrologers would crave a look at his notes. His own father was the royal astrologer in Tengal, did he mention? Yes, he'd mentioned. I got the feeling he wasn't doing this for our benefit, but as practice for when he saw his father again. A grown man, one of the most powerful in the world, fretting over what his babba would think. I suppressed a snort. I wondered if I'd be trying to impress my parents years from now when I was halfway to old age.

After the gaping hole in the marsh, our flotilla made a more or less direct line for the swamps. S'ami also moved on in his chatter, this time to rate all the excellent fish he'd been served so far in Ward Sapphire's dining hall and how surprising our thriving little port was when you got out to see it. The goods you can find here! Silk from his native Tengal, as refined as anything he'd wear himself, the heartiest aged wines from Primaria, filigree metal-work from Ferokor. He'd heard the food in our cantinas had no equal and was beginning to believe it. He joked about what fine illegal herbs must've made their way into our cuisine.

Even I knew that was meant to draw Mami out about her medicines. She let him talk, and I followed her cue. It wasn't much different from Mami smiling at the folks on our patio as they asked where she got this or that and was she sure she wasn't trying to poison them, body and soul. Only this time, Mami wasn't smiling.

I had time to study the Azwan more carefully. He wore sturdier clothes today, hemp broadcloth instead of spider silk, in teals and browns. His wardrobe's plainness didn't alter the snooty lift of his chin or the narrowing of his eyes as he studied us right back. I had to like his dark complexion. Saphirrans are a practical people in a sun-kissed land, and his ebony skin made him handsome by that and many other standards. He had a muscular build, even with a paunch. But his talking! My old aunties didn't gab as much at Sabbath dinners.

He eventually gave up on hints and instead peppered Mami with questions about her work. Mami hesitated, casting her eyes downward. S'ami leaned forward to catch Mami's soft diction and kept assuring her not to fear him.

Mami shook her head.

"It's my colleague, the Azwan of Ambiguity, then?" he asked.

Mami bit her lip and stared blankly at the sweaty, unhappy men all around us. "You said you knew about my mother."

"Her trial and execution made Reyhim's career."

Mami didn't look up. "They were lovers."

I must've gasped, because they both shot looks at me. S'ami scowled, and I bit my lip and fought back any other reaction. The possibilities roiled within me. Is this why we were never allowed to hear how Mami had no family? Because Reyhim was my grandfather? No, that didn't necessarily follow. There were other explanations for why I had no maternal grandparents. There had to be.

S'ami acted as if Mami hadn't said anything more interesting than that it was hot out. He began listing medicines he said he'd heard about, asked what they did, whether they were distilled or infused or whatnot. There ought to be a livelier trade in such things, he said, hinting again. Perhaps he would work on Nihil to lift some of the prohibitions.

I wondered if my grandmother had heard similar promises from Reyhim, or if she'd done something much, much worse than anything Mami and I had ever attempted. Her frown told me to keep quiet. I nodded. I didn't need any hints to avoid this man's snares, as if I couldn't see them for what they were. No stinging retorts were going to slip past my lips today. For once, I had control over my straying tongue.

After our party reached the end of the salt marshes and pulled up to the swamps, the soldiers left their boats to proceed on foot. This was the only time I gave myself a few moments to search for Valeo, but it was no use. In the murky half-light, all the crouching soldiers looked the same. Then the moment was gone, and Mami needed me.

Our work—Mami's and mine—began at that point. The Gek don't build canals, exactly, but they shape the swamp to their liking, pruning foliage and roots to create narrow streams where a small craft might pass. We knew these by heart, as the Gek leave no other markings to navigate by. Ours would be the only watercraft from that point forward, and the second part of our journey got underway with the sun only a half-turn past dawn. We were making good time so far.

With the soldiers battling the muck, the woods grew denser until the tree canopy let in only scattered patches of light. Between the dense clusters of smoky trunks, we could hear the rustling of the Feroxi units more than a hundred paces away on either side. They had fanned out far, and the Gek would likely read that as a threat. The soldiers acted as if hunting a human enemy that could be taken by surprise. Obviously they'd never seen Gek in their cold lands, or they'd have known better.

The soldiers' eyes scanned treetops and branches. Then they swept the vista ahead, on the lookout for something that resembled a snake with legs, or so I'd tried to describe Gek. Perhaps the men had an image of walking snakes so firmly rooted in their minds that they nearly missed the first signs of them. A branch cracked somewhere to one side of us. Mami and I knew that as a warning, not a misstep. The Gek aren't clumsy.

It worked. Several Feroxi heads snapped around, their gaze directed to the spot from where the sound had come.

At first, they would've seen nothing unusual, merely more slender branches, swaying foliage, and patches of sky. But this was a familiar spot to me. Further ahead, the narrow, porous trunks of waterwood trees with their spiny roots gave way to ancient, thick-trunked redbeams whose gnarled limbs stretched in supplication to the hidden sky.

We'd reached a forest island, essentially a massive hummock with dry, passable ground. The soldiers fanned out faster, spying up and down trunks, into branches, through layers of rippling leaves for any sign of life. After my own eyes became adjusted to scouting the contours of maroon-tinted trunks, I settled on the nearest one. I knew what to look for: a swollen brown bubble sprouted where the lowest and thickest branches intersected.

I had reached a mud-walled hut built into the tree itself, with vines and branches entwined as a roof. There would be no signs of life. If Mami and I weren't recognized, there soon would be no signs of life on the ground, either. Mami and I drew up to that first hut, S'ami behind us, and clapped out a greeting code. Two short, two long, two short. The soldiers halted, wary. We repeated our clapping, peering up at the sentinel hut for some sign or signal.

Guards took up positions around the tree and under several others, crouching low beneath their shields, spears at the ready. Mami looked close to panic, shaking her head, clasping and unclasping her fingers. I didn't feel any better. We should've come without the soldiers, and maybe the Gek would've told us what became of the falling star, if they even knew.

One of the guards nodded up at the hut and waved two guards beside us. Their eyes followed the outlines of the mud hut, their expressions cold and watchful under their helmets. I caught my breath. One of them was Valeo. He gave no flicker of recognition, fully intent on the sentinel tree. I pretended I hadn't noticed him, while my insides did somersaults.

He was here. Right beside me.

That was good, yes? We'd be going through this together. My heartbeat trilled.

Then again, he was someone else to worry about. And right at that moment, I had plenty of things worrying me.

Mami lowered her head and spoke in a hoarse whisper to S'ami. "We should go, Azwan. I don't like this."

"Aren't they always silent?"

"Yes, but not like this. It's *too* quiet."

"We'll press ahead. They'll make noise soon enough." He motioned the guards ahead, further into the forest. I noticed then the gold totem dangling from a chain on his wrist. He'd been conjuring.

"Mami, look. The Azwan's totem."

Mami gasped. "You mustn't, Worthiness. They can sense it."

"And I, them. They have what I need. There's no longer any question." S'ami turned to the men, and, with another nod, they were off. I'd never been further than the sentinel tree, but S'ami motioned for us to follow, and there could be no going back. We plunged into the forest, noticing other huts, in tree after tree, sometimes several at a time.

A whole city grew above our heads.

Behind us, more soldiers fanned out at a distance. They were loud, too loud, their wet boots squishing on the solid ground, the scraggly underbrush cracking and snapping underfoot. A commander held up a hand to halt everyone and then cocked his head to listen.

Far above us, things rattled. It wasn't the rattling of sticks or leaves or stones, but a tongue clicking rapidly against the roof of the mouth, only louder. We'd heard the sound several times before, and it always boded a quick departure.

Mami grabbed S'ami's sleeve. "It's their last warning to us."

"So noted." He turned to one of the guards. "Get me up there. The women, too."

He'd picked one of the more populated trees, a majestic hardwood probably older than Nihil himself, untouched by time except for a half-dozen clay bubbles bulging from limbs as wide as our boardwalks.

A guard knelt, and Mami stepped on his knee and onto the trunk. We'd worn flared, split skirts so our going would be easier. I clambered up after Mami, the Azwan behind me. My cloth boots found easy purchase in slippery areas. I reached the first branch as S'ami pulled himself up behind me. We landed on a limb as wide as the spread of a Feroxi's shoulders where we could stand without too much difficulty. Bile rose in my throat and then slid down, burning as it went, as I forced myself to calm. Breathe in, breathe out, steady. Steady.

There, better.

Valeo scrambled up after me, surprisingly light on his feet, as if all that leather armor were no heavier than crane feathers.

The first mud hut came only to my forehead. I bent my knees and craned my neck to peer in. Dried leaves covered the floor, which looked solid enough, and the walls felt thick and sturdy. The vines and branches along the roof let in little light and probably less rain. The hut was empty, except for the gnarled branches they'd trained into the shapes of rough benches and sleeping lofts. It looked much like human furniture, only lumpier and leafier. I backed out and made my way up another branch to the next hut, from where we'd heard the rattling noise.

Valeo pressed himself against the outside wall and peered through the hut's opening with a turn of his head. I hadn't noticed anyone else's arrival, but there were a handful of guards in the trees with us. At first I saw nothing in the hut amid the scattered leaves, which looked like they had fallen from the roof and were simply left in place as a floor covering. Then a breeze shifted the branches overhead, and a darting shaft of light reflected off something on the floor.

I let Valeo go first, and he crept into the doorway, searched this way and that, and knelt to reach for the shimmering object. He snatched it.

A skin. He'd grabbed a Gek's cast-off skin. It hung limply in his hand, gray but translucent, patches of light catching on iridescent scales like the scattering of glass shards. The hide was split down the back, with tattered shreds of what had been arm- and leg-skin. To anyone who'd never seen Gek, it might look like a woman's shredded, silk underthings. It slipped between the guard's fingers, oily and new. Valeo turned to S'ami: "If the Gek are like snakes, this creature has only just molted. Maybe it'll be nearby."

He handed the skin to S'ami, who rolled it into a tight ball and tucked it into a pouch at his side. Such pelts were hard to come by, even if it looked fragile. I tried not to obsess over what it might fetch among traders.

Valeo motioned toward the hut, and the other men drew their swords while he ducked under the low doorway. I tiptoed in after him. Valeo crouched, unable to stand in the low room. We both scanned the walls and leafy ceiling. In the corner by the doorway, half-hidden in shadows, huddled a shivering creature, its skin pink as if rubbed raw, still wet and oily, not yet iridescent like the hide it had just shed.

The Gek cracked a crescent slit of a mouth and emitted a high-pitched whimper. It stood on two legs, like us, despite its reptilian hide, and a short, stubby, vestigial tail it used for balance in the trees. It was cold-blooded, but this was mid-morning, and the Gek would have plenty of sunlight to keep themselves warm and active. Even coming up to my navel, it could cause plenty of trouble. But it trembled and cowered in the shadows.

"It's a juvenile," I said. "And it's terrified. It can't camouflage itself until its skin dries."

"Will its mother be nearby?"

I nodded.

"Then it's our hostage," Valeo said.

"No! How could you!" My shout startled the creature. It tried to dart between Valeo's legs, but he snapped his knees together. It slid to one side and dashed past him. He wheeled about as it ran into the opposite corner and began climbing the wall. Valeo grabbed it around its waist with his left arm. It writhed and thrashed, and I could see him squeezing in a vice-like grip.

"You're crushing it," I said. "It's just a child."

Whether Valeo dropped the Gek or it wriggled free, I didn't see. Valeo had already lunged toward the wall with his sword, piercing a clump of wall.

It bled. And screamed.

The piece of wall opened a pink mouth and let out a shrill, fearful yalp. It moved, becoming a torso and arms and legs and opening eyes the color of the surrounding leaves. The creature was another Gek, its hide camouflaged a dark brown. Valeo aimed another thrust at the center of its chest, pinning it to the wall. The creature's color went from brown to gray, the green eyes losing their radiance as its life drained away. A javelin dropped to the hut floor. Valeo pulled his sword away, and the Gek slid to his feet.

The child-Gek screamed, a shrill, agonizing cry that tore me to hear it, and flung itself on its dead parent. I ran to the body, feeling vainly for signs of life. I'm no healer and could offer no comfort. I made frantic hand motions to the child. That's how humans spoke to Gek, with gestures that right at that moment weren't springing readily to mind. My fingers were stuck, frozen, like I was stammering with my hands. I managed to say, "I'm sorry," as if that would help. Valeo tried wrapping another arm around the Gek, and Nihil spare that poor thing, it sank its teeth into his forearm and thrashed its head. It must have hurt like nothing Valeo had ever felt.

"Get it off me!" he shouted.

"Let go of it."

"It's our hostage."

I frowned. "Then I can't help you." Which was true; I can't help someone who gets in his own way.

"Nihil's balls, get out of here, then."

I bolted. A few short steps to the door. Two more Gek dropped from the ceiling to block us, shaded a dark green like the foliage. My long-ago first impression of Gek had been of spindly limbs and smooth bellies; now I noticed ropes of muscles beneath their pebbly skin. They aimed javelins at us, the wooden tips whittled and polished to razor sharpness. These Gek came to my chin. Valeo held the pink Gek in front of him as it kicked and thrashed, a sword edge at its throat.

"Tell them what we want."

I made motions. My hands moved more nimbly as if they'd gathered courage independent of the rest of me, though they visibly shook. I'd practiced some gestures the night before, and muscle memory took over. The signal for "star." For "sky." How about "I'm so horribly sorry"? I knew the gestures better than Mami; I was younger when I started to learn them. I'd even kept charts for a time, until a tearful Amaniel had begged Babba to burn such a heathen thing. My hands flew by instinct; I gave no thought to their rudimentary syntax or whatever courtesies usually passed among them. My pulse pounded in my ears; my breathing came hard and fast. They could sense I was terrified. Would such a show of weakness mean death?

They blocked the doorway.

"I need help in here," Valeo said, his breathing ragged, blood streaming from the gashes on his arm where the young Gek was gnawing his flesh. He pressed it closer to his chest. I recalled how powerful that grip was.

"Azwan! Commander!"

A commotion outside told us we would get no answer.

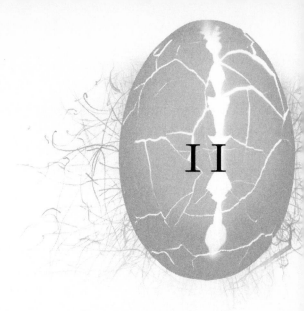

II

Your sharpest weapons are your wits.
—*Feroxi proverb*

It all registered at once: crashing and shouting, men's voices and Gek squawking, javelins clattering and arrows whizzing all around, the whine of steel slicing the air as men fought. I watched, helpless, as Valeo braced himself to fight one-handed from his low crouch. He rushed the doorway, working his sword to one side then the other. I huddled behind him as Gek parted and dropped, bleeding, the javelins splintered and useless. Valeo whirled and kept me at his back as we lurched out onto the branches. I stayed close and then closer, until there was barely air between us.

We kept our backs to the outer wall of the hut, me by his left side, one hand on the little Gek's head, hoping if I stroked it, it would calm down and maybe release Valeo's arm from its stubborn bite. A ways off, two dozen Gek surrounded Mami and S'ami and several guards who'd ventured into the tree. They bunched together where wide branches met

in a wooden tangle. S'ami waved his gold totem high overhead, and from it emanated a wide, bluish sphere. Javelins
and arrows burst into flame on impact. He had conjured
some sort of glowing shield to encircle the stranded party.
The Gek flung themselves at the nearly invisible barrier and
fell screaming, the smell of burning flesh clawing at my gut. I
couldn't bring myself to watch. They were no match for the
Azwan's magic, and they were being slaughtered.

A hush fell over the Gek. I peered through my fingers
to see them gathering in a half-circle around Valeo and
myself. They scuttled from the enchanted sphere, seething
and hissing, a few of them gesturing to me and pointing to
the Gek child. I tried to read the gestures as best I could,
but some of the signals were new. What I could understand, I didn't like. I quaked all over, and the Gek became
a blur. I confused the hand signals, unsure who'd said what,
until I tried to zero in on just one or two of the closest
ones. Mami shouted over to me. "What are they saying?"

"That we captured the shaman's daughter. I think
they're cursing us."

"The star, Hadara. I asked them—they have it."

I nodded and flexed and unflexed my trembling fingers,
rotated my hands this way and that, and flapped and waved
and gesticulated wildly. *We want the star. We'll let shaman-
spawn go. For the star.*

Several shook their heads. I suppose that gesture is uni-
versal. I tried again. I took a deep breath and tucked my
elbows by my side. That helped keep my hands steadier as I
gestured. *We do not want your swamp. Only the star.*

One of the Gek stepped forward, a big fellow with a
spiny crest atop his head, clearly some kind of leader. The

men had crests, the only way to tell them from females. This one's skin turned a mottled green streaked with angry crimson as he gestured:

You come with the big drabskins from long-ago memory. From before the lizards crossed the deep waters. The big drabskins trade only one way. Lizards remember.

Drabskins. That was their name for us. A one-way trade was basically a theft, or maybe meant looting. I shouted my translation to Mami and S'ami anyway. He nodded. "That sounds about right. They know the Feroxi well," he said. "Guardsman. Release the girl."

"Azwan, they'll kill us all." Valeo raised his sword, and the Gek fell back, hissing.

S'ami's tone hardened. The blue sphere deepened in intensity, grew more like controlled lightning, flashing silently around him and Mami. "Guardsman."

Valeo matched his controlled anger. "Cover me, then."

"Absolutely not."

I grabbed Valeo's shoulder. "I think it'll be alright." I didn't, but the Gek would definitely kill us if we hung on to the girl. The shamans kept all the tribe's Gek-lore in their heads. Even Mami didn't know how much that meant—all their herb knowledge, potion recipes, even the tree-worshipping that passed for a religion among them. A shaman's daughter wasn't someone they'd easily give up. As if to prove my point, javelin tips brushed our skin or hovered a finger's width from our eyes.

A quick release of the soldier's arm, and she revived, darting away and into the crowd. She was already regaining her ability to change color, and I had some difficulty picking her out. But now Valeo and I were alone, our backs to the small hut, our footing uneven on the tree limb. Valeo's left arm curled by his side, blood streaming from where she'd nearly gnawed to the bone.

He let out a short, angry exhale. "What do we bargain with now, Worthiness?"

I knew. I had figured out some of this when sleep wouldn't come the night before. I gestured again, slower this time, more carefully. I had to get this right. No blurting or blathering or fumbling for words. I wasn't in a classroom; here, the Temple was powerless, except for their weapons, and that wouldn't gain them what they wanted. Only Mami and I had that authority, and only I had the chance, likely the only chance. My mind and body trained on the crested Gek-man, honing in on him like an archer finds his mark.

I had a singular thought, sharp as a glass shard. They wanted a two-way trade, right? Well, while we trade for their medicines, they trade for our metals. They don't know how to work the stuff. Cups, hammers, nails, pins. And, of course, knives, axes, spades, saws.

Daggers. Spears tips. Arrowheads. Perhaps swords and battle axes if the Feroxi could be persuaded to part with a few. The Feroxi's mighty weapons were worth their weight in witch's wort and shadowroot—and, maybe, fallen stars. So I asked. *What do you want for the star? You've seen what the big drabskins carry. Tools. Weapons. Pick what you want. Name your price.*

I had no idea if the Feroxi would part with anything, but then it didn't seem like S'ami would walk away empty-handed if a few daggers and pikes would get him what he wanted.

The Gek leader edged closer to me, his long, forked tongue flicking a finger's width from my face. They smell that way. Fear has a smell, I remembered. So does desperation. Valeo edged his sword between the Gek and me and nudged him back. The leader began gesturing:

Lizards will get useful things from the big drabskin corpses. Big drabskins will learn lizards can trade one way also.

Only then did I realize I heard no sounds from the forest floor. Nothing stirred below us. No leaves or branches crackled. I couldn't see the ground from where I stood, but Valeo could. He could look down, through the leaves, over a branch, at . . . I didn't want to think at what.

I closed my eyes. Oh, by all three moons, what trouble was I in? S'ami was too far away for us to seek protection under his magic shield, and a score of Gek lay between us anyway.

"The soldiers." My mouth felt dry. "Where are the other soldiers? The ones on the ground."

"They took up positions," Valeo said. "Why?"

"There's no sound from them."

"They're there. From where I stand, I can see two dozen shields at least."

"Out of two hundred?"

"There's been no fighting on the ground. We'd know. What do they want?"

Mami and S'ami wanted to know that, too. Mami had been calling my name this whole time. And S'ami had been craning his neck for a glimpse through the rippling leaves. They would have to wait. I tried one more time. With that many soldiers unharmed, the Gek hadn't been eager for a fight. Maybe I could smell, too—a bluff. I threw up my arms and spoke, my hands pounding in what I hoped seemed like fury.

Bring the star now. No more trade. Bring it.

For one brief moment, my anger hung in the air. Then they scattered. Every direction. Gone. Only a handful remained, flicking tongues and bobbing their heads, looking shrunken and wary, very much like humans do when we're nervous.

I spotted the Gek girl, smaller than the others, her mouth ringed with Valeo's blood. She crouched behind one of the adults and hissed at me. Our eyes locked. I hissed back, hoping I appeared tougher and less remorseful than I felt. She shrank back behind the others. I pressed my lips together and toughened my stance, my shoulders arching back, my spine stiffening. Maybe I didn't smell like raw, heart-thumping panic.

"Ha-da-ra." Mami again. "By Nihil, girl! What's going on?"

"They're bringing it."

The blue sphere flickered around her and the others. S'ami was edging forward. "What did they say?"

"Nothing." I could explain later. "They're bringing it." I hoped. Oh, by Nihil's many wives and many lives, how I hoped.

Then it struck me. They were bringing me the star-demon. To me. Not to S'ami or a soldier or anyone else. I was going to get what S'ami wanted, what he'd sensed even from the deck of his ship. I didn't know if I could move.

I was no one's dunce any longer. I was everything those other girls—including my sister—could ever have hoped for. I felt again their eyes on me, waiting for my inevitable misstep, waiting for the chance to pounce and earn their smug expressions. Me. Hadara. The natural girl, the wild one. It was all up to me, and all the honor and glory I could want were being hand-delivered to my outstretched palm.

But I'm no student of theology. The Azwan of Uncertainty, keeper of all the doctrine that kept worshippers guessing, was under my spell. And the one thing I could think was this:

I had the biggest barter chit in all Kuldor coming my way.

Or a demon who would possess me and destroy me from within.

Ragged breaths ripped deep, achy pangs in my chest. I wasn't going to have very long to make up my mind if I wanted to keep this thing, whatever it was. A moment. A fraction of a moment. And still my lungs hurt, my knees wobbled, and I'd begun sweating. What to do?

I could seize it and hold it and demand S'ami and the Temple guards and the rest of them agree to leave at once. No, that wouldn't work. S'ami would shoot that blue arc into me. I'd be dead, and he'd have the star. I could graciously offer it to him and ask a favor later. *I'm delighted you love our cuisine, now could you please leave?* That notion, of course, had "stupid idea" tattooed across its face.

No, I knew what I wanted from the Temple: to survive with some degree of honor, and their respect, however begrudging. They were going to leave Mami and me alone, leave our island alone, let us go back to our own way of doing things, and be fine with it. No more ransacked houses, no curfew, no fear.

The Gek finally returned, or at least a few of them did, but my plan was only half-formed, maybe a quarter-formed, in my brain. But I wanted it, that much I realized. It was coming to me, and I wanted it. The leader was carrying a clunky metal box I recognized from a trade last winter. It had been a cheap, tin thing we'd picked up from a market kiosk, but the Gek had fawned over it like it was worth a hundred coppers. It was hinged, at least, and it locked. The crested Gek fumbled with the key. Gek fingers are dexterous, but sticky, and the tiny key became glued in half a dozen ways. I reached for it, not quite touching it, when I realized S'ami was screaming at me.

"Don't open that. I'll melt you myself on the Soul's Forge, you lay hands on it. Guard! Have them set it down."

Valeo extended his bloodied arm across my body and motioned to the Gek. He pointed downward. The leader snatched the box back, hugging it to his chest. I could see that chest heaving, even with the skin camouflaged. Maybe I can't smell fear, but I can see it. I let Valeo edge forward, more insistent, demanding the box through silent force of will. All the Gek backed away, every last one. A corridor opened between us and them, their eyes on Valeo. He didn't turn to me as he spoke, and his voice was low.

"Why have they lowered their weapons?"

Indeed, they had. It couldn't possibly be because they suddenly liked us. What had changed? The Gek pointed to me. To the box. To me. It's as if they knew my intent. We were in perfect agreement, the Gek and I. I wanted it; they wanted me to want it.

The leader-Gek sidled over and gestured directly to me. This time, I shouted a hasty translation to S'ami. *The star seeks one who knows to undo what must be undone. The star comes to you as you come to it.*

That made no sense but I didn't care. S'ami couldn't deny, to himself or Nihil or twice ten thousand guards, that the Gek meant for me to have it. The box was barely a hand-width from my outstretched palm. It was mine, almost.

"Don't touch that Nihil-blasted box!" The blue sphere flickered as S'ami shouted. "Have them lay it at their feet."

I did something I almost never do then. I'm a good girl, a kind-hearted soul—anyone will say so, except maybe my teacher. I have a little trouble with authority sometimes, particularly religious authority. But I did something that, even for me, was completely outside the ordinary.

I lied.

I told the Gek-leader the magic user wanted me to have the box. I hoped I was hidden enough that Mami couldn't see my gesturing and figure it out, but maybe by the time she did, it would be in my sweaty paws. I could try dodging S'ami's blue fire and white-hot anger later.

I paused for a beat and then added, without translating: *Is there a danger to me?*

The Gek throng hesitated. Traded glances. Shook their heads. But I saw a few nod. I signaled again. *Tell me what to do with it.*

Whatever they thought I was supposed to know, I became determined to use. With another furtive exchange of looks all around, the Gek holding the box reached forward, slowly, hesitating. If what Amaniel had shown me in Scriptures was true, a whole world, the end of civilizations, a conflagration to end all time, buffered in the air above the lid of that box.

Then, out of nowhere, a brownish streak. The box was snatched up, gone. The Gek girl, fully camouflaged, leaped on her leafy roof, box in hand, and leaped again toward a higher branch. A cyan flame shot from S'ami's sphere, arcing up in an instant, reforming around the Gek girl and sending her tumbling off the roof. The blue orb sliced through branches, setting leaves afire, throwing smoke in its trail. The Gek girl plunged downward with a throaty scream and slammed into the unyielding ground.

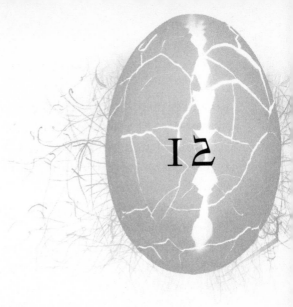

I2

Be judicious in bringing war upon yourselves. To consider your petty quarrels to be worth spilling blood over is a conceit I find hard to abide.
—*from Oblations 15,* The Book of Unease

Every tree limb burst into motion. Every part of the tree writhed or slithered. Branches snapped. The movement around us exploded as many more Gek shifted and started, in this tree and surrounding ones. I'd never had any idea of their true numbers. More clicking noises, and then chirps and croaks as branches and clusters of leaves called out to one another. Green eyes peered here, tongues flicked there.

Valeo's voice boomed above the commotion.

"Jump!"

He pressed backward, forcing me to creep toward the narrow tip of our branch. I jumped, my knees buckling beneath me. I sprang up and staggered off toward our punt, which seemed a million lengths away. Valeo jumped after me and pushed me toward the punt, his injured left hand pressed between my shoulders, hastening my pace.

Javelins landed all around us. Arrows whizzed past. One struck him between the shoulder blades with a thump and dangled there. He barely noticed.

"You left your shield," I said. "Is it in the tree?"

"No time for it."

I glanced back. The blue sphere, the Gek girl limp inside it, floated above S'ami's head. He, too, was hustling toward the punt as guards scurried around him, their shields raised to ward off a hail of missiles. They shouted directions and ordered retreats. Javelins pinged against their shields and fell away, but the arrows stuck by the score, and I could see the men laboring under the extra weight, crouching as they jogged away. None broke formation, and the shields moved above their left shoulders in bobbing waves like giant scales on a great, coiling beast.

I couldn't see Mami.

"Mami!"

"Hadara!"

She was further back, lost amid the soldiers. I tried to push my way to her, only to feel a hand grab my dress and drag me back. I fought to pry Valeo's fingers from my clothes, but he pulled, pushed, and hauled me, half-turned and struggling.

"She'll be okay?" I asked him.

"She's not my concern."

"But I am?"

"Keep moving."

We were almost running. Everyone else was, too, and I was so busy turning my head this way and that, anxious for a glimpse of Mami, that I missed the first body underfoot.

We'd reached the jagged shoreline where the tree island ended. The underbrush grew so thick, I stumbled over what I thought was a root. It was a leg. A guard lay beneath us, facedown, scores of tiny darts jutting from his exposed limbs. I recognized pins we'd traded to the Gek even as Valeo yanked me to my feet. Pins! With tiny, feathered flights glued on. And here I'd always thought *we'd* gotten the best of *them*. We'd traded pins when they never wore clothes or sewed a stitch, not even a blanket, and I couldn't figure why by all three moons and seven planets they'd ever needed a single one. They could barely manage to hold them with their sticky fingers. I swore never to underestimate them again.

The dead soldier had been left to guard the punt. They must've killed him early, or they'd used a poison more potent than anything they'd ever given us. Valeo had these pins all over his armor, and, worse, poking from the skin on his arms and the back of his legs. Blood trickled from them. I had none on myself, since he'd pushed me before him.

Our punt was tethered to a low-hanging branch surrounded by Gek. Guards cut them down, this way and that, clearing a path to the small boat, but not before being showered with more of the pin-darts.

"Get in," Valeo said. Was his voice thicker? His motions slower? I began prying the darts from him. "Leave it. Get in."

Before I could move, S'ami rushed past us. I tugged and yanked and finally shoved Valeo away before the magic orb seared off his head. It had left a blackened, smoking trail through the canopy's lowest branches as it streaked through them. Valeo teetered around me and clumsily regained his footing. Was that the poison, or just my worrying?

Two guards helped S'ami in the punt, and he lowered the sphere with the Gek into the boat, where the flames didn't seem to harm the wooden craft. Magic didn't ever work the way I expected, which is probably why it's called magic in the first place. The tin box was tight in the Gek's wiry hands, but she was writhing and moaning. Two guards clambered into the boat to pole S'ami along. They pushed off without Mami and me. S'ami's gaze was locked on his prey, and he didn't notice or care that the female guides he'd so amiably befriended only a half-day earlier had been left behind.

"Move." Valeo put his hand between my shoulder blades and nudged me into the water with him. I had acquired an unexpected ally. I didn't question it, or him. I might be on familiar ground, but battles were his business, not mine. He ordered; I obeyed.

The rest of the guards huddled under their shields, edging sideways, jabbing and stabbing at Gek on low-hanging branches. Darts and javelins sprayed in waves toward us. Still no sign of Mami. I hurled myself into the crowd to find her, only to be pressed back as the men swept toward the black water under repeated hails of missiles. Any soldier who fell was jerked to his feet and pushed forward by a comrade.

A brass horn sounded in the distance. We waded toward it, the water quickly reaching my upper thigh. Around me, metal and leather flashed through the foliage. All the men fought, but their pace was unrelenting. They'd gotten what they came for and made no secret of their rush to leave. I felt no different. It was time to go, and quick.

We staggered on, my feet working against the soft, sticky ooze at the swamp's bottom. The missiles followed us, but no more darts. Perhaps we were already out of range. After barely a hundred paces, though, Valeo stumbled beside me. He shook his head as if trying to startle himself awake and blinked his eyes. His movements slowed again, his whole body sticking in the muck. He stopped. Blinked. And lurched forward again. A foot caught in the muck, and he stumbled again.

It was entirely my fault. Mine. Trading those pins. I think all we'd gotten for them was a basket of itchvine pods, which we'd lost anyway during the raid. Poor Valeo, all sick and maybe dying because I'd thought, "What a laugh! Pins for the Gek!" I shook his shoulder. Another guard pulled him to his feet and shoved him along.

I pulled a dart from his leather armor and squinted at the slender point. It had been dipped in a bright magenta liquid that had dried in place. I never made poisons and was out of my depth with it, but I stuck it through my skirt in a way that wouldn't prick me. For later, when I had time.

Someone splashed behind us. A guard floated facedown in the black water. Another man tossed his shield away, hoisted his dead comrade onto his back, and kept plodding on, the waters parting reluctantly before him.

Valeo's knees buckled. Black water burbled around his chest. Blood dripped into the muck and slid away in crimson streaks. I had switched over to his right side some time back and found myself reaching for his elbow. He tried to brush me off and came within a hand-width of clipping me with the broad side of his sword. I reached more firmly for his bicep with both hands and propped him up. He felt solid and heavy.

A fallen tree stump provided just what I needed to make Valeo stop, if even for a moment. It was my turn to give the orders.

"Sit."

"No." His voice was thick and sounded groggy, but he did what he was told to, and wedged his bottom into the ragged stump. "Must. Keep . . . moving."

He was panting.

"Can you hear me?" I held up three fingers. "How many?"

"Moving."

"How many?"

"I don't know. Two. Four. Please." He shut his eyes.

I didn't like the way his body was hunching. "We need to find someone to carry you."

"I can walk."

"And you can die. Which I'm not going to let happen."

He opened his eyes. "Why? Why do you care?"

"Because I do."

"I frighten you." He made eye contact, and I could see at least a glint piercing through the fog there.

Good. He had something to concentrate on besides his muddled state.

"Yes, so don't die. Someone needs to scare me."

"Nihil doesn't scare you?" His breathing grew ragged again. "He should."

"I don't know. He's far away. You're here." I had to keep him talking. Somehow, I had to keep his lips moving and his mind focused until I could stop one of these men and get him to carry Valeo. But every man I saw either was stumbling along, similarly stricken, or helping another man already.

I turned back to Valeo. "Tell me about your family."

Bad idea. "The guards. Are. My family."

"Alright, let's try again. Tell me your favorite song."

"Song?"

"Anything. Your favorite story, song, prayer. Something."

He squinted at me and tried to focus. "Markden. Woolass."

"Start from the beginning."

"Can't."

I saw a familiar head scarf dart and weave around the men and close in on where I stood, hovering over the seated, wobbly Valeo. I shouted with relief and a whole new fear. "Mami, grab his arm!"

"They weren't aiming for you and me, Hadara."

"This one's hurt." Wait, what had she said? *Not aiming at us.* It didn't register.

"They're loyal to us," she said. "I don't know why."

The star comes to you as you come to it. I wondered if Mami would know what that meant.

Mami and I reached around Valeo from either side and propped him up and half-dragged him through the mud.

Between his heft and his armor and the heavy wetness and thigh-high muck, the going was slow and tiring. I shouted at him to lean on us, keep going, don't stop now, another step. Another! Keep going!

He slowed and teetered in place, about to crash over like a chopped-down tree. Mami shouted across to me. "We have to leave him!"

"No, we don't." I was panting. If we dropped him, we were giving up on him. I couldn't do that.

I whipped around to the nearest soldier. "You have to help him. We can't hold him."

The guard waded beside me and shouted something in Fernai to the others, and they crowded in beside Valeo. I fell back and let them take over the burden of dragging Valeo along, as he'd nodded off, right there on his feet. There wasn't anything I could do. I realized I'd likely just watched a man stagger to his death, but then all around me, soldiers were falling and not getting up again. I clutched at Mami, like she was the one safe spot in all the swamp, and she held back. I kept my eyes riveted on the men dragging Valeo forward, even as the tall grasses of the border marsh loomed into view. All the rowboats and punts were still moored. Safety was at hand.

For me, at least.

Then far behind us came an ear-splitting boom and a roar of sudden fire. My ears ached from the popping rush of air. The force threw me forward, Mami landing in the water on top of me. All that stopped me from sinking below the surface were the upright roots of the water-wood. I wedged between them, stuck, gasping.

The Feroxi renewed their yelling, and their tight formations evaporated. Men threw down shields and ran, even tried to swim, from the billowing flames that swept toward us. Smoke singed my nostrils. The intense heat sucked all the air from our lungs. Mami and I grasped at roots and bark to regain our footing, grabbed hands, and ran as best we could, not knowing if even the boats could get us away in time.

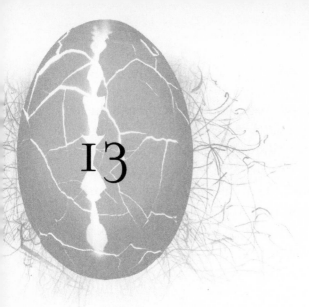

13

*I planted among the giants' frozen realm a magic
seed that yielded a bitter harvest. All the male
children born that year never learned to walk, their
limbs withered in the womb. The priests could not
cure them, nor would I spare any.*

*Know that I shall scatter such seeds throughout
Kuldor, I told them. They are watered by your
excesses, and you cannot cure them except by my
mercy.*

— *Verisimilitudes* 7, The Book of Unease

From his punt far ahead of us, S'ami shouted.

"A seed, a seed!" he said. "The demon's cast a seed
among us."

Without Amaniel here, I had only a vague idea what
that meant and no one to ask. Mami and I reached the
boats, most of the long-legged Feroxi having passed us all.

I'd lost sight of Valeo the instant the fireball burst. My own safety mattered most now.

Mami grabbed at a rowboat as it pushed off, loaded with men.

"Don't you dare leave us," she said.

"One only," a guard said.

A soldier from another boat called out, "We'll take one."

The men in the second boat helped me aboard, and we pushed off, with four of them rowing in hard, long strokes, their pace brisk. I squeezed next to a guard but kept my eyes on Mami, wedged into the next boat over. She squinted back toward the swamp.

I followed her gaze and stiffened as the first orange licks of fire shot above the treetops. The swamp burned. I didn't understand why. I know the Gek can make some things explode, but no one risks such massive harm to their homes, do they? The blaze roared through the tops of trees, sending thick, roiling smoke bending skyward. I rewrapped my scarf so it covered my nose and mouth, though it let some hair show. I didn't care. Modesty was far down on my list of worries at the moment. Many of the men had fished out rags or torn off chunks of their togs to create a similar face mask. The smoke was blinding, choking—and everywhere.

Were the Feroxi responsible for the blazing swamp? I couldn't see how. The swamp flooded so thoroughly in summer that the boles of trees were no longer visible beneath the inky waterline. Setting that kind of fire would be more of a job than the Feroxi had had time for.

The last guards straggled single file from different points along the swamp's border, their faces sooty, many of them carrying the limp forms of other guards. For all I hated the Feroxi, I found myself rooting for their safety. I tried to think of what Babba would have to say about them had he been here. They only raised sword or spear when under attack. They'd retreated in order, quickly, methodically, and aided one another. There was much to admire about them, now that I had a few moments to reflect on it.

I shifted in my seat, squished and overheated, but pretty much in cozy luxury compared to my battered companions. A more bedraggled, hard-bitten, grubby bunch hadn't drifted through these fens since the first settlers, I imagined. The cramped space and teetery boat didn't bother them at all. They didn't even look tired. I could only hope Valeo was made of similarly stern stuff and would ride out whatever the Gek had hit him with.

The singed guards wore a steel-eyed alert look that probably came standard issue with the rest of their gear. I figured I must look like I'd swum up from the murky depths myself, some brown-tarred, red-eyed creature in limp rags and soggy boots. Plus, I stank. It's one thing to admire the musky aroma of the swamps and another thing to wear it. I needed a hot soak and a cool drink and time to reflect.

The soldier next to me shifted and surveyed the boats ahead of ours. His rangy frame fit tightly into the narrow space, and he was all elbows and knees and sharp angles that I could only avoid by not budging a finger-width.

Another man in our boat said something in Fernai. I caught a word—Valeo—somewhere in the sentence.

"What is it?" I said, remembering my manners only afterward. "That is, if you don't mind my asking."

The soldier beside me looked down as if noticing me for the first time. His startling blue eyes locked on mine for an instant until I remembered to look away out of modesty. No staring. Manners were a pain even when I wasn't recently spared a harrowing death and overcome by stink and soot and worry. Right then, courtesy was a downright irritant, another pit in the path to safety.

"The guard who protected you. These men are in his unit." The man's thick accent was lilting and musical, giving his basso voice an unexpectedly soft edge. "He is in a boat far ahead."

"He's alright then?"

"His Highness is unconscious or dead. We cannot tell from here."

My breath caught in my throat. *His Highness?* "I don't know if there's an antidote."

"Antidote?" The guard sounded out the word to himself.

"The cure for the poison."

"You mean a potion. His Highness would rather swallow his sword. The Azwan will cure him if he can."

"But if he can't?"

"There is nothing the Azwan of Uncertainty cannot do if Nihil permits it."

A quick glance over my shoulder told me the Azwan had other things on his mind. The punt radiated pale blue light from where the Gek girl was imprisoned with her treasure.

"I hope you're right," I said.

The man bristled and clamped a massive, filthy hand on my shoulder. The other soldiers in our boat glared as one.

"There is no Azwan like the Son of the Second Moon," he said. "We are his men, and we will suffer no doubts on his behalf."

145

I gulped back the first stupid thing that came to mind and stammered an apology. "I meant no disrespect."

He shrugged and released his grip. "It seems to come instinctively to your kind."

I had to let the insult pass. We had drawn up to the Azwan's punt by then, and I had a clear view through the crushed reeds of both that boat and Mami's just beyond. All the soldiers were watching, too.

S'ami rubbed his gold wisdom knot in his right hand, his brow knit in concentration. Beads of perspiration glistened on his forehead. The Gek girl lay curled, limp and unconscious, within a haze of bluish light at the bottom of the punt, but I couldn't see the box from where I sat. It could be on the other side of Kuldor for all it mattered just then. The Gek may have wanted me to have it, but there'd be no getting it with S'ami hovering beside it.

He called out to Mami through the wisps of smoke and ash that sifted angrily all around us. Coughing fits interrupted him, but he managed to call out to her.

"It shouldn't seem that I abandoned you, Lia, wife of Rimonil. You mustn't think the Temple ungrateful."

Mami bowed her head from her boat on the other side of him. Her face always went blank and passive around clerics. "I understand, I think, the importance of your mission, Azwan. I wouldn't presume to preoccupy you at such a dangerous moment."

"In other words, you can fend for yourself." S'ami flashed a quick grin, while not taking his eyes off his prize. My sunburned face stung as it scrunched into a scowl. Fend for ourselves, indeed. Many fine thanks for that.

Mami only said: "If need be, sir."

"For someone who makes her living defying the Temple and allows her daughter to grow up half-wild, you are a paragon of grace and modesty, Lia of Rimonil."

"If it pleases you, Azwan."

Mami was covered in muck and soot, as we all were. Even so, I could see her make her fiercest "be quiet" face at me beneath her soiled head scarf. She wasn't having any of it, but I was silently being warned not to open my mouth. I nodded, like hers only a slight movement, and kept my gaze steady. Half-wild. I didn't feel any shame about it. Mami had done the best she could, considering I would've had to have been tied to the boardwalk not to follow her out to the fens.

The Azwan's right hand jerked then, and he grasped his totem with both hands, steadying himself. It was as if the odd little gold weight had startled to life. I heard it as a buzzing, almost a tinny, shrill sound, distinct from the hum of insects around us.

One of the guards poling S'ami's punt paused. "Azwan?"

"I'm alright." S'ami nodded. He glanced over to my boat, but not at me. He nodded toward the man beside me, who'd angled around to face the Azwan. "All your men off, Commander?"

The guard with the ice in his eyes placed his fist, thumb-first, in the middle of his chest by way of salute. His elbow nearly knocked me out of the boat. I tried to make myself as small as possible.

"Guardsman Makkio signaled from the last boat. All are accounted for, Azwan."

"Casualties?"

"Thirty-three dead so far."

"Wounded?"

"Unknown. The poison isn't slow. For those still living . . ."

"I'll take care of it."

The Commander looked down his nose at me with an I-told-you-so grimace. I took a sudden interest in my ruined boots, until the Azwan's hand jumped again. He had trouble wrestling his own wrist back to his lap, as if he'd caught a wriggly fish intent on returning to the marsh. His hands went high, then low, then up and to the side. The grating buzz grew louder.

Our boat and Mami's and several others drew closer, the guards drawing weapons. The men who'd kept their shields raised those as well. Their helmets glinted dully in the sun beneath clusters of plumes angled toward the struggling Azwan.

"Back off," S'ami said. "You're in more danger here than me."

The Commander signaled the boats to back away, and we floated off a body length or so, but no further. No one had spoken; we were all riveted to S'ami's struggle. S'ami was too chatty to keep from us what was happening.

"It's a seed," he said. "I'd know if it were Nihil's, but it isn't. It tries to reverse my theurgy. The conflagration . . . the fire in the swamp. This is its handiwork, distorting my own."

A seed? All I knew of seeds were the kind we planted in pots. I had some dim memory of learning about chaotic spells, but this was not the moment to ask. S'ami wrestled his own right hand back to a spot between his knees, moisture fanning out from his armpits and in a jagged line down his back. His chest heaved, and he closed his eyes. The Gek hadn't stirred in her transparent cage.

"Lia of Rimonil," S'ami said.

"Great Azwan."

"What do you know of seeds?"

"Nothing but what the priest tells us."

"And that is?"

"Nihil sows the seeds of random discord among us. They sprout in the fertile soil of our perfidy, Worthiness."

"It isn't our fault this time. I must leave off guarding this Gek child and her prize if I am to douse the fire in the swamp. You'll sit with me, Lia, and keep your eyes on that box."

My mother straightened up at that. "Azwan, wouldn't your guards hold her better? What if she escapes?"

"It's not the Gek, but what she carries. The demon is in that box. I can feel it. If Scripture is any guide, it'll seek a human body so it can walk among us. You'd be easier to defeat than one of my guards."

My hands flew up to my face. "Mami, no!"

An enormous, sooty hand clamped over my mouth. The Commander's great paw held my silence, his meaty arm locking me in place against his armor. A dagger pressed against my lower back. I stiffened my spine and bit down hard on my lip.

S'ami turned in the punt to face backward, his eyes riveted to the giant plume of smoke that rose overhead. Hot ash swirled and sizzled into the water around us. Would the marsh catch fire? I realized that we might've been in danger all along. Mami's boat pulled up alongside his punt and guards helped her aboard. She sat at one end by the Gek, taking pains to keep from stepping anywhere near the blue light. It faded and flickered out.

For a moment, nothing happened. The Gek huddled unconscious on her side, but I could see the gentle rising and falling of her chest. The tin box lay beneath one arm.

S'ami sat across from Mami, eyes squeezed shut, his breathing heavy. He began incantations in the lively rhythm of Tengali. The wisdom knot danced in S'ami's hand, and he tightened his grip. Slowly, slowly, he raised his arms, his sleeves falling back to reveal muscled forearms. His chanting turned to the common tongue again for the spell I'd heard the Ward's high priest use to summon Nihil's power when all else failed. It was the incantation of last resort, unmistakable in its desperate tone:

From the void I come, through the abyss I fall;
My place is nowhere, and from naught comes all.

An explosion ripped across the faraway swamp. Flames shot into the sky. The force sent ripples through the marsh waters, rocking all the craft and sending men headlong into grass. The Commander released me as we both lurched sideways.

S'ami let out a shout. "An eldritch power. Like I've never seen." His face shone.

Men scrambled back into boats. Behind us, treetops burned to the horizon. Smoke obliterated the sky.

Mami hovered over the Gek, her angled features twisted in horror. At her feet, the tin box glowed a bright orange.

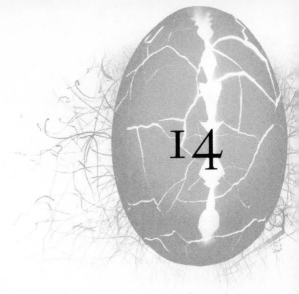

14

Nor shall you abide those who abandon faith; I
am god, you shall follow only me.
  —from Oblations 10, The Book of Unease

Our crafts drew toward a boat launch and a rickety dock
near the tail end of Port Sapphire. A crowd began shouting
and waving as they spotted us. Several healers in the blue
smocks of the sick ward milled with constables in their
yellow coats. Dockworkers scurried to pull our boats in,
tying scarves around their noses and mouths to block the
fingers of smoke that trailed us.

My boat went first so the Commander could leap out
and give orders. He transformed what had been a loose
mob into purposeful teams. At his direction, workmen
pulled wounded and dead Feroxi out of their boats and
loaded them onto a scow. They pulled Valeo up, too, and
I thought I heard him moan. I watched until I could see
only the soles of his muddy boots, the ones I'd stomped
on. I kept watching for him until the crowds and smoke

combined to block my view of much of anything. I choked back dry, scratchy sobs, my eyes watering freely.

Valeo had looked after me in the swamp until he needed looking after, and I couldn't be sure those were only orders. I had to remind myself he was a bloodthirsty, lusty idiot with a bad shave. And he was dying. I suddenly had trouble breathing, and it wasn't only the swamp fire to blame. I should flush in shame. The Gek were burning in their tree homes back there while I got all giddy about a man, even if he did have shoulders the width of the mainland and answered to "His Highness."

I stood around not quite knowing what to do with myself, until I saw guards clambering from the boats with darts jutting from exposed skin. I waded into the crowd toward the first healer I saw. The Commander's booming voice ordered my halt. I turned back. "The Gek poisoned them," I said.

The healer brushed past me. "We'll get them all," the woman said. But she didn't know the poison. I carefully pulled out the pin I'd saved and grabbed another healer's sleeve, a man.

"Look, it's a Gek poison."

He squinted at the tiny point between my fingertips and the pinkish blot. "You know it?"

I shook my head.

The healer shrugged. "It's not much use to us, even if you did. Nihil's theurgy should get most of this solved. Thank you, though your weeds aren't much help here."

He hustled past as if I'd delayed him all day. Why did he treat me as if the poison were something *I'd* gathered? I stewed and pushed forward again, only to have the crowds press me back. More elbows and shoulders found their mark on my torso; I was being sidelined when that little pin could've meant saving someone's life with the right herb-lore.

Everything I'd done out in the swamp didn't matter at all to anyone here; I would always be the know-nothing, out of place and in the way.

Alright, let them cast their magic, for what good it would do. I tucked the pin back into a corner of my dress and felt contrary doing so. Sure, let them come to us when they ran out of other options. Maybe I'd jab that tiny bit of steel where it hurts most.

I hated being wrong in school, but it was so much worse at times like this to suspect I was right and have no one listen.

Soon, the Azwan's punt was the only craft left in the water; all the others had been emptied and loaded onto racks by the boat ramp. Guards poled the punt in and helped S'ami onto dry ground. He turned back toward where Mami huddled beside the tin box and the gray, limp Gek. The pleasing music I'd heard on the pier that day his ship landed sounded again, sonorous and low. An answering buzz came from the boat, from where Mami hugged her knees to her chest. Poor, brave Mami. She didn't budge at all, and though her eyes didn't move from the bottom of the boat, she didn't let on how terrified she must be. But I could see her face tighten, her lips pursed.

The buzzing—the same grating sound I'd heard earlier—grew louder as the box levitated and began spinning. S'ami's sound matched it, and the two noises dueled, one chiming and sweet, the other scraping and bitter. I know which I preferred. What I didn't know was which one to root for. Maybe they'd destroy each other, and we'd all go home, tired but triumphant. I imagined a sad ballad for the tragic hero S'ami, sung in our Ward by a dour-faced choir, everyone weeping whether they'd witnessed his fall or not.

The ballad would have to wait. S'ami wrapped his protective sphere of light around the box as it shot forward, rotating corner over corner, tumbling in a crazy, twirly, nonsense way within that sphere. The box didn't open, and nothing spilled out, but the entire crowd ducked as the sphere sailed past, barely clearing the tops of our heads.

The guards parted the crowd and led S'ami through, falling in behind him as the tin box flashed ahead. The barge pulled out as soon as S'ami was aboard, with workmen rowing in long strokes. Soon, the constables were gone, too, and the healers had left with the main party. Even the dock owner was off tying up his boats with his crew.

I helped Mami out of the punt, and she collapsed onto shore, resting her head between her knees. I rubbed between her shoulders and took a deep breath. I fixed my head scarf back around my mouth again—it wasn't terribly secure, but it didn't seem to matter at the moment.

"We made it, Mami. We got lucky."

She peered up at me. "I don't feel particularly lucky."

"What do you suppose was in that box?"

Mami stared at the roaring fire on the horizon. "Something worth destroying a civilization for, I guess, and risking even the soldiers' lives. I'd have thought he'd care more about them, at least."

"Their Commander said thirty-three were dead," I said. "The box must hold something S'ami can't do without."

Mami nodded. "It's hard to know what to believe. All I can say is that we were all very, very wrong to presume it was just a lump of rock from one of the other planets or a spark from the sun. I don't know that anyone really wanted it to be a demon. Except the Azwan of Uncertainty, that is."

I gave a quick glance around to make sure no one heard her. The dockworkers were straggling away in twos and threes. Even so, I kept my voice low. "He did seem proud of himself."

"It's his moment," Mami said. "Some history scroll somewhere will carry his name someday."

"And us?"

"Lucky to be alive. Like you said."

She leaned into me and let out a few short sobs. I held her and let her cry softly into my shoulder for a few moments. I swallowed back the lump in my own throat, but I let her take her time until she was ready to draw a deep breath and sit up again.

When Mami spoke next, her voice was raggedy. "We are lucky to be alive, Hadara. It just bothers me that I ought to feel grateful to the Azwan who put us in harm's way."

"I know, Mami," I said, feeling useless. What else was there to say?

I hesitated before I asked my next question, staring at the small creature huddled in the boat, her chest rising and falling but otherwise motionless. There was something I had to know, and I thought I'd earned the right to know it. "Is now a bad time to ask about my grandmother?"

Mami exhaled sharply. "No, I guess it isn't."

"You said something to the Azwan about her and Reyhim."

Mami gave me one of her sidelong looks that told me she was weighing how much I ought to know. "Ask away."

"Is he my grandfather?"

Mami shrugged. "I never wanted him to be my father, so I never asked, to be honest. It stopped mattering to me long ago, and it clearly never mattered to him. I thought you were interested in my mother?"

"Yes!" I nearly shouted. "Everything, please. The herbs, the heresy, everything."

She launched into her story: Her mother had gathered herbs and made medicines much the same as her mother before her and on down since the island had been settled centuries earlier. Mother to daughter, generation to generation, a world of herb-lore passed on by word of mouth alone. Ward Sapphire had always taken what it wanted but otherwise looked the other way. The women of my mother's line had always obliged—until my grandmother refused.

"I don't know what set her off, really," Mami said. "Whether it was the end of her affair with Reyhim, or something else. I was a child, remember."

"I know, but I think I'm confused," I said. "Are you saying the Ward turned on her after she *stopped* gathering herbs?"

Mami coughed and gagged from a sudden puff of smoke that hit us. I helped her unwrap her own scarf so she could hold it over her face. It made for a flimsy mask, but it was better than breathing the ash directly. We'd left a water jug in the punt, and I fished it out. Mami continued after we both took a drink, easing the searing soreness in our throats, and splashed some of it into our stinging eyes.

A fever had broken out in Port Sapphire, Mami said, probably brought over in one of the merchant ships. It had spread in a few six-days from one end of town to the other, killing the old, the very young, and anyone already sick. Then it began killing those in the prime of health. Mami's voice caught as she spoke. It had been a painful time. The healers went from home to home, and when stronger magic was needed, the priests went, too. Water was purified, food was blessed, entire canals were emptied and refilled. Nothing worked.

"And through it all, your grandmother refused to grind a single root or steep so much as a leaf."

I sat in shock. "How could she sit by and watch people die?"

"She told people if they believed in the Temple of Doubt's teachings, they should let the Temple cure them."

"And that didn't sit well with the Temple, I'm sure." I was having trouble swallowing this. I'd have her hanged, too, I decided.

Mami propped her chin on one elbow and stared off at the distant fire again. "You think the Temple likes to be seen failing at anything?"

Something occurred to me, a connection forming in my brain. I reversed what Mami had said, about teachings and cures. "Was your mother saying that, if they wanted her help, they had to stop believing in the Temple? In Nihil's power?"

Mami whipped her head toward where the dock owner had lashed the last of his boats together, except the one at our feet. "Shhh . . . yes, that's exactly what I'm saying."

157

I turned that over in my head a few moments. How could someone not believe in Nihil's power? He was Nihil. He was god. He put us here and gave us life and the Eternal Tree for afterward. How could someone tell everyone to just forget about him? I may be a bad student, but I wasn't stupid. I believed in a Nihil that other people had seen and talked to and even lain down with and whose magic was tangible and real, even if the priests and healers couldn't always make it work, even if it did nothing at all but was just for show, which is what I'd suspected for some time.

I didn't budge. "I really *don't* understand. How could she tell people not to believe in Nihil's magic? What were they supposed to do instead? If they don't go to the Temple, where do they go?"

Mami grinned. "You're getting this much faster than I did. I was already married to your father when I started hearing stories about my mother and the things she said and what she was trying to do."

"What *was* she trying to do?"

Mami laughed. I was shocked. We were talking about my grandmother's terrible blasphemies that had rightly gotten her hanged.

"You're laughing," was all I could manage to say.

"I know I shouldn't," Mami said. "But I think I'm entitled to say what I want today, considering what the Temple just put me through."

"Me too, then."

"Yes, you, too. So, talk. I know that look, Hadara. You have a hundred things whirling around in that busy mind of yours."

I inhaled, deep and long. Best to start with something small and solid. The not-believing part was much too huge and shapeless to wrestle to the ground just yet. "Why do we keep doing it? The herbs. It's blasphemy, right? Or something like double-triple blasphemy to keep gathering them if grandmother was meant to be an example."

Mami nodded. "Alright, that's an easy one. The elder women all around me insisted on it. My mother and grandmother had taught a number of the local ladies a little herb-lore, just bits and pieces, here and there, in case the worst happened, which it did. So the other women taught me. One knew a few salves, another could make tinctures, a third had some tisane blends I should know. Imagine if all this knowledge vanished; imagine no way to treat all the aches and pains and diseases for all those times Nihil's magic falls short.

"Even the Ward priests never meant to carry their threats too far. Reyhim was the only one who seemed intent on following Scriptures down to the last detail, and no one else was going to stand up to him. But once Reyhim got his promotion to Azwan and left us, Ward Sapphire went right back to tolerating the herb-lore. Nihil had made it clear more mass deaths from a natural cause wouldn't be tolerated, but they couldn't muster up the magic to cure so many. I suppose the priests had to weigh the greater and lesser evils."

This was what it meant to be a woman in my line, then. Mami carried on the family business despite its danger. She didn't dare stop. She had to keep balancing along the edge of that invisible, ever-moving line between what the priests said and what they really seemed to want. And I'd likely have to do the same.

We didn't get to pass along a name, like my father's house was known by his name because of his high standing in Port Sapphire. Mami and I passed along our store of knowledge, and it stretched across generations. People would depend on us even if it cost our lives.

"But the healers pushed me out of the way just now," I said, my voice insolent. "They had no use for anything I could offer."

Mami shook her head. "What I saw was you looking irritated and hurt. You were thinking more about yourself, Hadara, while the healers rightly focused on the injured. That's a hard lesson, I know. It's one that only experience can teach you."

If she started on the you're-too-young part that I sometimes got, I was going to boil over. I decided to steer the conversation back to where I'd started.

"Why am I hearing this now for the first time?" I sounded like a little girl throwing a tantrum, but I couldn't stop. "You held this back from me. All of it."

Mami gave me a shrewd, calculating look, the kind she levels at Babba when she wants something he's not prepared to give. "Would you have listened?"

I had no answer. Probably not. Maybe thinking it was all a grand, vaguely daring adventure was the part that had appealed to me. I sighed, letting some of the tension seep away. "Why does the Temple both reward and punish us?"

"I don't know, blossom. It's the Temple of Doubt, remember, not the temple of faith or compassion or even wisdom. And we really must go—here comes that dock owner."

I wasn't nearly ready to leave. I hadn't gotten to the larger questions yet.

I grabbed her arm. "It's not good enough. I'll have to spend my whole life doing as you have. You can't simply say, it's the Temple of Doubt, so hide your doubts and live with it. How do you live with it?"

She patted my arm. "Time for that later."

The dock owner had turned and was waving at us. He called over, "You still need the boat?"

Mami shook her head, and we stood up and dusted ourselves off as best we could. I leaned into the craft and scooped up the Gek. It didn't seem right to leave her.

"Hadara, no," Mami said.

I hesitated. We were likely in enough trouble already. "If you really think I ought not to . . ."

"How would we hide her? What do you think the high priest would say? Besides, what do you think we'd do with her?"

"Take care of her," I said, realizing how feeble I sounded.

"She's not a pet."

"I know. Really, I do. She'll go when she's ready."

We both took a long look back at the burning swamp. The flames were dying down, but smoke singed our nostrils, even through our scarves. The Gek child might never go home again from what I could see, but I didn't have any other answer.

Mami paused and then spoke haltingly. "Alright. You did say she's the shaman's daughter. Maybe we should take care of her because we owe them at least that much. And I suppose one more by our hearth won't change much. I'll think up something to tell the priest."

We got ready to go, Mami giving a final wave to the dock owner as he stared slack-jawed at the Gek in my arms. "Suppose you got the Azwan's alrighty for that? They make awful pets, though. Mind you—feed 'em their fish, or they'll be into your pantry."

Mami thanked him, and we made our goodbyes. I'd tethered our canoe far from the boat launch that morning to stay out of everyone's way. I was happy I'd picked an isolated spot at the end of a fat stub of dry land, covered with trees and brush but within easy sight of the city. I lay the Gek in the canoe, where she turned over soundlessly.

"They don't take much to magic, do they?" I asked. "It does things to them."

"Us, too," Mami said. "They just show it sooner."

"How does it harm us?"

"It makes us rely on easy answers, for starters," Mami said. Her soft features hardened into a sneer that wasn't typical for her. "Can't do something for yourself? Get the priest to wave his talisman over you. Maybe it'll happen. Maybe not. If it doesn't, ah well, maybe your doubts are too strong, and Nihil can't bother with you. For the privilege of possibly having Nihil's brief attention, you get to let the priest have a say in every aspect of your life."

With that, Mami snatched several canvas sacks from the canoe.

"Wait a moment," I said. "It's not that you don't believe in Nihil. It's the Temple that bothers you. I can see that. I want them gone, same as you. I do! Was my grandmother like this, too?"

It was as if Mami were a full waterskin and she'd suddenly deflated. She seemed smaller, frailer. "No, I'm sorry.

I do get cynical. It's a feeling far beyond doubt, maybe all the way into despondent."

"Was this how . . ."

"No, she was hopeful, your grandmother. She was all sunshine and hugs and 'There—don't you feel better now?' And I know Reyhim adored her. But he saw a chance to further himself, and my mami's corpse was his stepping stone."

I threw my arms around her. "I'm so sorry. Oh, Nihil's earlobes, I'm the sorriest person ever. I wanted that tin box for myself, I did, so I could get the Temple to leave our island for good. I thought I could help in some crazy way."

Mami hugged back. "Hadara, that's terrible. Noble and selfless and kind, but truly terrible. If that thing is what the Azwan says it is, it would destroy you. No, Hadara, we stick to what we know, you and I."

She shoved an armload of canvas sacks at me. I groaned, knowing what she intended. We'd left before dawn and it was then sometime between high heat and latesun, with no break for meals and no rest from the heat or soot. I was tired and eager for home. Mami had other ideas and patted a sack for emphasis.

"We're out," she said. "Of everything."

"What if someone sees us? There are guards everywhere." Being aware of the Temple's hypocrisies didn't make me any less fearful of crossing that invisible line they kept redrawing.

"We've been with the Azwan today," Mami said. "That'll cover us. I reason this is our only chance for a while. Let's make the best of it."

Imagine if all this knowledge vanished.

But then another voice rang in my ears, that of the Commander: *he'd rather swallow poison than a potion.*

On the mainland and closer to the Temple of Doubt, there was no room for what Mami and I did. My heart pounded in my rib cage thinking of Valeo stretched out, unconscious, possibly dead, with no way to help him. Yes, something in nature cooked up by the Gek had done that to him, but something in nature could be curing him, too, perhaps. Deep within, I'd always had more faith in Mami's wild harvest than in magic, but hearing her say it aloud confirmed it for me more solidly.

Her words rang in my ears as we hiked north, beyond the end of the marsh, toward one of Mami's favorite spots for herb gathering. We hit solid ground lush with every sort of blossom and berry. It felt like a crime trampling the intricate floral lacework underfoot or swatting away tapestries of spider silk. I did know what to look for and when it was ready for harvesting, be it blossom or berry or root or stalk. Mami had made sure of that.

To her own mother, this simple act of rooting around and plucking things had been sacred in its way. It could be its own Temple of the Wild, or Ward Fens, with its sanctuary of prickly grass and swaying palms. But what good was all that knowing if my grandmother hadn't used it for anything? If all this herb-lore was mine to gather and guard, it would have to go to good use, too. I thought of the girls who singled me out in school for mocking. Yes, them, too. The guards who'd ransacked our home. Valeo. Oh, by all three moons! How much I wanted to help him. If I prayed to Nihil for Sami's magic to work, would it help? Would it hurt? Was there any way to know?

S'ami—could I ever bring myself to come to his aid? Yes, S'ami, even. I couldn't imagine withholding so much as a cup of tea from the man, even if handing it to him made me cringe. That's how I'd been raised. That's who I was.

But there would be no more sick, weak Valeos someday, not if there was some way to help it. Someday, the Temple would have to value what Mami and I did. Somehow.

Such thoughts helped me tap a reserve of strength even as I resisted the temptation to eat everything I plucked. I was famished. We pulled up swamp root with small spades and plucked callousvine leaf. My fingertips smarted from sweet nettles, my eyes burned from onion weed. I wrestled thick hydrocanth pods out of their tough bromeliads with all the solemnity of Sabbath prayers. I trimmed stalks and separated vines from tree trunks with a knife I kept in our boat.

When I was with Mami like this, I was no longer the overly tall, awkward girl with the permanently skinned knees. These wiry arms could lift a wooden pole to harvest citrine from a treetop or grapple a palm root out of the muck. These scarred fingers could sift the tiniest stamens from flowers smaller than my pinky nail without losing a single one. And these long, twiggy legs seldom tired even on a day like today that had seen so much violence and turmoil. I didn't have the soft, padded figure that I'd been told men liked, but what I had, I used.

We plodded through a thin stand of trees until we came to a clearing where we knew moonblooms some-times grew. We were lucky: the ground swelled with the prickly succulent, its fist-sized, pale flowers tightly bound until the sun went down. Each fat petal was packed with nectar that settled tummies, eased fevers, and cured a dozen other complaints. More than a few lives had been saved with moonbloom. It fetched a high price among those brave enough to trade in such things. Finding it's rare, and keeping it secret is rarer. I'd have been thrilled at our discovery even if I hadn't been newly convinced it was about as holy as something in nature could be.

I pulled out the pin again. Most of the poison had rubbed off. There was only a dab of magenta at the very end. I tugged at Mami's sleeve and showed it to her.

"What do you suppose it is?"

She bent and took a closer look. "I didn't think to grab anything, Hadara. That's very clever of you. That bright color comes from a salamander, if I remember correctly."

"A salamander?"

She nodded. "Those little purply salamanders that skittle everywhere? Their skin has some sort of odd toxin. The Gek make some sort of dream drug from it, but it mixes badly with Feroxi blood, it would seem."

A dream drug? Such things are extra banned by the Temple. The Temple teaches we're not supposed to dream unless Nihil scrambles our sleeping thoughts himself. Strange the Gek would want such a power for themselves.

Mami glanced around at the moonblooms. "Well, look where we've landed. Never mind poisonous salamanders, we've got a cash crop to pick. I shall dream of the new slippers I plan to buy."

We dug up the shallow root balls by hand for repotting, stuffing our satchels until we couldn't fit so much as another stem. My arms were scratched and bleeding from the effort.

It took until after dark to get back to our canoe. The Gek girl lay there, more obviously sleeping instead of unconscious. We loaded up and paddled our way home through byways and shortcuts to our peninsula clear on the opposite side of the city, too tired for more talk. The muscles in my arms knotted until I thought I'd no longer be able to lift them. Inside, however, my mind floated along on Mami's explanations to some far shore where my life was starting to make sense and my choice to follow her began to feel wiser, even fated. I felt light, airy, even happy.

My mood didn't even lift at the sight of Babba pacing the boardwalk, my sisters sitting cross-legged on our small dock. They spotted us at once, jumping up and waving enthusiastically in the dim torchlight. Babba stopped pacing, his relief obvious even in shadow.

Mami and I picked up our pace, paddling forcefully with a last burst of energy. My arms felt ready to drop from their sockets.

"We're alright!" Mami shouted.

"Mami!" screamed Rishi. And then she kept repeating it: "Mami! Mami!"

Babba stood over us, his face dark, as we moored the canoe and unloaded. Our neighbors and friends had already gone home, and stars twinkled where clouds of smoke had begun to dissipate.

My sisters hugged Mami, then me, then each other, then Mami again.

"I'm so happy you're back," Amaniel said to me. She'd been crying, and so had Rishi. "We heard only bad news. The swamp and the fire and that many of the guards had died. But no one knew anything about you and Mami."

Mami glanced around. "Where is everyone? I'd think at least your sisters would've stayed with you, Rim."

"I sent them home," Babba said. "Their fretting wasn't helping anyone."

That was Babba—he hated all that female crying stuff. I felt the same, mostly. Sometimes I wondered if I wasn't secretly the son he'd never had, but one who liked dresses and long hair.

Babba took one look at our full satchels and began fuming. "You didn't."

"I have no stores," said Mami. She gave him a pleading look, but Babba wasn't in a mood to stop.

"With the entire Temple out stomping around, you had to pluck your Nihil-blasted flowers," Babba said. "With me at home thinking you dead, you did this."

He snatched up a sack and undid the string. The next moment, the bag was upside down and its contents dumped in the canal. Mami grabbed the next sack as Babba reached for it, and a tug of war ensued.

Amaniel gasped. "Mami, but the guards are everywhere!"

"Will Mami get arrested?" asked Rishi, starting a fresh round of wailing.

Babba turned to my sisters. "Take Rishi inside. Everything will be fine, girls. Just go."

After another few sobs from both, Amaniel carried Rishi into our house. As soon as the door had shut, Babba ripped the bag from Mami's hand. But Mami was unfazed.

"The Ward won't like that when they come calling," Mami said.

"Did they order this?" Babba's voice sounded skeptical. "Is this suddenly the kind of thing the Temple of Doubt comes all this way for?"

"No. But they will. They have sick men and some queer demon that messes with everything the Azwans do. The priests will be furious if I can't help them."

Father's eyes roamed to the Gek panting in the canoe bottom. She'd been hidden in the canoe's dark bottom, and all but invisible as she lay there, unmoving.

Babba let go of the sack, and it plopped into Mami's lap. "The demon. I can't even think about that. By Nihil's eleven incarnations, you'll end up like your mother, Lia. I'll be fishing your body out of a canal. And Hadara's, too. The two of you are filthy. You look like witches. You smell like witches."

"Rimonil, love, you don't know what witches smell like."

"Like a sewage canal."

Mami's shoulders sagged. "Please, love, I'd like a bath, some supper, some tea."

Babba's jaw worked back and forth in muted fury. He pointed to the Gek. "Dare I ask what heathen beast that is."

I piped up. "The shaman's daughter. She's orphaned. She's important."

"I know what a shaman is," he said. "And it's of no use to me. She goes."

Mami shook her head. "Hadara wants this. The Gek child stays."

"Who makes the rules in this family?"

Mami scowled at him. "You just tossed away pea-tea leaves it took a quarter turn to pick. The Gek stays."

"And just what makes you think . . ."

"I'm still alive, that's what makes me think."

"Lia." He scowled.

"Rimonil." She flashed a lopsided, wicked grin.

That was it. Mami won. Whenever they got to the name part of the argument, it was over. I could've danced in relief. I'd be missing those pea-tea leaves in the morning, though. Pea tea was like my personal wake-up horn. At least Mami had defended the rest of our haul.

She handed the Gek up to Babba, who gingerly adjusted the creature in his arms. He carried his load easily enough up to the house, shaking his head the entire way. After we'd downed a bowl of reheated beans and scrubbed off at the bathhouse, dousing ourselves with whatever remained of the day's hot water, Mami and I went home and slept, lulled by warm blankets and soft pillows. I slept all through morning prayers and so missed the first rumors of the natural girl, the Azwan's favorite, with her odd new pet.

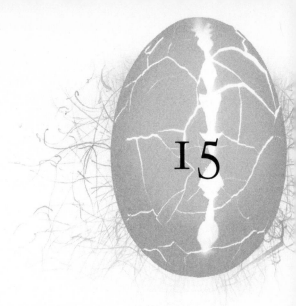

15

There is a Valley of Spite where resentment roots
in the barren soil, its pods frothing seeds that latch
onto the frailest breeze, infecting the unwary with
its whispers of discontent.
—from "The Fall of B'Nai," Verisimilitudes 13,
The Book of Unease

A scream sounded outside near the hearth. Our door,
newly repaired since the Feroxi raid, crashed open again.
Amaniel tripped over the doorway, screaming and pointing
outside.

"That, that *thing* is eating insects!"

I sat up in bed. Broad daylight streamed in from beyond
the mangled door. The stench of charred wood and soot
hit me at once, but what I noticed was Amaniel standing
over me wearing a dress of mine. My nicest dress! It was
flowing and bright, and I'd only just finished embroidering
it. Ocean waves tripped along the hemlines, with silvery
fish darting between the folds and around the arms.

"That's my dress," I said.

"Did you hear me? It's eating bugs."

"Where's your school uniform . . ."

"It's. Eating. Bugs!"

I pulled a loose robe over my nightdress. Whatever was out there obviously had to be handled. This wasn't the more pleasant part of being designated the nature-loving child in the family. Amaniel got praise for sitting in a hot classroom without fainting, and I got to chase away swamp rats and birds or whatever was foraging at our hearth.

Mami was on the patio with Rishi repotting yesterday's haul of moonblooms. Other herbs had been bundled and hung upside down from a drying rack, and a pile lay at Rishi's feet, looking far less fresh than when I'd picked them. We'd been too tired to prepare them the night before. I breathed deeply. The charred smell hung in the air, but there was no trace of smoke from the swamp's fiery end.

Amaniel trailed behind me. "It's in our oven. With bugs."

"I got the bugs part. What's in the oven?"

Rishi waved and blew me a good-morning kiss. "The Gek. I named it Bugsy. It likes beetle larvae. There's lots in with the swamp roots."

Sure enough, the Gek girl had wedged herself in an empty clay oven propped beside the hearth. I kneeled and took a closer look. She was wide-awake and fully recovered, her skin a ruddy color to match the red clay of the oven. Her round eyes peered out and blinked translucent eyelids; then they rotated at opposite angles to study me and take in Amaniel, who hovered behind me. A croak escaped the Gek's open mouth.

Bright day, I gestured. *You alright?*

She nodded. She was old enough to have learned some hand language, at least.

Amaniel leaned in. "I hope you're telling it to go away."

"I'm telling her no such thing."

"It's disgusting." Amaniel folded her arms over her chest. "It peed in the canal."

"Will you shut up?" I returned to the Gek. *Do you have a name?*

She held up fingers and motioned. *Shaman-spawn. Only Shaman is dead.*

She whimpered. Tears gathered in the corners of her bulbous green eyes.

I didn't know how much she knew of her home.

Many of your people are dead. The swamp burned.

The whimpers became wails and then sobs, the Gek spreading slender fingers over her face and weeping. I tried to reach in and hug her, but she withdrew, hissing and signaling. *Only drabskins destroy nests.*

"What's it saying?" Amaniel peered over my shoulder. "Is it leaving?"

I motioned hastily to the Gek. *Come out when you're ready. We aren't the kind of drabskins who hurt.*

I whipped around to Amaniel. "*She* has nowhere to go. And get out of my dress, or I will cut you apart and let the Gek gnaw your thieving bones."

Amaniel grinned. "Not if you want my help."

"Help for what? Being a useless, inhospitable thief?"

Mami cut us off. "That's enough, girls. Amaniel, you'd promised me Hadara wouldn't mind."

Amaniel's grin faded. "Well, she won't. Eventually."

I put my hands on my hips and waited for Mami to straighten this all out. She patted a spot beside her, and I plunked down, feeling out of sorts and sour. "So why am I giving her permission to steal my best dress?"

"You're not. Amaniel is, however, going to make it up to both of us, since she fibbed to me."

"I can't wait."

Mami chuckled. "And to think your father wanted boys. He'd miss all this fun."

"Not funny."

Mami's face grew serious. "They closed the whole Ward."

That grounded me again. There were bigger goings-on than larcenous sisters.

"The demon? Did they destroy it?" I asked. A new hope rose within me.

Mami shook her head.

A million details came rushing back. We were alive, so, obviously, the end of the world hadn't come, but there was no one at our hearth besides my family. The gossiping relatives had stayed away.

"Any news at all?" I asked. "About the demon, about the poison, anything?"

"Not yet," Mami said. "By evening, I expect."

I couldn't sit here and wait for news to come to me. "Maybe they'll know something on the wharf. That is, if you can spare me."

Mami seemed to read my thoughts. "We already have it worked out. Rishi can help me. Amaniel's going with you. Listen to her. She knows how to get past the priests better than you."

If that was designed to make me feel better about my missing clothes, it didn't. I made a face at Amaniel and slipped on a dress to nearly rival the one she wore. It covered me chastely from elbows to mid-calf, with just enough showing for a few anklets that jingled cheerily when I walked. The top hugged my narrow waist before flaring out at my hips, which was about the best I could do with my stringy shape. I'd sewn the dress from aqua-colored broadcloth with wide umber and orange meanders that had taken many six-days to stitch. That should impress the priests more than any uniform. We both knotted our hair beneath lacy headscarves, draping them loosely behind our ears as we did on the Sabbath. A pair of dangly earrings later, and I felt like I could impress Nihil himself. If we didn't learn anything, it wouldn't be because anyone snubbed us.

After all, the last time any of these guards had seen me, I'd been a mud-soaked mess. That wasn't the real me. I wanted them to know that. More importantly, I had to remind myself of that. What did it mean to be civilized? Scriptures taught us that magic, belief in the supernatural, faith in Nihil, lifted us from the lowest, meanest creature that crawled. And that creature wasn't going to be me. I needed to be someone the guards, at least, would accept.

I tucked a stray curl into place and grabbed Amaniel's hand.

A few twists and turns of the boardwalk connected us to a stretch of mainland and the cobblestone square by Ward Sapphire's wide gates. Feroxi guards armed from top to bottom patrolled every handwidth of it. Sentries paced by the gates and beyond, far into the grassy courtyard and all the way to the Ward's magnificent carved doors. Archers roamed atop walls and roofs. They carried bows as tall as themselves and long, fat quivers of arrows.

A guard near us grunted, and we stopped. Amaniel bowed, and I followed, holding my right hand to my dress top and with my left hand lifting a corner of my skirt. It required some choreography, and Amaniel pulled it off gracefully. The guard directed his attention to her.

"Move along, mistress. This part of the city is closed today."

"Nihil's theurgy upon you, Pious Sentry of the Temple," she said. "We come but seeking news of the Azwan's great deeds."

The scowling guard didn't bother with the proper response to her salutations. "There is none. Move along."

Amaniel bowed again and turned to leave. Since when did she give up so easily?

"Wait," I said. I found a spear tip against my chest. That wasn't the reaction I wanted, but I couldn't go back without knowing at least one thing. "Valeo. His Highness. He's a first guardsman?"

The spear lifted to my throat. I'd caught the man's attention, but probably Valeo wasn't worth being beheaded over. I wasn't even sure what Valeo looked like under his clunky helmet. I ought to go home and not worry about a short-tempered half-Feroxi with grabby hands. Who'd defended my life, more than once. Who was fiercer than a mash cat. And made sure I wasn't left behind in a burning swamp. And, and—I didn't know what else. Everything else.

I placed a fingertip on the spear and tried to push it away. It wasn't budging. The guard took a step forward and glowered. I took a step back and held my breath. "How is he? Did Valeo survive? Please."

Three more soldiers strode over at the second mention of Valeo's name. I soon found their spear tips leveled at me, too. I wondered how far I could push matters before they closed their distance. Amaniel tugged on my sleeve to go, as if my errand couldn't be as important as hers had been the last time we'd had to get past guards. The first guard gave me a once-over, up-and-down look.

"You know His Highness?"

"I accompanied the Azwan yesterday to the swamp."

"You're Lia?"

"I'm Hadara, her daughter."

The men exchanged words in Fernai, and one strode off. A moment later, he returned with a guard I recognized as their Commander. Except for his sunburned face, I couldn't tell he'd been through battle the day before. Even the bronze on his armor gleamed anew. The cold blue eyes held me in the same low regard as ever.

"You clean up well," he said. "The men didn't recognize you."

I bowed again. "I thank you, Pious Sentry of . . ."

"He struggles."

"Valeo?"

"The Prince of the Realm, to you. Unless you know him better than I think you do."

I bit my lip. Maybe I only wished I knew him better. I could feel my face growing hot. *He struggled.* I didn't know what that meant and tried to ask.

Amaniel interupted. "Please, Righteous Guardians of Nihil's Person, you must forgive my sister. Her speech is unworthy, but her soul is pure. I know she's grateful to hear your prince yet lives."

By Nihil's wives, she was good. I wanted to elbow her in the lip though. My speech is unworthy? I'd show her unworthy speech later. I smiled through gritted teeth at the Commander. He waved the spear tips away and nodded toward Amaniel. "Then explain to your sister the injured were moved to your Customs House. There's nothing else to tell."

We left with another deep bow and sped toward Pilgrim Bridge, where guards waved everyone past so long as no one paused for too long a look back at the Ward. There was nothing to see anyway, not a single sign of life besides the many patrols. The star-demon had obviously brought this on.

I wasn't about to forget that the tin box was meant for me. At least the Gek said so, and it seemed to have spoken to them. They weren't afraid of it. S'ami insisted the demon caused the fire in the swamp, but how did I know that was so? Maybe its clash with S'ami had destroyed the swamp. The Gek certainly wouldn't harm their own homes. Nor would they have harbored a creature who threatened to destroy them, and they hadn't seemed like they were being held hostage or under some sort of spell.

Maybe I was rationalizing to myself. I didn't want anything to do with any demon if it was a killer. The very idea made my flesh crawl. What would I do with it? I at least wanted to know what it wanted from me. Was that too much? A few moments to hear its mission for me might be all I needed. What did it mean by getting something undone? And what did it want undone so badly it would ravage everything around it in the process?

And why me?

I had no standing in the Temple, that was for sure, and that probably was reason enough for the Temple to keep it from me. It wasn't right. The star, whatever it was, might have nothing to do with Nihil at all.

Then again, maybe the Azwans could get rid of it, and then they'd leave Port Sapphire and life would go on. Maybe that could happen without anyone or anything leveling the whole town the way the swamp was all but gone. Maybe I could get close to it without it jumping into my head, or whatever it was that people were so afraid of.

And maybe I could get Kuldor to rotate backwards and make day into night.

I sighed, and Amaniel nudged me.

"You going to stare all day at soldiers again?"

"What?" I turned toward her, momentarily thrown off.

"Like you do with sailors. I don't know what you see in them, honest."

I scowled. "You will. Wait a year or two. And just so you know, my speech isn't unworthy."

"It is," Amaniel said. "No one was threatening to poke a hole in *my* throat."

"We weren't in any real danger." I was going to throttle her. "Not compared to yesterday, anyway."

"Oh, so sorry I didn't go to the swamp and get all filthy with you, big sister. Y'know, back here in civilization, you have to keep your mouth clean, too." Amaniel sniffed at me. "You should be glad I helped you."

"You should be glad I didn't snatch my dress off your ungrateful back while the guards were standing there."

"You wouldn't."

"Would."

We stormed along without speaking after that. Was it so difficult to get my own sister to respect me even a copper-weight's worth?

Not that it mattered what I wanted—no matter how much I'd given the Temple yesterday, I'd gone right back to being nobody today. Amaniel would always be the one everyone preferred, even soldiers who wouldn't be able to pick us out from a crowd.

The humiliation burned, as it always had.

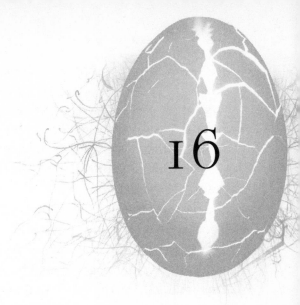

16

A dram of good gossip's worth a crate of gold.
—Meridian proverb

On Callers Wharf, people went about their business but in hushed fear. More Feroxi archers held their rooftop vigils, and foot patrols eyed activity in every kiosk and stall.

Two new merchant ships had berthed since yesterday, and longshoremen were unloading their holds in silence. Their work songs were usually smutty and made my ears burn, but I found myself missing their raucous sound. The bazaar was as packed as ever, but I needed no prodding today to make straight for the Customs House until a woman called to us from a market stall. A cousin of ours waved us over to where she sold spices and pungent teas— all certifiably without any natural medicinal properties whatsoever—out of burlap sacks and wooden bins.

She leaned in close and whispered.

"Hey, loves, what's the word by your hearth?"

Amaniel patted our cousin's pregnant belly. "You look beautiful, Dina. Maybe you can give us good news soon."

"By Nihil's whim, the baby will come any day," Dina said. She glanced about as if one of the soldiers might take it away. "Anyway, you're just about tearing up cobblestones in your hurry. I figured you had word of something. Especially you." She pointed at me.

"You mean about yesterday?" A day ago could've been a decade ago from the way I felt about it. It hadn't occurred to me that I'd be the day's main gossip as, mentally, I'd already moved on to needing some new piece of news about the Azwans barricaded in the Ward or the wounded Valeo. Dina would probably hand over her whole stall to hear what had happened in the swamps yesterday.

I'd guessed right. She could barely contain herself.

"Listen, cuz," she said. "You go nowhere without the full story."

This was exactly what I needed—a salve for my bruised pride. Sure, I'd gone into the swamp, but I'd come back with the rarest, most refined gold any gossip-starved person might want. I had returned with a story that no one else had ever heard, and it was so out of the ordinary, they probably couldn't imagine the slightest detail, either.

I grinned. "I divulge nothing without a glass of tea."

"You don't haggle very well. I was going to offer."

I sat down on a worn rug that served as the stall's floor, Amaniel beside me. Dina waved over a small throng of other vendors and bystanders. I relished the attention, sorry to say, and forgot all the maidenly modesty I'm supposed to show on such occasions. Not that anyone would've endured a sweet demurral; I was peppered with questions before I could take a breath. A few kept an eye out for guards, and others shushed me if my voice rose above a murmur.

The glass of tea eventually turned into a midday meal. Someone produced a plate with flatbread piled with fish stew from one of the many food vendors. I washed it down with some of Dina's best tisane blend, making sure to praise its quality.

"Never mind that," Dina said. "Drink up, and tell us more. The Gek tried to give the box to you? What did they say?"

What had they said? I tried to recall word for word, seeing in my mind their hand gestures and translating them again.

The star seeks one who knows to undo what must be undone. The star comes to you as you come to it.

The crowd reeled. Amaniel gasped. I hadn't realized until then to what degree those words indicted me as an enemy of the Temple. It did make it sound like we'd chosen each other, the demon-star and me. That wasn't the case. Not exactly. The fish stew churned uneasily in my stomach. I could choke on the flatbread. It wouldn't be much of a reach for anyone here to consider me the opposite of all that was pious and wise. I fidgeted with the lace on my head scarf, tugging at a loose thread, my insides beginning to bubble unhappily. This isn't what I had wanted at all. I was right back to saying the wrong thing. Would my wayward tongue be the only talent people knew me for?

Amaniel turned to the crowd. "I know she didn't get the star. My mother told me so. The star's with the Azwans."

Several nodded. The fish-stew vendor waved a dish towel at me. "Them Gek are nasty creatures. I been hearing what they done to the Temple Guards. Lucky all Nihil did was roast their scaly bottoms."

Another man shook his head. "Sent their souls back to the forge for remaking, I pray."

I didn't correct them on the reason for the swamp fire. Dina was perched on the only stool, cooling herself with a reed fan. "Never you mind that prophecy, Hadara. S'long as you stay away from the Ward till the Azwans are done with their business, I'd think."

The crowd buzzed in agreement, and I didn't tell them that finding the tin box had until recently been a goal of mine. Now my only goal was to finish my story and the stew, and relish both, if not necessarily in that order.

The fish-stew cook was an older man, grizzled and lean. "Mind you stay away from all that natural business for good. A fine man like Rimonil should have a pious family."

Dina kicked him. "Meaning?"

He rubbed his leg. "Ain't nothing on you, Dina of Faddar. But Lia sure is a strange one, for all her beauty."

"That's my uncle's wife you're insulting," Dina said.

If Amaniel hadn't intervened, I thought it might come to blows, and I didn't rate fish-stew man's chances against Dina.

"We know, kind sir, what others think of our odd little family," she said. "I assure you, Nihil has no more faithful servants than my mother and sister."

Dina motioned toward Amaniel. "See? Pious. Nothing to worry about."

"Let's hope so." Master Fish Stew didn't sound convinced.

"Listen," I said, hoping to change the topic. I didn't like the idea that both Mami and I needed apologizing for or that Amaniel was the one to do it. "I've enjoyed this man's cooking. I should give him what he bartered for and finish the tale."

That brought a few smiles, at least.

I took my time with it, getting to the part where S'ami battled the swamp fire, and found my throat drying despite the tea. There's nothing quite so satisfying as having a story you're the very first to tell, and knowing all are itching to repeat it until they're as hoarse as old Reyhim.

Two guards burst through the crowd, shoving their way inside, though there was no room for them in the narrow space.

"What goes on here?" said one, his accent thick. My audience fled.

Amaniel gave a bow-curtsy, distracting a guard, who tried to peer down her blouse. "Kind sirs . . . "

"Just break it up," he said.

Amaniel and I set out again with renewed haste. Over my shoulder, I glimpsed one of the Feroxi draining the tea from one of Dina's glasses and crushing it underfoot. They moved on wordlessly, and so did we.

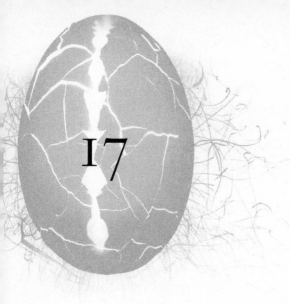

17

What a strange and rare gift, to see parts of your life before you have lived it. Yet for every seer whose visions come true are a score of pretenders who perceive only vapors.
   —from Oblations 12, The Book of Unease

The Customs House bustled with its usual commerce and another score of Temple Guards around the entrances. We bowed and announced ourselves as the Chief Port Inspector's daughters and were shown to the back staircase, out of sight of the main floor. Babba didn't look up from his desk when we approached. He was fingering an abacus and jotting figures in his ledger.

"I told your mother to keep you home," he said. "Amaniel, too."

"She wanted news," I said.

"Did you get any?" He kept his focus on his abacus, fingers flying.

"No. Mostly I did the talking."

"Which is why I wanted you home. Best not to go bragging about this dybbuk business."

"But, Babba, I . . ."

"Should keep out of sight. And act humble if asked. You were flattered to have been of some minor service to the great Azwan. That's all."

"Yes, Babba."

"That's not what you did, is it?"

I hung my head. "I'm sorry, Babba." This was idiotic. The whole immediate world gathered by our hearth to gossip on a normal day, so why all of a sudden was I the one person in all of New Meridian who should shut up just when I had the piece of news everyone wanted? Act humble. Minor service. So pleased to wade hip-deep in muck, get fired upon, and watch men drop like stingflies around me. Not to mention a star-meteorite-creature that talks to Gek and wants to make my acquaintance.

Why did everyone around me always try to keep me down? I thought I'd done something right—many things right. I was entitled to the right kind of attention, for once, and some dignity.

Act humble, he said. I could snort. Maybe I should go back to school and have them whack me a few more times. That's humbling. All I said was, "Yes, Babba."

Babba kept going. "The head of the sick ward has asked to see you if you should come. You'll remember my warning."

"See me?" That meant going downstairs. That meant seeing Valeo—maybe. What warning had Babba given me? It had flown straight out of my head.

Then, I realized, so had any thoughts of the sick men.

"Whatever she asks, politely refuse until she's talked to me," Babba said. "A healer has no say over a man's daughter."

Babba looked up, his eyes immediately roaming over our fine clothes. "Did someone declare this a Sabbath? I feel quite outclassed in my uniform."

Amaniel and I both smiled in relief, but our humor was short-lived. Babba escorted us to the front staircase that spiraled to the main floor, where merchants from around the world would barter over cargo and currency. The vast trading floor had been roped off for an impromptu sick ward.

Before we even got there, shouts and moans from delirious men carried across the room. We turned the corner as healers and orderlies scurried around us in complete pandemonium. Both healers and priests huddled over thrashing bodies, waving gold totems and casting spells to no obvious effect. Healing spells often did at least a little something, ease an ache or a fever, but that didn't seem to be the case this time, not even slightly. Amaniel clutched my hand, and the two of us stood there, wordless and tense, as frantic healers begged their charges to get better. Some were even weeping.

The giants had been strapped down on cots that creaked and bowed beneath those bulky bodies. They thrashed and screamed, their complexions a sickly green. I realized I didn't know what Valeo looked like without his armor, so I scanned the cots looking for one with darker skin. They all looked too pale, too wan, too bloodless.

If only I'd gotten there sooner. I'm not sure what I could've done for them, but guilt washed over me just the same. I'd been gossiping in the marketplace, bragging about my haughty self out there in the swamps, while these men seized up and died. Mortification crept across my skin in hot, tiny pricks of self-loathing. If there was any truth to the old saying that judgment makes the giant, I was the smallest person in the room.

I recognized Healer Mistress Leba Mara as she swept toward us, a bosomy woman with a loud voice and firm manner. "I was about to send for you."

We all bowed, and Babba spoke. "I lend her to you in all pious trust, Leba Mara."

"I won't harm her."

Babba gave me a stern look, a reminder of his warning that I'd forgotten but could easily guess at, and led Amaniel back upstairs. Leba Mara tugged my sleeve and guided me to where one man murmured in his fever, draped only in a loincloth. Beneath his pallor, his skin carried a faint bronze tone. There were scars on his chin. Valeo. He may've taunted me cruelly, but any last thread of hatred or fear slipped away at the sight of him so thoroughly debased.

My gaze roamed up and down his glistening body. I had never seen this much of a man unclothed before, except for the dead Portreeve, and that hadn't really counted. This man was alive. All that skin, stretching along that taut frame. He looked strong, even laid low like this, as if he could pull a barge single-handed, barely straining the muscles that roped along his upper arms and thighs. The idea that anything, especially a tiny pin, could've pierced those mighty limbs struck me as terrifying. If he was vulnerable, who was ever safe?

And his stomach! It was flat as a serving platter, with thick curls of hair—did every man have that? I lingered on the way it tufted around the indent of his navel; then my gaze traveled further to the first fold of the loincloth.

I inwardly recoiled as my mind wandered and looked away. Shame on me for taking advantage of a sick man to stare at his body.

Leba Mara pointed at him. "What's he saying?"

"I'm sorry, I don't speak Fernai," I said. Fire raced up my cheeks. I was sure Leba Mara knew what I'd been thinking.

"No, it's the common tongue. Listen."

I bent closer, until my ear was nearly to his lips, my eyes on his chest and the uneven way it rose and fell.

Golden eyes, he whispered. *The city. Burns. The city.*

"He's been saying that since they brought him in."

I backed away, smoothing the folds of my dress, again and again, anything to distract me from Valeo's ranting. "You don't think it's about me?"

"You have golden eyes."

"With all deference, Healer Mistress, so does my mother. So do a lot of women." My stomach felt like a flock of birds was practicing aerial maneuvers in it.

"And the fire could be the swamp yesterday. Yes, we considered all that. Come."

I looked over my shoulder as I followed her. Poor Valeo. I didn't want to leave him, but Leba Mara had other ideas. With a clattering of beads and a swoosh of her wide skirts, she motioned me to the next bed, where a Feroxi convulsed and pulled against leather tethers. An orderly rushed over to pin him as he shouted in Fernai at an unseen foe. Even tied down and feverish, the giant easily tossed the man off. I helped the orderly up, and he skirted around me to sit on the soldier's chest.

Leba Mara checked the sick man's pulse. "They tell me he's been shouting, 'Nihil is god. There is no other.' Something he's seeing is shaking his faith."

"Are all of them this way?" I glanced around at the thrashing, gyrating, struggling men, the guilt rising up in me again. I remembered the pin and something about salamanders. "Is it the Gek poison?"

"Is it? You'd know, not us. It's why I sent for you. You or your mother, but you'll do."

The healer didn't stop mopping men's brows or forcing a few sips of water through their lips as we talked. The disquiet in my stomach settled itself. There was work to be done.

Sure, I could blame the healers for not listening to me on the pier when I'd first shown someone the pin. I couldn't have told them much then, though, and Mami had warned me about thinking too much of my own poor, misunderstood, self-pitying self. Nihil spit on me, if I hadn't once again wrapped myself up in my own need for glory, or fawning praise, or to be at the center of things, or whatever it was I'd thought I wanted.

Here, I could be of some help, at least. I could be truly useful, not to mention mindful of who really needed attention. I followed Leba Mara on her rounds without waiting to be asked, tucking blankets around those too feeble to resist or squeezing out wet cloths in basins set by every cot. I wasn't sure if that was what I should be doing, but Leba Mara didn't correct or scold, so I kept at it. Tuck blankets, dampen foreheads, refill basins. Every part of me moved to an imaginary drumbeat—steady, swift, but cautious and gentle.

When the orderlies nodded a hasty thanks here and there, it was a better compliment than all the flattery in the marketplace. I picked up my pace, and so did Leba Mara, until we were racing as fast as any of the other healers. Tuck, dampen, refill.

The sick Feroxi weren't any better for my feeble efforts, and there was no convincing me their misery wasn't partly my fault. If I'd kept a few more pins so we could be sure of the poison. If I'd stayed up later to make an antidote. If I'd known to ask the Gek girl about it. If I'd gotten here right away and offered my help. If. A thousand ifs.

I tried to keep my mind on my tasks and on Leba Mara's rapid-fire questions. I related to her what I knew of Gek potions, what herbs we'd seen them use, and what few recipes they'd agreed to share. Leba Mara listened intently, nodding at times or shaking her head in wonder.

In turn, she filled in what she knew. The Azwan had struggled with the demon box the entire way back from the swamp, she explained. It had spun and shook, floating over his head, as if trying to get away. He'd strained to keep it in check, until the healers begged him to take some water, at least.

A laborer whose life was considered expendable held it while S'ami rested. I chafed at that. Who decides who is expendable? S'ami, probably, but I didn't ask. While in the laborer's lap, the box rested, too, not moving or making its grating sound. Its quarrel seemed to be only with S'ami. That jibed with its reaction to Mami; I recalled her alone in the boat with the glowing box, a memory that jammed in my head with the sight of the sick, restless men.

Leba Mara went on. The Azwan used the hiatus to heal the guards' wounds, and there wasn't so much as a scratch afterward. Their journey continued without trouble, save for the Azwan's grim contest with the unseen demon in its container.

The poison, well, that was another thing. The guards walked away fine at first, but began shaking and having visions before they'd even sat down to supper. The sick ward was soon filled to overflowing, but there was no chance to treat them. Orders soon came to evacuate the whole of Ward Sapphire. No explanation was offered. The priests shooed their families away; the whole place emptied except for both Azwans and that mysterious tin box.

"And then this." Leba Mara made a sweeping motion with her arm. "A room full of dying visionaries. This one sees the Temple itself covered in weeds; that one screams of Nihil bleeding. A dream drug, you say. These men'll die of their nightmares."

"Won't the poison wear off?"

"We've lost three. Their prince is next, unless I'm mistaken."

I spun toward where Valeo lay motionless. He'd been so full of life, so sure of himself. I tried not to stammer and to retain some shred of formality. "May I ask, in all humility . . ."

"Why I'm telling you any of this?" Leba Mara wasn't one to mince words.

"It occurs to me I'm only . . ."

"The humble daughter of a port inspector, right? Whose family quietly deals in all kinds of Gek witchery.

If you know anything at all that could help us, now's the time."

I swallowed hard. If I uttered a single syllable about moonblooms or anything else Mami and I had nabbed, it would be seized, and we might be arrested. There was no shortage of Temple Guards stomping around unharmed. If I said nothing, the men around me would succumb to the Gek's terrifying toxin.

Leba Mara gave me a mean squint, the corners of her mouth set. "You do know something. You're too sweet to keep it inside. Alright, out with it."

It was all I could do to draw a deep breath and buy myself a moment to compose my thoughts. I'd seen Mami deal with the priests enough times and knew neither side could ever say outright what they wanted. It was a little like Callers' Wharf, where you pretended you didn't want some knickknack so you could whittle the price down until you sighed and said, *Oh, alright. At that price I guess I have to take it.* Only I was the seller this time, and I'd have to haggle my way out of a noose.

"There might be a way," I said. "But there's no promise it'll work. At best, it would only ease the convulsions. I don't know about the visions."

Leba Mara nodded. "That could buy us enough time for the visions to pass on their own, if we could settle down their bodies."

"I cannot promise it'll work as you hope. There's no telling. There's also the small matter of my safety."

"Ah. Of course. Get your father. I'll work that out with him. Whatever you have planned, it better be good. I can't defend you if you come up with some concoction and they die anyway, you know."

I glanced around the room. Leba Mara was a big woman with a loud voice. Who had heard? I wrung the rag in my hands until my knuckles whitened, my nerves jangling. I remembered what the Commander had said: they'd rather swallow poison than a potion. Then again, my grandmother had refused to help, and that hadn't gone well, either.

"Forgive my impertinence," I said. "But even if it works, the men likely won't drink it, will they?"

Leba Mara wagged a heavily ringed finger in my face. "Everything we've tried has failed. The Gek clearly set this up so that nothing magic will work, Nihil curse them. You say you've never seen this poison either. What does that leave us?"

I couldn't shake the image in my head of the Commander's contempt. "How will you persuade the men to drink it? What if the Temple finds out?"

Leba Mara shook her head. "I run the priests' sick wards. No one dies on my watch if I can help it. If you're worried, I'll work out something with your father. You'll be safe if the men survive."

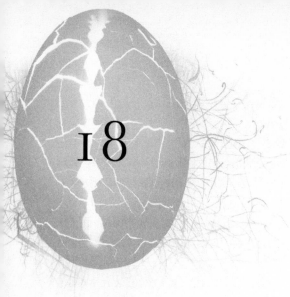

18

*Make no bargains with a demon that you'd ask
a god to keep.*

—*Tengalian proverb*

I'd be safe if the men survived. I suppose that was more
lenient treatment than my grandmother got. I took a deep
breath and nodded. An orderly went for Babba, who pulled
Leba Mara aside as soon as she opened her mouth. They
stood as far from the cots as Babba could drag her. I tried
to read their lips, at least.

I sat on the nearest stool I could find, realizing too
late it was by the dying Valeo. I didn't want to be here. I
couldn't watch him die. I wasn't that brave.

He began to twitch and turn his head this way and that.
I fought to avoid looking down at his fevered face, which
wouldn't have been handsome even when well. Then again,
how could I treat him any differently than the other men? I
reached for a cloth in the nearest basin and got it good and
wet, wringing out only just enough to keep it from dripping.

I mopped the brow that wasn't quite as pronounced as the other Feroxi, the nose that looked like it'd been broken more than once, and along the scar that ran from chin to cheek, now that his helmet was off. Some men have chiseled features; Valeo's had apparently been pounded into existence with a hammer. I should've felt repelled, I suppose, but I'd never minded ugly men. Mami would say Nihil must have put all his handsome on the inside. Though I hadn't seen much of that, either. There must be something attractive about him, or why was I so attached to every finger-width of him?

I worked my way down his torso, pretending I'd have done the same for any of the other men, given the chance. I'd have paused along those shoulders for anyone, had anyone else had shoulders the approximate width of a doorway. At least, that's what I told myself. After another moment, I abandoned any thought of being too generous with my time.

The curls of hair that tufted along his chest gleamed with sweat and obviously needed me to gently swab them all back into place. His head thrashed as I bathed along his arms, but I kept going. The left forearm sported a new scar, gnarled and angry red, from where the Gek girl had tried to chew herself free. S'ami or one of the healers had obviously gotten to it, and I wiped the grime from his hands.

I rinsed and squeezed the cloth again, giving me a moment to clear my head. The air was getting much warmer, which was odd, since it was evening, and a cool breeze would be coming in off the harbor. No, it was me. I was once again having thoughts about the sort of thing a woman does with her husband, wanting to feel his skin against mine, enjoying the sharp contours of his body beneath the damp cloth. What was wrong with me? I was in a sick ward, not a brothel.

This wouldn't do at all.

Valeo shivered and convulsed, but it was feeble, as if he hadn't much fight left in him. That jarred me back to reality. It's not that I couldn't watch him die—I couldn't sit and do nothing, and that impulse gave me more bravery than I felt. He wouldn't remember me doing this, I was sure, but that seemed beside the point. I would remember him this way forever.

It wasn't love, exactly.

I reached for his blanket and tried to tuck it around him, but he kicked it off. I laid it atop him, draped over his middle, and this time he let it stay, still shivering.

No, it wasn't love. It was something much deeper.

All the times I'd seen him, he radiated authority and confidence. I'd always felt silly and small around anyone having to do with the Temple, including my sister. I was so obviously inferior, always saying the wrong thing, every misstep noted and pored over by the schoolmistress or classmates, even Babba.

But Valeo had been different. We'd gotten off to a bad start, to be sure, but he hadn't cut my tongue out for standing up to him, and there was the mash cat and the Gek and the swamps, and, through it all, I'd been something of an equal, as if the possibility of me being equal wasn't a completely crazy idea.

And he was a *prince* and treated me that way.

If he died, I might never know that feeling again.

From across the vast hall, I could see Babba suddenly gesticulate as if a spark had set him off. He scowled and stabbed one finger in the air. Opposite him, Leba Mara had folded her arms across her chest and pursed her lips into a firm line. That didn't look promising for Babba. They were discussing me, and my suggestion for making a moonbloom tonic of some sort, or my safety, and from the looks of it, Babba wasn't hearing what he wanted.

I couldn't overhear them from this distance, so I squinted to see if I could make out what Babba was saying. I'm no lip reader, though, and his mouth formed words rapidly in obvious anger. I kept my focus on what my father might be saying until I felt a tugging at my dress.

"Golden eyes," Valeo said, his voice grating and uneven.

I looked down. His eyes were slits, but they were open. He clutched a fold of my dress.

I wrapped both my slender hands around his meaty one. Please, Nihil, don't let this be his last rally before his breathing stops. I peered into his face to see if there was still fire in his gaze, or a spark, anything. But his eyes had dulled over, his pupils dilated and unfocused through his fever.

"You are half-human and half-Feroxi and all-over fierce," I told him. "And you are going to fight this, yes? You're not going to let a bunch of lizards take you down."

I squeezed his hand harder. "Squeeze back."

Nothing.

"Squeeze, Nihil damn you."

He squeezed. Hard.

Several of my rings bit into my fingers. I winced.

"Alright, you proved your point. You're fighting, yes?"

199

He nodded, ever so slightly, his eyes finding and fixing on my own.

"Well, don't stop on my account. You need to keep going. That's an order."

He didn't smile. His eyes closed.

"Stay with me, or I'll think up something else to call you. Something terrible." I was so close to tears, I didn't know what terrible thing I could say just then.

I wished I knew how to help him. None of the healers knew either, but at least they'd know better how to identify what was wrong. I wanted to be good at healing. I wanted to be them, even in all their panic and racing around. The healers had purpose, and their purpose had a certain purity to it. I wanted to know how it felt to see men get up off their cots and walk away, as fine as ever.

I could do this, if I knew how. But I didn't. All I knew was how to brew and concoct and ferment and distill. So I simply stroked the back of Valeo's hand as I watched Babba confer with Leba Mara. It was something, at least. Babba's expression hardened from stern to furious, his jaw setting in that way of his, his neck coloring.

"Golden eyes," Valeo said again. His grip was loosening on my hands.

"I'm here," I said. "Everything will be alright." Wouldn't it? If there's truly an Eternal Tree to shelter us in the life beyond life, wouldn't everything come out right? I bit my lip.

He struggled to raise his head, and it wobbled as he whispered to me.

"Your sister's at the gate," he said.

"What?"

"Beware." He let go, his head rolling back on his pillow, his eyes closing, his hand sliding from my own. I choked back a sob.

There was nothing more I could do.

I paused long enough to check that his chest rose and fell again, and then again. Then I tucked his blanket around him and fled over to Babba.

"Amaniel, where's Amaniel?" I was almost yelling.

"Upstairs," Babba said. "Did you agree to Leba Mara's terms, Hadara?"

His glower told me I'd done something wrong. I hadn't remembered agreeing to anything. All I'd done was nod my head when she said I wouldn't die if the men lived. Had that constituted an agreement? Was this another of the Temple's tricks?

Leba Mara shrugged. "It's a deal as far as I'm concerned."

"Hadara, you've made this more difficult," Babba said. "I told you to leave any negotiations to me."

What difference did it make? What difference did anything make any longer?

"Their prince is dying," I said, choking back a sob. "He's slipped into the dreaming world."

Leba Mara exchanged a surprised look with Babba. "I shall take care of this."

Babba shook his head. "I'll get that letter first."

"Letter?" I asked.

Babba gave me a nasty, sidelong glance, as if wondering what I would mess up next. "Leave us."

Amaniel. I had to find Amaniel. What gates would she be at? What did Valeo's words mean?

I bounded up the spiral stairs and nearly flew off the balcony before I realized the landing faced the wrong way, toward the outside. I reoriented myself and weaved back through the many hardwood desks. Had Amaniel gone to the Ward, with its wide gates? No, of course not—there she was at Babba's desk, practicing her calligraphy with his inkbrush and scraps of hemproll. She seemed shocked at the sight of me. I was, after all, entirely out of breath and in an utter state of panic.

"Whatever's wrong?" she said.

"Don't get ink on my dress."

She smirked. We both did, but for different reasons. There was no truth to Valeo's vision; it was just a fever rant. I hugged Amaniel tight and tugged at her head scarf. I couldn't hug Valeo, but I could hug her, and she returned my hug with some of the same intensity. I knew she had worried about me this entire time, and all yesterday, too.

"You raced up here to tell me that?" she asked.

"And don't go downstairs."

"They want some other mission for you. It's so unfair. I get the good marks, and you get the favors."

The man at the next desk cleared his throat and pointed to his work. We were bothering him.

I whispered in Amaniel's ear. "You don't want this favor—trust me."

She whispered back. "Oh yes, I do."

"Can't. If Mami and I get arrested, you have to raise Rishi."

"Nihil's earlobes! Then I don't want to know."

"Thought so." She was Babba's daughter to the core. She'd blow all bad news out to sea, if she could.

Babba returned, but I couldn't tell his mood from his stern face. We stood respectfully and curtsy-bowed when he got to us. "A nice display of manners, girls, thank you. My colleagues shouldn't think I'm raising swamp rats."

Amaniel and I exchanged glances, unsure if he was joking. Babba talked to the man at the next desk, giving him instructions about two new ships in the harbor and their tariffs. He'd be back tomorrow, he promised, after sun-up.

Then he walked us toward the back staircase, giving his excuses to the other men as we left. They stared at us—at me, especially—but not in the appreciative way they had on that day when the Azwans first came. This felt sullen, angry even. They nodded toward Rimonil out of respect. None smiled. They were normally a cheery lot, full of jokes and quips, but not today. I don't suppose having a trading floor full of delirious soldiers struck anyone as funny. Yet I was the girl who'd gone to the swamp.

I had the nagging feeling the brunt of their unease was aimed at me.

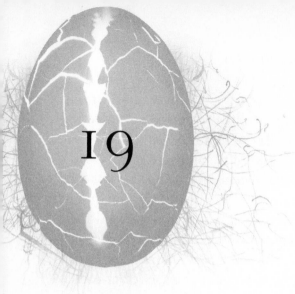

19

Be wary of those who heal by Nature. Would you drink some potion made from the soil, from insects, from dead things plucked by dirty hands? I do not bless such low and common things, and without my blessing, what may ease an ache may scar your soul.
—*from* Oblations 13, The Book of Unease

"Will they make you Portreeve?" Mami asked. It was after first moonrise, and we were outdoors. My hands flew over trays of flower petals, placing them side-by-side, none touching, while my parents talked. Babba sat across from Mami and me, the glow of the dying hearth casting his face in sharp relief. He'd propped his lanky legs on the hearth's tiled edge, but his tone of voice was curt and tight.

"The merchants haven't talked of it yet," he said. "I'd discourage it in any case."

"Because of me?" Mami asked.

He shrugged. "We can't joke it's the worst-kept secret any longer. You defy the Temple, the Temple asks another favor. No one knows what to make of it."

"You're a born statesmen, love. Make the most of it."

Babba humphed. "You'd be Lady Lia, the city's official hostess. You'd have to set an example. No more crazy herbs or medicines."

"Just delicious teas."

"You've promised such things before."

Mami sighed. I had a newfound appreciation for what Babba was asking of her. She'd have to give up generations of herb-lore to stand by her lordly husband's side if the Merchants Guild picked him. I had no idea what she'd choose. Lady Lia! The Lia whose hearth was always packed with neighbors and friends and friends' neighbors would love that role. Imagine the parties and celebrations and Solstice feasts! I wasn't sure even moonblooms were worth defending in that case.

I hoped she wouldn't make any such promise tonight, though. Too much depended on us doing what we did best: break taboos and save lives. Just a few more lives—one in particular—and Mami could surrender her sunhat and work gloves for a spider silk wrap and silver rings for good. That meant I'd have to join her as the Portreeve's eldest daughter. I suppose that meant more eligible men for me.

Men! Who had time for such distractions? And just thinking the word to myself—men—brought up a singular image, one that brought back the flush to my neck. Memories of skin, of muscle and sinew, of his fevered face, burned bright in my imagination, blinding me to the delicate, frail flowers. My mind raced, my fingers flew. I pinned my attention onto the petals and their aroma, pushing memories of Valeo down, but they floated just beneath the surface, glinting with the hard promise of heat and sunlight, when what I needed was the moons' soft radiance for the task at hand.

We were nearly finished laying out the moonbloom petals and stamens on metal trays. I'd somehow managed not to burn or lose any of them. Even so, it was too dangerous, for so many reasons, to keep letting my mind bask in thoughts of Valeo.

Mami hadn't hesitated when I'd told her my plan and had brought out the trays. First dehydrate, then decoct, she'd said. Or let the sick ward make the decoction as they see fit. She said we wouldn't have the time to boil anything down to a syrup. Whatever we did have time to do would have to suffice.

It was a bright night, at least, with Lunyo still full and Qamra waxing gibbous and bathing the city in a silvery sheen. The potion would be stronger because of it, the petals plucked and prepared beneath broad moonbeams. It was a beautiful night to be by a hearth. Every breath filled my lungs with aromas of citrine and spice flowers heavy on the breeze and the fresh slap of air after a summer shower. Hearth fires dotted the canal banks on either side of our peninsula. People wandered on a night like this, and the boardwalks groaned with comings and goings as distant chatter drifted toward us. It belied the terror that lay around a few bends and beyond the Ward's gates and gave no hint of the febrile men in the sick ward.

Amaniel had finally agreed to Mami's strict orders to stay indoors with Rishiel while we worked, but not without a last backward frown in my direction. I'd ignored her, but it stung anyway. I'm sorry she's the good girl, and I'm not. I can only do what the priests seem to want, and she ought to be happy she's headed for a less eventful life, anyway.

For her part, Rishi hadn't wanted to leave the Gek girl alone, until I pointed out the creature was sound asleep. She'd curled up in a corner of the patio, where she snored softly through her slits of nostrils. She had refused a blanket and ate only fish she plucked from the canal or insects. She'd also refused to wander more than a few body lengths from the hearth, always scampering back at the first noise or movement. Rishi had to be coaxed out of the idea she could poke and prod the creature into friendship.

As Mami and I finished our work, we placed a mesh cover over the trays so the drying pieces wouldn't blow away in any sea breezes. We set everything atop the iron grate over the hearth with its dying embers. Our goal wasn't to roast the petals but to gently dehydrate them and concentrate their strength. That would take time and patience, both things I lacked. But for all my fretting, the moments went by only just so fast and no faster.

All the while, Leba Mara's words echoed in my head. No one died on her watch if she could help it. Those words filled me with purpose. I hadn't forgotten my ransacked home or the brute force with which those guards had taken over our city. But they weren't going to die if I could help it.

If there was any chance of seeing Valeo on his feet again, I would take it. Leba Mara hadn't needed to threaten my life. I knew it was at stake, even if Babba thought there was room to negotiate. Mami and I had run out of options, no matter which way we turned. There was no escaping who we were, and it had led us here, to this clutch of flower petals and the people who both needed them and hated us for it.

I rattled a few pans to re-scatter the petals and checked everything again, just to be sure, and to keep from fidgeting.

I also couldn't wrap my mind around why, after all we'd gone through, the vast, many-limbed creature that was the Temple of Doubt, with its hundreds of Wards and thousands of priests, would care about two women at a lone hearth on a tiny island at the center of the world. We'd escaped their notice for so long, hadn't we? And we were always there when they needed us, for whatever they wanted from us. It had felt perfectly right to be in the makeshift sick ward, busy and distracted and blending in with everyone else, helping out as another set of hands among many.

Besides, drying herbs seemed so minor, so everyday. If they were for cooking, no one would notice or care. I couldn't fathom that the Temple would ask this favor of us, only to turn on us. I assumed they would thank us in some quiet, discreet way, and then vanish once their demon was found and their men cured.

I was, of course, wrong.

I was even the first to spot the danger as a gray form approaching from the mainland took shape as a cloaked figure. He could be another neighbor out for a stroll before moonset, wandering along the boardwalk past our avenue. It was when he paused and leaned against a railing shortly before the intersection, where our wooden street met the mainland, that I decided something was vaguely off about the man.

He had a perfect view of our hearth, and he bided his time watching us: Babba with his feet up, Mami chatting about the Portreeve's job, us sifting the trays of petals and fanning the embers. We could be making one of the more common teas, for all anyone knew, just an innocuous, flower-scented brew for breakfast tomorrow, that's it. The man didn't move for a long time.

"There's someone watching," I said. "A man, I think."

Babba rose and walked toward him, offering a respectful nod. "Our hearth is yours, friend."

The gray man stepped out of the shadows but didn't reply. A hood hid his features except for a patch of cropped white beard. Few people cloak themselves here; he was no doubt a traveler from a colder clime. He was older but vigorous, his shoulders somewhat stooped but his stride confident. He closed the distance between Babba and himself with ease and grasped the hand extended to him. Two other cloaked forms, much larger, glided in behind him. Feroxi. Babba drew back. "Is there something the matter, sir?"

"That all depends," said the man. His voice was raspy and thin, but it carried across the quiet street. "On what you're serving."

"Your voice sounds familiar," Babba said. "Whatever we have, good traveler, is yours for the sharing."

"I find I'm in the mood for an infusion of moonbloom."

I gasped. My aunties always warned me that Port Sapphire was small, as cities go, but it had just gotten much smaller. Someone had turned us in. We weren't making an infusion, but that was beside the point. He knew about our moonblooms.

Babba's voice was measured. "I'm not sure I heard you, friend."

"I think you heard me just fine." The man turned to the two giants. "Moonbloom tisane? This is the only place in the world for it."

One of the giants grumbled from within his cloak. "I'd not swallow it for gold, Great Azwan."

I already knew. The Azwan of Ambiguity. Reyhim. I'd heard his voice before, and so had Mami, but we'd both corrected our expressions to be unreadable and calm. Even so, my heart raced, and my stomach churned. I reached for the trays to dump them into the ashes. I acted on instinct. That instinct said to burn. Burn it all. Mami held my wrist and murmured. "Let it play out."

Babba bowed to the man and cupped his palms beneath his chin. We did the same as Reyhim approached us. He seated himself by our hearth on one of the many stools. The two guards stayed further back and cast suspicious glances at our drying racks. Reyhim drew back his cloak to reveal a lined and thoughtful face and eyes that missed nothing as he took in his surroundings and assessed his hosts. With a forward flick of his fingers, he motioned for us to sit around him. He leaned over the trays and inhaled with gusto. But his tone was wry.

"There is nothing, and I mean nothing, that matches the aroma of this flower harvested when the moons are just

right. It invites, it teases, its perfume pulls you into a flir-
tatious dance under the stars. It wafts under the nose and
then darts away laughing. It is said to cure what Nihil cannot, a thing therefore of great danger, and greater beauty."

We said nothing. No priest I knew ever spoke this way.
No sermon had ever sounded so poetic—or threatening.

Reyhim glanced up at Mami. "A strong batch, from
the smell of it, but a pity Qamra wasn't full as well. Petals
picked under a double full moon are immeasurably stronger, as I recall. It's Lia, isn't it?"

Mami nodded, her face drawn and pained. "I'm flattered you remember, Worthiness."

"You were a child. Nine or so."

"A long time ago, Azwan."

"We have some catching up to do." Reyhim motioned
to the trays. "These don't look nearly done. Surely you
have some in reserve."

I didn't trust the way he eyed us. He was laying a hunt-
er's trap for us, a device of hidden coils and nasty spikes, one
that our own words would spring. S'ami had laid a word-
trap the day he announced our mission to the swamp, and
my teacher had done it to me for years. Anger twisted in
my gut, and my familiar nausea returned.

"Your soldiers were thorough in their inspections,
Azwan," said Mami. "We've been purged of our wayward-
ness except what you see here."

The Azwan's tone grew cold. "Not terribly repentant,
were you."

It was Babba's turn. You didn't insult Mami around
him, not even if you were Azwan. "Surely you bless us with
the uncertainty of your intent," Babba said. "If this is a

lesson, you'll find us good students. Yet my wife does as the Temple itself has asked."

Babba pulled a short scroll from a pouch at his waist and handed it to the Azwan, who tore its string and read it. It was the note Leba Mara had written after promising me some small measure of protection for making contraband items. I had to hope it would be enough.

Reyhim waved something gold over it, and it burst into flames and fell into the hearth. From somewhere in the corner, the Gek croaked. She must've felt his spell. Reyhim didn't seem to hear her and addressed Babba. "The word of the healers of Ward Sapphire carries no weight with me. And I should still like some tea."

Mami turned to me, out of breath. "Did you bring anything back from Dina's?"

"No, I'm sorry. There's some callousvine leaf in the cupboard, I think."

Reyhim interrupted. "Moonbloom is, I believe, what I requested. Is it now the custom here to refuse a traveler what you have already promised?" He turned to Babba. "Well?"

"If it's moonbloom you prefer, my wife and daughter are pleased to prepare it for you." Babba sounded more accommodating than I felt. I didn't blame Mami for not wanting to know if he was her father. It chilled me to think his blood might be running through my veins. We—Mami and I—were nothing like him. We'd serve him tea, though, even if he weren't Azwan.

Our kettle is always full, even this late, but to make the coals hot enough to heat the water would in turn burn the trays of petals. I didn't know what to do. I began fumbling to remove them and make way for the kettle, but Mami again stopped me.

"We'll have to simmer the petals with a tight lid on the pot," she said.

"Whatever for?" said Reyhim. "You mean to say you don't have any reserves?"

Mami shook her head.

"Then I do apologize. I'd assumed much contraband had escaped the guards. The Sapphirans are a wily people."

"But not dishonest, Worthiness." Babba said, his voice carrying an edge of caution. "We've never hidden who we are or what we have."

"A brave man, to speak that way to me." Reyhim returned Babba's stare. "But I've made a mistake. Your household's out of this medicine, and there are men in need of it."

My jaw dropped. That was the first glimmer of compassion I'd seen from either Azwan. Maybe there was a chance the Customs House wouldn't become a boneyard tonight.

"But Azwan," I said, before I could stop myself. "Would they even drink it?"

Babba spoke sharply to me. "Hadara, inside please."

"Hadara? Is it so?" Reyhim looked at me with renewed interest. "I knew someone named Hadara once."

"I'm named for my grandmother." The trap was being set, I could sense it, and there was nothing I could do. I lacked my parents' wisdom for knowing where not to step.

"Of course, you are," Reyhim said. "You're every bit as impertinent, too. But I'll answer your question. No servant of Nihil's would take a curative that lacked supernatural properties. Satisfied?"

I paused. Make this good, Hadara, as if your life depends on it. Because it does. "And isn't it a sin to administer a natural medicine without their knowing?"

Babba's tone darkened. "Hadara, this is an Azwan you address."

"He can help," I said. "He can solve this."

"Is this some riddle, then?" Reyhim leaned toward me. "I've no patience for it."

"Azwan, please. Isn't there some way you could dry these herbs? Then they'll be done quicker, and they'll have Nihil's theurgy upon them besides. The healers wouldn't need to coerce or trick anyone to take it."

No one spoke for what seemed a long time. We all waited on Reyhim, whose eyes narrowed as he considered what I'd said. "Clever. Just a short, tender kiss of Nihil's. A tidy way to get your family out of trouble, too."

"Were we in trouble?"

He rose and stretched. "My plan was to drink some so none would declare it profane. After all, an Azwan had some, it must be alright. But your solution is better."

The relief that spread across Mami and Babba's faces must've been mirrored in my own, because in a moment we were all smiling, even Reyhim. He wasn't my family in any true sense of the word, but I could suddenly feel grandfatherly affection radiating from him. His grin, his relaxed air, it was as if he wanted us to like him. I wondered if my grandmother had found much to love in him when he was like this, with his silk-spun words and quiet dignity.

We lifted the mesh screens on the trays, and he fished his totem from a pouch. It was in the shape of a crescent moon of solid gold. Its face was frowning.

"Which moon?" I asked.

Reyhim glanced up at his guards standing off at a distance. He winked at me and whispered, "I tell the guards it's Lunyo."

I laughed, but he gently shushed me and raised his hands over the trays. A moment later, the petals and stamens shrivelled, without any sign of browning. He was merely dehydrating them. Mami beamed at me, and I returned her smile. The victory felt sweet.

A loud squawk, a flash of green eyes, and the Gek pounced on the trays, shouting and croaking. The spell must have startled her. She flung trays this way and that, sending delicate tendrils of dried herbs in every direction. Breezes picked up the rest and soon we were in a swirl of feathery light petals, Mami and I frantic to collect what we could, Reyhim and Babba shouting and struggling with the creature. The guards leapt forward, swords drawn from beneath their cloaks, and the real bedlam began.

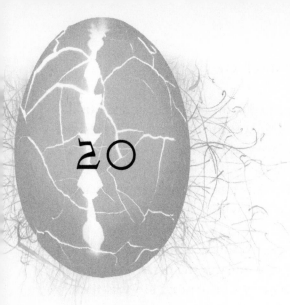

20

Giants forge a lovely ring
Humans lift a voice to sing
Lizards dart from thing to thing
                    —children's rhyme

The Gek raced under and over and around, hissing and squawking.

"My totem," Reyhim said. "That creature has it."

Neighbors filed out of their homes at the commotion, people paused on the boardwalks, even boats out on nearby canals rowed closer. The sudden crowd gave the Gek an endless source of legs to weave through and heads to leap over. The neighbors looked like they were doing some insane new dance, up, down, twisting, tripping, clutching their hair.

The guards pursued, but, for all their strength, they were clumsy against the agile Gek. She darted out from under their blows, untouched. She zigged before they could zag, her slender fingers wrapped around the only thing that could get all that tea back in one spot again.

What few pots and urns had survived the soldiers' wrecking were overturned and emptied. Neighbors rushed to right this and catch that before the calamity got any worse. At last the Gek fled under our house, where she disappeared into the dark save for the glow of her eyes. I knelt between two stilts, the guards crouching behind me, a complete knot of frustration.

A soft, little-girl voice called out from underneath the house. "Bugsy, it's me!"

The voice belonged to my youngest sister, who must've snuck out when she should've been in bed, asleep.

"Rishi," I said, silently cursing the stupidity of little sisters. "Get out of there."

"It's okay. She likes it in here. Bugsy, are you okay?"

I heard hissing. "Rishi, we need that gold totem back."

"Okay," Rishi said. "Bugsy, give the gold toy back."

So much for Rishi translating. At least I could see the Gek's eyes. Maybe it could see me. I motioned.

Shaman-spawn. Were we hurting you?

I couldn't see a thing. "Someone get me a light."

A torch was passed to one of the guards. Reyhim held another over me. "So, this is the famous Gek translator? I might've known it was the same young woman."

"I'll do my best, Azwan."

"Or we burn the house down to get it." He was no longer smiling, no longer grandfatherly.

I turned to the Gek and my sister and motioned again with a renewed sense of urgency. *Can you see me?*

The Gek croaked and crept forward. She nodded and motioned back, the talisman in her hand. *This metal is natural, but what it does is not.*

It belongs to this drabskin, I replied. I was careful to translate aloud this time, with everyone peering over my shoulder.

Such unnatural things destroyed my nest, she signed.

The bad box destroyed it, I replied.

The Gek shook her head. *The star does not make bad. It unmakes. It promised.*

Reyhim nudged me. "Tell it you'll go and get the star."

"Will I?"

"Say it."

I translated for her.

She cocked her head. *Right now?*

I glanced up at Reyhim. He shook his head and held a finger to his lips. He was lying, in other words. Traps and lies—it was what the Temple did best. I seethed but translated anyway. I told myself it wasn't my own lies but the Temple's, and I had to translate accurately. Mami was standing close by and would know if I didn't pass along every last untrue word. We both wanted Reyhim to have his totem back for our own reasons, I suppose.

I made the last gesture when I heard a squawk and some tussling. Rishi shouted, "I got it! I got it!"

"Get out of there—she bites," I said.

Rishi tumbled one way, and the Gek scrambled the other. A guard reached for Rishi and pulled her up by her curls. Reyhim plucked his totem from her hand and patted her on her head. She ran to Babba and buried her face in his legs. The Gek darted out the other side of the house and into a patch of tall grass, where I lost sight of her. Several neighbors applauded as Reyhim held up his prize.

"We averted disaster," Reyhim said. "That's all that matters. Well, now, everyone, I do believe you've gotten your entertainment for the night. The Temple bids you all a deep, dreamless goodmoons."

People bowed and filed back indoors. Amaniel appeared in her nightdress to lead Rishi back to bed, but not before gazing wide-eyed at Reyhim, the second Azwan to come to our house in only a few days. Reyhim didn't even see Amaniel, which made me feel guilty even if it wasn't my fault. Poor Amaniel, so pious, left out of the biggest event to ever happen to us. Well, she could have all this history being made and then some. I'd prefer to be indoors in my nightdress if she wanted to change places, so long as she used her fancy language to persuade the Azwans to go—and take all their fear and suspicion with them.

As that wasn't likely to happen, I followed Reyhim and Mami back to our hearth, where petals lay scattered in the dust. With a wave of Reyhim's totem, everything on the floor became airborne. He asked for a small urn, which I held out for him. Gradually, bits of sand and dust and old crumbs settled back down, leaving only the precious petals and a few stamens that spiraled gently and precisely into the urn.

The relief was palpable. A happy sigh escaped my lips, and even Babba nodded as if agreeing. Mami capped the urn and handed it to Reyhim, who turned it over to the guard. "I believe you'll have no compunction now about your comrades taking this."

"Your word is Nihil's," the guard said. They did their chest-thump salute and strode off, leaving Reyhim with us, which I hadn't expected. Traps and lies. I waited to see which it would be.

Babba's voice also held a note of suspicion. "Surely it's late, Azwan."

"I ask but one other favor from you, pious Rimonil, and then it's you who may request favors from the Temple."

"That's a gift we couldn't possibly redeem," Babba said.

"You will. We'll owe you much."

"It's our pleasure to serve."

"Not this time. Your daughter must come with me."

I squeezed my eyes shut. Oh, dear Nihil. Dear, capricious, unknowable god of whims and wishes and all things dubious and strange. Reyhim was going to take me into the Ward, straight to the tin box. What other explanation could there be? I almost hugged the man. I'd get to talk to the star-demon, if it hadn't been destroyed yet. I'd ask it what it wanted and why it was here. I'd promise to help, though maybe not in front of the Azwans. Even if that's not exactly where Reyhim was taking me, I could figure it out. I'd be inside the Ward compound. It had to be easy after that.

What an amazing night it was turning out to be. I had every hope in the world suddenly bloom in my head. The star-demon, Valeo's cure, everything. It was all happening.

Reyhim even seemed more kindly in the radiant moonlight. I warmed to the feel of his hand on my left arm and closed my eyes to savor the moment. "Come, child."

I opened my eyes to see Mami and Babba trade worried looks. Babba placed a hand on my right shoulder, as if to stop me from going. "She'll be back by morning?"

"No."

"Azwan?"

"We don't ask such a sacrifice lightly. Her body will be returned to you for burning."

Mami gasped. Wait. Sacrifice? On an altar, that type of sacrifice? But Nihil wasn't here. A sacrifice couldn't happen without Nihil present to consume my soul. The Temple had said so. The Temple. Traps and lies. I snapped my head away from Reyhim with a fraction of a moment to spare before I puked suddenly and miserably onto the patio tiles. There wasn't much in my stomach, fortunately, and a quick check told me I hadn't soiled my dress. Babba's sandals had gotten the worst of it, though. Poor Babba. He squeezed my shoulder by way of comfort.

I didn't dare look up. I shut my eyes again and tried to think of something to be optimistic about, a way out or an excuse or something else I could try or say.

Nothing came to mind. A sour, acrid taste lingered on my tongue.

Babba's grip hardened on my shoulder. "Why a sacrifice? Azwan, have we not . . ."

"Don't ask, Rimonil. It's through no shame of yours or sin. I could've left without the tea, but not without her. Our reasons remain our own."

"This has to do with the demon?"

Reyhim's voice lowered to a growl. "Our reasons. Remain. Our own."

Something was wrong, then. They hadn't defeated the tin box creature; that much I could've guessed anyway, or Reyhim wouldn't be here. But something had gone wrong, I could tell by the desperation and anger in his voice, the rigid way he had begun to hold me, the urgency with which he wanted to be gone. All pretense of family warmth was gone.

Mami wedged herself between us, sheer hate rising from her twisted features. "You're not doing this to me, Azwan. You can't take everything from me *again*."

The expression on Reyhim's face went dark, as if he'd retreated into himself. "The Temple understands your anguish."

"Do you?" Mami peered into Reyhim's hood, but there was nothing there to read but shadows.

"It'll be much worse for you if you resist," he said.

"At least let us be there," Babba said. "The parents are always there, aren't they?"

The hood shook from side to side. "Not this time."

"Is there nothing . . ."

"Nothing."

Babba released my shoulder as he choked out a reply. "Then I lend her to you in all pious trust."

I cried out as the Azwan pulled me away. Mami and I caught hands, but Reyhim's pull was stronger than our grasp. I slid away from her as she began wailing and shrieking my name. I grabbed at the flimsy hope I was headed toward the tin box and whatever was in it was as benevolent as the Gek girl promised and that it might be waiting for me, and all would be well and the Temple would go.

It was an impossible hope, maybe beyond impossible, one it didn't do any good to harbor, but it was all I had.

Reyhim's grip was firm. Even for an old man, he was too strong to resist. I glanced back to see Mami try to claw and fight her way out of Babba's arms, reaching for me, straining, calling my name.

My name. It echoed along the street, shrill and piercing, and out across the water, on up into the night sky.

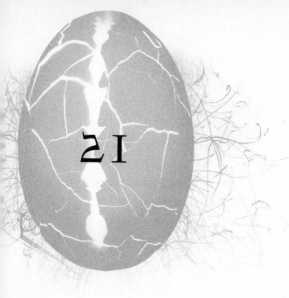

21

Therefore you must assume that your life unfolds
as I planned it. Do not curse me if your life does
not take the path you desire. Instead look to your-
self and the direction you chose.
    —*from* Oblations 9, The Book of Unease

We paused before Ward Sapphire's wide, carved doors.
Reyhim placed his arm around me as if I were a beloved
niece instead of a sacrifice. I bristled at his touch. We'd slowed
our pace as we neared the Ward gates, and the guards had
let us past with crisp chest-thumps. The long yard had been
empty except for the rooftop sentinels, but even they kept
their distance from the double doors of the sanctuary. I'd
been right about our destination, but it was small consolation.

I removed my sandals inside the vestibule. On the
Sabbath, it'd be stuffed with shoes. Reyhim placed his on
the men's rack beside mud-soaked boots I recognized as
S'ami's. Mine were the only pair on the women's rack.

My bare feet landed on the cold tile floor. I realized I was trembling.

Reyhim pulled me close again. I couldn't meet his gaze and stared instead at his gnarled toes. "Don't cry, whatever you do," he said. "God is within. He scries from his home in the Abandoned City on the other side of the world. You'll be in his presence, so keep that in mind."

I shook harder. As a child, I was taught that Nihil could scry on anyone, at any time, and to always behave as if he had me in view. To remove all doubt of it only made me more uncertain. I knew then what I hated most about the Temple of Doubt—it stood sturdily on human infirmity, it pulled the legs of reason out from under you and offered you the wobbly crutches of faith instead.

Even the name of his home—Abandoned City—was supposed to remind us that he could thrive amid desolation. And, it implied, we could not. He did not give up as easily as his followers.

Had I given up on faith? I reminded myself of what I'd said in the swamp a few days ago with Mami—I believed in a god I could see and hear, or whom others had seen and heard. I believed even as I chose every path of rebellion that opened to me. If I didn't believe in him, it would not bother me so much that I blasphemed. I wouldn't care.

And I cared. A lot.

I hesitated as Reyhim pulled open the inner doors. Beyond this vestibule was my god and his enemy. Not just any enemy, but one who'd tracked him here from someplace beyond our world. Who hated Nihil that much? And what did it want with me?

My bare feet stuck to the floor. Reyhim placed his hand on my back and gently guided me into the sanctuary, shafts of moonlight sifting through the slatted shutters and oil lamps glowing from sconces along the broad walls. We passed the rows of prayer mats laid end to end around a raised wooden dais with carved railings. In its center stood the priests' thrones, flanking a wide altar that glowed a faint orange. I recognized our high priest on one of the high-backed thrones. He was praying, fervently, his eyes closed, his body rocking back and forth with almost violent passion. The incantations were low but rapid, again and again:

From the void I come, through the abyss I fall;
My place is nowhere, and from naught comes all.

It was the prayer of last resort.

We stood by the first row of rugs, where a man lay sleeping. It was S'ami, unmistakable in his amethyst robes again, soundly snoring. Reyhim woke him with a single shake, and he bolted upright.

Reyhim motioned toward me. "The girl."

S'ami rubbed his eyes. "None too soon. A moment or two to relieve myself, please."

"We'll wait."

S'ami wandered across the sanctuary toward a side door that led to the priests' quarters and their bathhouse. Reyhim removed his gray cloak to reveal a pale longshirt over loose trousers, like something a common clerk would wear on his day off, except it, too, looked to be made of finely wrought spider silk.

The other Azwan returned, looking more alert. By then, I'd guessed the orange glow from the altar must be where Nihil was scrying from, and that was why the priest prayed so fervently there. I stared at the glowing spot and felt waves of raw fear wash over me.

Not my fight. Not fair.

How had I been dragged into this?

It was no use trying to fix blame elsewhere. There had been plenty I'd done to make sure this day was inevitable. It wasn't how the schoolmistress had described it, but it was coming true anyway. I had been chosen because I was the bold and curious one, and those were somehow bad traits. And here was my chance to make up for it all and presumably die to prevent a conflagration or some other horrible fate. Others would live. All my loved ones, and Valeo, and all the ones who'd never had much use for me at all, they would all live.

And I'd promised, back in the swamp, that I'd never, ever withhold my help from anyone for any reason.

Even if dying on an altar wasn't what I'd had in mind, exactly.

Neither man looked at me as they conversed in hushed tones. Reyhim spoke first. "You've addressed our Master?"

"I promised we'd wait for you," S'ami said.

"He's likely seen her already."

"Let's be sure."

I was led to a large mirror that graced the wall a few body-lengths beyond the altar. It ran from floor to ceiling, made of pure glass backed by real silver and always kept polished and fingerprint-free. Its gold-leaf frame swarmed with intricate, bejeweled insects to symbolize the plague Nihil had inflicted upon our island when we first colonized it. We were to remember his reach. Biting, gnawing, stinging vermin swarmed the length and breadth of it, refracting the dim light into thousands of glittery pinpoints.

The mirror held our faint reflections and blackness beyond. I had been wrong about Nihil's scrying locale; of course, this mirror would be it. The Azwans sank to their knees, and I followed them. We cupped our hands beneath our chins, bowed our heads, and waited. My heart beating against my ribs drowned out any other sound to me, save for the priest's chanting. I was caught between two ageless enemies; one was my god, and the other was some unknown creature from the stars. I had only the Gek's word that it meant no harm. Scores had died already.

And here was Nihil, whom Scriptures taught had shaped our world, brought all its warm-blooded peoples here, given us a common language and the written word, who'd instructed us to build cities, to care for each other and heal the sick and mind the old. He'd promised us life after death, and we promised him our bodies if he required them and any sacrifice he felt he deserved.

Yet I wanted that fallen star so desperately, like nothing else I'd ever craved in my life. I wanted the truth with my own eyes and ears. I wanted to know if every beating and switching I'd ever gotten in Nihil's name had been worth it. I wanted some sort of reward out of all this, but not money—no, it'd never been about money. I wanted some kind of elusive power that I didn't know how to name or describe but that would make these desperate men look at me with something resembling respect. I wanted them humbled.

And I wanted proof of Nihil's goodness on behalf of all the people who died because healing spells only did half the trick or nothing at all, and on behalf of a Tengalian girl I'd never met, whose father was standing beside me, seemingly immune to grief—his or anyone else's.

If I was going to learn anything and live to tell it, I had to summon every scrap of protocol I'd ever managed to master and hope I didn't mangle it. If there was any chance at all of saving my own life, I wanted to grab at it.

Maybe that was a terrible failing, to want to live. If I was meant to avoid a conflagration, I ought to be willing to die. Valeo had been willing to die. I corrected myself—he'd been willing to die as a soldier. He had the right to die on his feet with a weapon in his hand, not the way I'd seen him last.

He didn't deserve the death the Temple had dragged him to. All the lies, recited with such self-righteousness, such smug disregard for those of us worshipping at Nihil's feet, had been piling up, and the punishments, the humiliations, the tramping through the swamps and trying to leave us there, even then, the way S'ami had ordered Mami into the boat to surrender her life, even then. It all spun together, a cyclone of hate and resentment.

A man's voice filtered through the mirror. It was a tenor, rich and pure, the consonants perfectly articulated, the vowels long and soothing. It was the voice of a god. The rolling music of that voice found the eye of the storm within me, giving me a peace I knew wouldn't last. Yet my heart trilled at the sound of it. "Hadara of Rimonil. Explain this to me. 'The star comes to you as you come to it.'"

I peered into the mirror's darkness and tried to keep my voice steady. "Great Numen," I said. "I know not."

"You have some sense of it, perhaps."

This was my chance to explain some of what I hadn't translated back in the swamp, how I thought the Gek were afraid of it, how they wanted it for me, how most seemed to think it was harmless. I had lied to S'ami then, but I would do something worse in front of my god, and tell him as little as possible.

As I paused, Reyhim answered instead. "There was a Gek at her home, Fey One. It told her something about unmaking."

He tapped my shoulder, which I took as my cue to speak. "She said, 'The star doesn't make bad. It only unmakes.' Forgive me, kind Master and shaper of all Kuldor, if my words offend."

Or if what I don't say and won't reveal offends, too, I thought to myself.

The mirror answered: "As long as you translate accurately, the offense is only with the speaker."

"I praise your incarnations, may they be infinite," I said, bowing my head. I remembered at least some of my schooling.

"Very well," the mirror replied. "Let us see what we can unmake."

The Azwans raised me up and, after another bow toward the mirror, pointed me toward the steps to the altar. My brief audience was done, and he hadn't thought to ask anything about my family or grandmother or what I thought might be in the Gek box. He'd sooner notice the dust drifting up from the prayer rugs than a simple island girl. My knees wobbled the entire way to the dais, where we joined the high priest, who stopped chanting and rose as the Azwans approached. The orange glow faded.

The altar came to my waist and was ornately tiled in a shiny, elaborate sprawl of meanders and geometric shapes in dazzling hues, few of which I could make out in the orange half-light. The priests usually burned nothing more than incense here. Since Nihil had never visited us, no one had ever climbed atop it to be sacrificed to him. It hadn't occurred to me until this moment that this might be the kind of rite Reyhim had in mind. It certainly was what my parents had pictured.

It didn't seem right to be alone with these three men, to have no family here to wring their hands or beg me to be brave. I had to invent them in my head, Mami seething at the Temple's betrayal, Babba keeping his chin up, Amaniel whispering explanations to a teary Rishi, the prayer mats filled with everyone I knew, praying for my soul as it shredded before them.

Imagining this way gave me a few drams of courage as I faced the three men across the altar, my back toward the mirror and the god who watched from within. Each cleric held up his totem. The high priest's was a two-headed fish, a favorite symbol of seafarers. Not that it mattered. All that I ever bothered to learn about constellations or anything else had amounted to nothing in my short life. I'd be dead before I'd ever used another jot of it.

"What must I do?" I asked.

"Wait," said S'ami. "Patience."

My eyes adjusted to the dim light. I could make out the tin box atop the altar, its lid torn off, its hinges mangled. The Gek had woven a dense cushion of grass and leaves inside it. Nestled into the matting lay an egg larger than any I'd ever seen. It could easily fill my cupped hands. No bird I knew could lay something that large, unless it had somehow enlarged its casing. It emitted a vivid, orange glow from deep inside the shell. That wasn't at all what I'd expected. There was no meteorite or rock of any sort.

The unease built up within me, and my breathing came in choppy bursts. I didn't know what this meant. I hadn't fully understood what the Azwans had meant by possession or how something could leap inside a person. I'd pictured swallowing a talking rock. This was an egg that shone from within, and I felt as if the ground shifted beneath me before I had time to rethink my ideas and adjust my bearings.

I waited for it to do something, anything. It lay there, its glow fading, its light dying. The men began their incantations, the same as the high priest's, the one used only for the most desperate situations, when other spells and divinations fail. The egg fired to life again, piercing the darkness. I shielded my eyes.

"Don't turn away," S'ami said. "Take a long look."

I put my hand down. The egg had risen out of the grass matting, leaving an oval impression behind. It levitated above the altar at eye level, spinning top to bottom, gyrating and whirling in a crazy, nonsensical way. Its motion made flashes and arcs of orange, and its grating whine began to drone. My ears stung as much as my eyes, but my back straightened, and my balance steadied. I had nothing left in my stomach, so my insides achieved a sense of calm even if my brain kept whirling. It was so much like being in the fens with a snake or a stingfly swarm on the loose. If I couldn't escape it, then I had to face it with my mind working instead of panicking.

The men kept up their chanting, except for S'ami. "Brave Hadara. Sweet Hadara," he murmured. "I don't believe you brought this on yourself. The Gek have played you, for some reason. They've suggested, through your careful translation, that the demon chose you specifically.

"In all other contests through history—you've read Scripture, you know this—no demon has targeted someone this way. It raged from one body to another until someone found a way to kill it. But this creature has stolen some sort of bird's egg, a mere egg, and it confounds us. It can't be destroyed. It rests when we rest, fights as we fight, and as fiercely. Our strength has gone into keeping it from doing to Ward Sapphire what it did to the wilds beyond your city, a place, I believe, to which you are partial. We understand it better for our trying, but that knowledge is incomplete. Is there something, anything, you haven't told us from the Gek? Something about your role in all this?"

The good girl in me wanted to recount every last moment ever spent with the sprightly tree-dwellers. The doubter in me realized with a shock that the Temple was admitting failure. Nihil didn't know everything. Nihil could no longer even guess what was going on inside that egg or how to get at it and kill it. I'd been told that Nihil stayed away because, if he encountered it in person, it would destroy the entire world. The two couldn't battle face to face. So here were two Azwans, sent in his stead, forced to improvise.

I was seized by the wonder of it all. Great warriors had been infected by other demons and had finally died. Yet a fragile egg was stumping the mighty Azwans. Did I want Nihil to win this, even at the cost of my life? Or the unknown and apparently unknowable egg monster?

"Hadara?" S'ami asked, in a gentle voice I imagine he might've used on his daughter.

I froze. A brief squeak of air escaped me. Whose side was I on?

Think, Hadara, think. Maybe I didn't have to decide just yet. I could talk this through a little.

"My family has had dealings in the fens and swamps for generations," I said at last. "The Gek knew us better than any other humans. They didn't say why they wanted me."

"But they were anxious that you take hold of it?" S'ami said.

I nodded. "That was my feeling, yes."

"What might it mean 'one who knows to undo what must be undone'? That was the other part of their prophecy to you. And tonight a Gek told you the star unmakes? Undoing and unmaking, these mean anything to you? They have some context in Gek culture, perhaps?"

I shook my head. "They hate anything supernatural."

"We know this."

"Spells harm them."

"Nihil's theurgy is a poison to them; we know this, too."

"Perhaps, I don't know, perhaps . . ." I fished in my memory for anything that could keep me alive a few more moments. When memory failed, my imagination would have to do.

"Go ahead."

"Perhaps they mean undoing or unmaking magic." I thought that sounded sensible and safe.

"This was our guess, too. But why you?"

The high priest stopped chanting. "I have explained about her family, worthy Azwan."

S'ami kept his gaze on me. "Worthy brother, keep praying. I wish to hear the girl's own account. She's already mentioned her family of her own accord. Hadara, you're very brave for doing so. You mustn't think you're betraying anyone. There's little you and your mother get up to that we don't know about anyway. It's just your dealings with the Gek, some shading or nuance we're missing that might help us."

"And you know about my grandmother," I said, sneaking a sidelong glance at Reyhim. He snapped his head toward me and leveled a fierce stare. "I was forbidden to speak of her."

S'ami nodded. "You may speak of her now."

I took a deep breath. I was stumbling into a murkier swamp than ever. I wanted to talk to the egg and find out what it wanted, but I didn't want these men to know that. I wanted to hear what it had to say, but that meant keeping my own mouth shut. So I had to think up something to say about ol' grandma that said nothing at all.

"I only know she chose nature over Nihil. And maybe the Gek knew that, somehow, or sensed it, and picked me as the next in line."

"Why would they do that? Do you agree with her choice?"

I hesitated a half a moment too long. Three pairs of eyes turned toward me. A flash of light from the mirror told me Nihil had overheard. "No, no, of course not. People are more important than plants."

"I see. Then why bother with the plants at all?"

"Because. Sometimes. They, uh. They can help. I just want to help. I hate seeing people sickened." I want to help them even when Nihil doesn't. But I couldn't say that, not with my god watching. I was panting, from fear and nerves and a feeling I was about to be stripped naked again with words instead of an enchanted gaze.

I was right.

My hesitation and stammering had done me in. I could see it in the pure contempt in Reyhim's eyes and even the high priest's. S'ami regarded me coolly, as he had looked over the Gek he'd killed with his blue light shield.

"A few things to consider, Hadara." S'ami's voice took a more commanding tone. He was again the priest, and I was about to get the sermon of my life. "This is a demon. Not a rock or a star-creature or a friend of the Gek's or nature or anyone. Do you know what a demon is?"

"The opposite of a numen?" I felt like I was in class again, getting the answer wrong.

"That is correct. It isn't here to enlighten or uplift; it won't build any civilization or heal the sick you care about so deeply and movingly. It has its own ends, and it seeks its own means to that end. You're the means. We don't know why, but it wants you, and we don't intend to let it have you. We intend to destroy it, but you must do what we say without wavering."

I remembered what S'ami had said in the swamp when he'd asked Mami to watch over the tin box. She'd be easier to defeat than a Feroxi guard. I'd be even easier than that. I fumbled for a little more time. "Are . . . are you sure I have to die?"

Reyhim cut in. "It's heresy to question us."

S'ami held up a hand to Reyhim, and the fatherly voice returned. "It's natural to want to save your own life. But this isn't nature; it is a higher endeavor than mere instinct. There is little we can say, however, without risking the demon understanding us. It's time, Hadara. Know that we shall honor your family, and they'll remember you with love, always, no matter what happens here."

He would know. He must remember his dead daughter after all. I nodded, unable to speak. Tears trickled down my cheek, but I didn't try to fight it. I felt entitled to them. I'd earned them. But I wondered if my father would grow as hard as S'ami after losing me. At least he hadn't lost Amaniel, his favorite. I gulped back a sob, my tongue jamming the back of my throat. Babba's favorite. His pious, sweet Amaniel. Not like me, the stubborn doubter.

What would Amaniel do, if she were me?

And then I knew. She'd do whatever they'd asked of her, without question, and beam with joy about it. She would fill herself with the warmth of conviction, knowing there'd be an Eternal Tree, and god's love, and all the love in the universe, just sitting there waiting for her to pluck and savor forever and ever.

If a doubt had ever crossed her mind, she would not have nurtured it, and it died of thirst.

I loved my sister. I adored her. She was everything I could never be.

But she was weak, even fragile, despite the strength of her faith, or maybe because of it. I had always doubted, and I'd never surrendered my doubts—and here they were, giving me hope when I ought to have none.

I had hope, and it wasn't something faith could give me. Faith could only take it away and make my death a certainty.

And I was sure it wasn't wrong to want to live. Yes, it was natural to want to save my own life. A stingfly wanted to save its own life. It's not that S'ami was wrong. Maybe sacrificing myself for the benefit of others was a higher endeavor, and I was simply rationalizing, conjuring up reasons that made sense only to me. And maybe, being something more than a stingfly, that reasoning is what made me think my life worth living.

The three men waited without speaking while I sniffled and cried softly for a few moments. Let them think I was afraid. I had my hope, I had my reasons, and, most importantly, I had my doubts. I gulped some air, straightened my shoulders, and met S'ami's gaze through blurry vision. I was ready.

His gaze never left mine and held something I imagined to be pity in it. "Hold your hands up, and count to three to yourself. Don't make contact. You—and we—are safer if you keep a few fingers-width distance from it. We will attack if it tries to leap to you. Ready?"

I immediately forgot all my numbers. Twelve, one hundred forty-seven, four million, a billion jillion; they all came before three. I lifted my right hand and tried to keep it from trembling. I failed. My fingers quailed like twitchy spider legs. I hadn't known what a hard thing it is to do, to reach a few head-lengths in front of your face. It took long moments, all eternity, until Nihil's own doom, to reach the glowing sphere. My fingertips hovered beside it as the men chanted louder, faster, more earnestly, their eyes riveted to the crane's egg, to my fingers, to the thin strip of air between fingers and egg and whatever came after.

All my life had come down to this one moment. In another moment, would I be beneath the Eternal Tree? Perhaps Valeo would be waiting for me beneath its endless canopy. But no—how stupid could I be? If he were waiting there, it wouldn't be for me, the ignorant island girl he'd met only days ago. He was a soldier doing his job. And I would have to do mine.

Hope. Reason. Doubt.

The egg grew brighter and gyrated in the direction of my hand. Its compass adjusted to find its version of true north, and I was it. I heard the vibrant, chiming hum of S'ami's magic and a lower register of tones for the other two men. The room filled with sound and light, no longer orange but a heated amber, the egg rotating perfectly on an axis, its small end appearing to spin off my middle finger. Yet I didn't touch it. Not quite.

S'ami had said not to.

So I did.

My middle fingertip made contact, deliberate and quick, barely a poke.

The shell shattered.

An explosion spewed hot egg in my face, searing my flesh. I screamed. I could see nothing. I'd been blinded, my eyeballs scorched through. My right hand was on fire. I could feel flesh melting away. My shoulder thumped against the hard floor. I'd fallen. I thrashed and clutched my right hand, then my eyes. I shouted and wept. A thousand searing needles stabbed into my eye sockets. I could feel the hot wetness of blood on my face.

The air roared with an extended, sharp crackling. The noise crescendoed to a fury and then fizzled out like a doused fire. Then the only sound was my own screaming, and I could see only black. The chanting had stopped, and so had the music. S'ami's voice echoed in the quiet hall from directly over me. "Let's finish this."

I felt a jolt.

Then nothing.

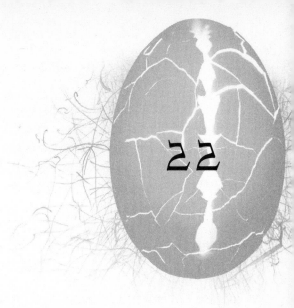

From our dreams be gently shaken,
Now we to our chores must go—
The sun's first rays bid us awaken.

Farmer, bent, with scythe and hoe
Plant this day tomorrow's bread,
Kuldor's largess on us bestow.

Fisherman, casting nets ahead,
Should currents and the moons align
We'll feast on silvery stars instead.

Let weaver spin her yarn so fine
Our shrouds will be of woven gold
And thus shame Death with her design.

If, by our labor, we grow old
Our tired limbs will surge with power
When Nihil's garden we behold.

There, beneath a fragrant bower,
We'll revel in our souls' repast,
As heaven's nectar we devour.

This sun shall set; our souls shall last.

—*"The Dance of Life,"*
traditional dawn prayer

I wasn't aware of movement or light, only sounds, mostly snatches of conversations in hushed tones that hovered about my ears and then winked out. Other times, I could remember drifting, cold and alone, high above the dusty continents that straddled the graceful arc of the planet. Mountains nosed above tree lines, and rivers cut downward to craggy coastlines and jostling seas.

I fell in that memory, or maybe it was a dream, the falling, when the biting cold gave way to a sudden heat. I gathered speed, and the heat rose above boiling to some point where the air itself melted around me. It seared every scrap of flesh from my bones and then the bones, too. I disintegrated, dropping as ash into a marsh, feeling the mud kick high around me, the cooling mud. My mind traced the outline of that memory, feeling its sharp edges, dwelling on the serrations of fire and pain and loss.

I dreamed Gek voices, high and nasal, and human ones, urgent and shrill. I thought I had answers for all their questions, but I couldn't recall what they might be. That bothered me. I ought to know. I knew what they were asking, or thought I did. I should have the answers, too.

That part of the dream lost shape and sifted away even as I reached for it.

I gave up and pushed aside the memory of the dream, or the dream of memories, whenever it surfaced. It sat in the back of my head, jagged and dangerous, waiting.

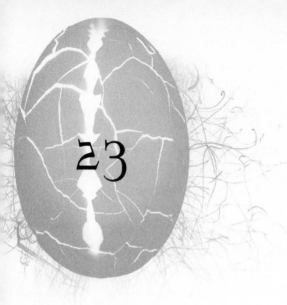

23

Will you choose my enemy over me? I am your only friend among the heavens; trust no one who says otherwise. He will only tell you what it pleases you to hear.
—*from Oblations 14,* The Book of Unease

The morning horn blasted closer than I'd remembered, as if the horn tower were beside my house. I shuddered awake. I wasn't at home. I didn't recognize the small, airless room or the scratchy blankets tucked around me.

Deep, manly voices chanting their morning prayers filtered through the thick stucco walls. Giants. Something sounded familiar about their words. They sang in Fernai, but, then again, it couldn't be. I don't speak Fernai. Yet the "Dance of Life" sounded so lilting in their tongue. How could I know this?

I realized I must be in Ward Sapphire's sick ward, with its musty smell tingling my nostrils. I lay on a canvas cot in a threadbare nightdress I'd never owned. I didn't know how I'd gotten there. Probably I'd been sick, maybe with a fever of some sort.

The door creaked open, and someone peered in. My eyes took a moment to focus on Leba Mara's round, smiling face. Her relief was palpable. "Didn't think you'd ever rejoin us."

I closed my eyes. I struggled to form words, in too much of a fog to know what to say. When I opened them again, she'd placed a tray on a low table with a bowl of soup and some tea.

"An Azwan'll be here after dawn prayers," she said. "Said to make sure to fetch them if you awoke."

My parched throat didn't allow for more than a thin gasp to escape. "What happened to me?"

"Azwans won't say. Nor am I allowed to ask."

I could see the curiosity reflected in her kind features. She touched warm fingertips to my neck, feeling along my glands, and across my brow. She examined me like this for long moments, checking my pulse, listening to my breathing. I closed my eyes through much of the exam and focused only on slowing my breath, in and out, fighting the weariness that pressed me downward into the coarse bedding.

"Where am I?" I asked.

"In the sick ward, of course," she said, fluffing a scroungy pillow as best she could. "We're all back at Ward Sapphire again, and apparently we have you to thank for that."

Thank me? My memories faded in and out. Valeo in his cot, dying. The altar. An egg of some sort. Falling. Pain. I clenched my eyes shut again. More falling. Valeo. "How long?"

"A whole six-day. You missed a Sabbath and your own Keeping Day."

My eyes fluttered open. My Keeping Day—I'd turned sixteen without even knowing. But I was alive at least. I had to focus on that. "My family."

"We turn them away when they ask after you. No news of you leaves this room."

My throat felt dry. I tried to swallow and couldn't. A grating whisper emerged from my parched lips. "But they know I live?"

"Not even that."

My spirits sank again. My family wasn't being encouraged to nurture hope. I could disappear or die still. I tried to imagine my fate, struggling to remember what had happened, as Leba Mara fed me and held a glass to my lips. The last I knew, I was making some sort of tea for the soldiers. Moonbloom tea, and Mami and I were in some sort of trouble. No, only I was in trouble.

Yes, that was it. I was in trouble, and one of the Azwans was leading me away. To Valeo? No, not that. Whatever had happened, I was fairly certain it involved only my family and me.

I strained to figure out what came next and couldn't. Bits and pieces floated to the surface but refused to stay, and there was nothing to hold any of the images in place. My memory had simply melted away.

I expected the tea brought to my lips to taste like the soft, sensuous nectar of moonbloom, but it didn't. I nearly gagged at the syrupy sweetness of the tisane Leba Mara poured down my throat. It served its purpose, though, and quenched a thirst that must've been building for some time. I'd dehydrated, and the over-sweetened tea sent strength seeping into tired limbs. Leba Mara left as soon as I could show her I could hold the tea glass without trembling. That took more effort, I think, than I let on.

I didn't want to worry her. She could get word out to my family. Even if she couldn't tell them anything, they'd see in her face signs that she'd stopped fretting over me. Mami would be skilled at reading such signals, and she'd tell Babba. I sank back into my pillows and let relief wash over me. Yes, Mami would see Leba Mara's face, and there'd be communication of the half-winking and quarter-nodding sort. Leba Mara could make a huge speech that way without the Azwans overhearing a word.

She left to make her rounds, leaving me listening to the fading chants outside that either were or weren't in Fernai, I was too weak to ponder it, and I got stuck again on my death that wasn't, or might yet be. There was only a blank after I'd left my home, when I had to answer for the moon-bloom petals we'd prepared. I could feel Reyhim's coarse hand tugging at my own as we walked, wondering how a priest could get calluses on his palms, and wasn't that an odd thing to have my mind get stuck on. Calluses. Maybe I ought to have remembered his raspy voice, and then I could've recalled what he'd said. When that didn't work, I listened to the footsteps in the corridor outside my room.

They belonged to Reyhim. I wasn't surprised by the coincidence. I wondered if my punishment was finished yet. Reyhim sidled in, bringing his own floor cushion. His thin voice was artificially cheery. "Can't stand the stool. Bad for the back."

He arranged his seating as I finished my tea and set it aside. I knew this encounter was coming; Leba Mara had said as much. That didn't mean I was ready for it. Reyhim propped himself against the wall and leaned one arm on my low cot. "Well, well, if Nihil's ambiguities aren't the best salves after all."

Then S'ami barged in, sweating in his prayer vestments. "You ask her anything yet?"

Reyhim shook his head.

S'ami turned to me. "What's your name? You remember it, yes?"

I told him. Then he asked after my family, their names, ages, and all sorts of trivia about myself. How well I did in school, where my family usually sits at Sabbath prayers, and so on. They were all things he could've learned within Ward Sapphire's walls. I wasn't sure why I was being tested but knew better than to protest. I answered calmly, slowly, gliding past any tremor in my voice by keeping it low and soft. The questions seemed simple enough, with the men unusually eager to question a mere schoolgirl. Wasn't I being punished? It didn't sound that way. The whole situation was starting to seem curious.

Both men produced their gold totems and waved them over me with more chanting. I could feel odd tingles wherever the totems passed, and each left a faint trail in the air of glowing dust. I hadn't noticed that before, and I watched them work, more fascinated than ever. Sparks flew out of the totems and intertwined before fizzling out or fading. I wondered if they knew I could see all this or if they even knew it was happening. I got a sense they didn't; they kept passing their hands through the dazzling wake their magic left as if oblivious.

The two men finished their work and fell silent, glancing from each other to me and back again. Reyhim cleared his throat, but his voice was its usual rasp. "She knows who she is. There's never been a case of possession where the victim was left with any sense of self."

"That we know of," S'ami said. "There's also never been anyone who's survived a deathcast."

"I still say you threw a faulty spell."

"Leave off." S'ami's words sounded clipped with anger. "This isn't the time or place."

"Will you be giving it another try?"

I held my breath. S'ami had tried to kill me and would try again. Though, wait, they just agreed his strongest spell didn't work. I steadied myself. S'ami barely acknowledged Reyhim's suggestion. "Our Master has bent my ear on this enough."

Reyhim patted my arm. "Nihil's grateful for your help. You're safe now."

I managed to find my voice. "I can't remember."

"What can't you remember?" Reyhim's voice was kind.

"What happened that night."

It was as if I'd held up a straw dummy that soldiers use in their practice. Both men fired off more questions, united in purpose again, asking at what point I'd stopped remembering and prodding me further. At last, I thought I did remember that the moonbloom petals had gone to the sick ward, while I'd gone to the altar. I had a vague recollection of talking to Nihil. The mirror and its jeweled insects loomed before me again, and my attention drifted as I lingered on the beautiful voice that had come from it.

"But that's it, then?" Reyhim peered into my face and anxiously took my measure. I shrank into the bedsheets and meekly nodded.

"I remember Nihil's voice," I said. "And the . . . maybe the altar."

"What happened there?"

I closed my eyes and shook my head.

S'ami cut in. "Then let's leave it at that."

Reyhim chuffed. "Didn't think you cared for her suffering, exactly. Just the opposite."

"Let's take this discussion elsewhere, brother."

"The girl deserves to know."

I sat up at that. I was going to hear what happened to me. I could fill in those blank spots. But why would Azwans take pity on me? Maybe they were grateful for my help in the swamp. When we'd gone to get the tin box with the . . .

Oh.

With the demon.

The night at the altar blasted back into my consciousness. The insect mirror, the ornate altar, the glowing egg, my decision to disobey S'ami and touch the thing—it was all there, rushing past in no particular order and making no sense yet. Further back, there were moonblooms and the Gek, and petals everywhere, and the sick ward, Valeo clutching my hand, Valeo convulsing, Valeo warning me about my sister.

Valeo dying.

I shrank back into the bedsheets, wanting to disappear or at least make myself much less noticeable. I needed time and space to sort the mess of details.

A few things I knew for certain: I hadn't gotten my chat with the egg-demon. That plan was probably stillborn the moment I set foot on the altar.

And I wasn't dead. And the Azwans were arguing over keeping me alive. That was a change, even if their quarrel was filled with their usual bile.

Reyhim scoffed—but not at me. "Were you going to get around to telling her how, exactly, you tried to crush her young soul into nothingness?"

"Get out." Beads of sweat popped from S'ami's brow.

"I go nowhere," Reyhim said.

"Then leave off arguing in front of this girl."

"*This girl* may've saved the planet, or at least this corner of it," Reyhim said. "We're to protect her so long as she shows no sign of possession. She's entitled to know who's on her side and who tried to argue she be put to death some other way."

"It's not as simple as that, and you know it." Angry flecks of spittle dotted S'ami's mouth. Had I been one of the men in the Customs House, I'd be selling seats to this spectacle. I could make a fortune with what I was over-hearing, and I sat up, fascinated.

Reyhim sneered at S'ami, all coolness and cruelty. "Ah, yes, talk to me of ambiguities, shall you?"

Finally, I couldn't take it any longer. If they kept on this way, I'd start laughing, and that wouldn't do. They could still kill me. And I wanted to go home. "Pious servants of Nihil, I'm sure I don't deserve all this fuss."

Reyhim patted my arm again. "You do, sweet girl. And I shall tell you."

S'ami interrupted. "No, you shall not. Leave us."

"I don't recall you moving up the ranks to give me orders."

"Or she'll know more about you than you'd like her to."

Reyhim blanched and sputtered. "You wouldn't dare."

"Wouldn't I."

With more sputtering and flailing, Reyhim rose with difficulty and gave S'ami a hard stare. The younger man only folded his arms across his chest and waited. Their battle had turned in S'ami's favor, and here was Reyhim, suddenly in retreat, fuming and shoving the door with such force that it squeaked on its track.

My mother sometimes talked about manipulative people, how they worked, what to watch for, especially in men. How they could love-talk you out of your clothes and into trouble. S'ami was as manipulative as a catapult. One moment, you could be standing there, fine as could be, never better, and the next moment, you're a pulpy lump without ever having seen what landed on you.

No sooner had the door clicked shut than S'ami plopped down on the edge of my cot. My body remembered his invasive stare from the pier before my mind did, and my legs clenched by instinct. My whole body huddled into a ball.

"He didn't see you touch that egg."

I fumbled for something to say. "Nihil sows doubts and reaps discord."

"Such an idiotic response, I might concede it's actually clever. I honestly cannot decide if you're so impertinent because you're stupid or brilliant."

"Um, which would you prefer?"

"Stupid. No, that would irritate me. Brilliant, then. As hard as that would be to deal with."

It was an odd compliment, but I liked it. I'd settle for being brilliant and hard for a priest to deal with, and also quite alive. Which reminded me to ask, "So why am I not dead?"

"Because you lived."

"By accident, I assume."

He sighed. "You are bright, as I suspected. A curse. If you were stupid, I'd have less to fear. I could pat your hand and assure you that you'd been forgiven and give you my best smile."

"And instead?"

"I'll tell you as little as you'll let me get away with." One corner of his mouth lifted into a half-smile. He must be the only man who could reek of dignity with a smirk on his face.

I thought about his statement, really a challenge. The Temple was setting another trap, wasn't it? I was supposed to ask him questions that he'd refuse to answer, or he'd ask me things and twist my answers. The latter was how it usually worked. This new twist was a challenge I'd normally avoid like a thundercloud, but it had to mean something that an Azwan, of all people, was asking me to test him. I was either stupid or brilliant, after all. I was tired of people, particularly holy people, thinking me stupid. It took a half a moment, not even that, to decide I'd accept his challenge and try my hardest—weakened and bedridden and all—to pry my story out of him.

"Did Nihil see me touch the egg?"

"He felt it." S'ami's eyes locked onto mine. I knew he was looking for any reaction from me, and I wasn't going to give him the satisfaction. Let him be the one to keep guessing.

"How did Nihil feel it?" For a moment, I considered what a stupid question that would be. I expected an answer my schoolmistress would give: that Nihil was god and could do anything. But S'ami wasn't her.

"He's aware of his enemy, probably in a way similar to how you knew the Gek were watching us in the swamp."

That sounded reasonable enough, and a flicker of gratitude went through me. I'd had a question that someone in the Temple had taken seriously and answered without talking down to me or swatting me. I must've come up in their esteem, and all I'd had to do was to not die when they'd wanted. "Am I in trouble then?"

"You should be. But what's done is done. We killed the creature, we're absolutely sure of it, especially with you awake and not possessed. This is good. Nihil will be pleased. I have to say, you came out of this like a thistle rose, a mite prickly but smelling sweet."

I grinned. "Thank you, I think." Really, what does someone say to a compliment like that?

S'ami kept going. "Your behavior on the altar was outstanding. You didn't beg or whine and showed a quick grasp of what was occurring. Did you have doubts? Well, yes, but you've overcome them, I trust. You should be filled with certainty of the Temple's rectitude after your ordeal. Are you?"

My jaw opened and closed a few times, but I couldn't manage a sound. I remembered telling myself about hope and reason and doubt. Did I have all three? I couldn't think like this. My head was starting to throb. I was only certain I wanted to leave this room and never talk to an Azwan again.

He shook his head. "Ah, doubtful even yet. Only Nihil is allowed the privilege of skepticism, even if you find yourself overwhelmed by events. But . . ." S'ami leaned in close and dropped his voice. "You might secretly harbor doubts, mightn't you? You did all along, yes? And that's why you reached for that egg?"

An instinct to nod gripped me, and I stopped my chin before it could bob down even a fraction. No, no nodding. No agreeing. I wasn't going to say I held doubts and get myself in trouble all over again. But it wasn't an accident, either—I wouldn't use a child's excuse for wrongdoing.

"You were going to tell me what happened," I said.

"You didn't answer my question."

I didn't budge. "Did you win against the demon?"

"We're all still here."

"So I'm alright? I can go home?"

"Well, not yet. Maybe not at all. No one's ever survived the way you did. All of this is new to us."

"Please, Azwan, I want to know if I'll ever walk out that door again." If he wanted me dead, I needed to know that, and I figured he'd never tell me outright. Azwan of Uncertainty, indeed. Uncertainties hovered around him, like a buzzing swarm of nettlesome questions that stung anyone who came close.

S'ami drew a deep breath and shook his head. "Six days ago, I stood over what I'd hoped was your lifeless form. And now, here we are, all cozy and chatty. It's touching, really. Even if you're clearly not going to tell me what doubts you still harbor."

I must've won the challenge, because he began unwinding the entire story of what I'd missed, from the moment I'd entered the sanctuary and knelt, trembling, before the scrying mirror. More came back to me as he talked, until I thought I could see the amber light again, and I tensed, recalling the whine of the spinning egg.

The Azwans and the high priest had rehearsed in advance, he said, and Nihil had described previous disembodied spirits to them. Though the egg-as-vessel was a new idea to them, they were ready when the time came. When I touched the shell, it released a fiery spray of sparks. Reyhim and the high priest saw only the explosion and not my fingertip tapping the shell. The fire had been hotter and far more intense than they'd predicted, but it shot straight at me, and that left them free for the spellcasting they'd planned.

The three men had focused solely on the cloud of sparks. They cast spells to surround and contain it within a fraction of a moment. It had been doused, like any other flame. Not so much as a single glimmer of demonfire had reached me, as far as they could tell. Yet my fingertip tingled. Perhaps it was only my imagination.

"All over with a flash and a fizzle," S'ami said. "There were no signs of any other entity when I went to finish you."

I didn't buy the friendly tone. "But you don't know if I'm alright or not. I don't get to go home, and my family doesn't know whether to have any hope. Can't you tell them?"

"You've dropped all pretense of formality. I could almost like that from you."

"You're going to watch me for signs of possession."

"Of course. And you're going to tell me about why you doubt Nihil or perhaps me or the Temple or something. Maybe you doubt the weather. Something made you disobey my request, and I intend to find out what it is, sooner or later."

"Or you'll kill me?"

"Dropping formality is one thing. I'll not tolerate impertinence. To think, I almost killed you on the spot that first day on the balcony, with that mouth of yours. A demon could be the least of your worries. Though if you're possessed, there won't be anything of you left to destroy."

Did he seriously believe I'd find that idea consoling? There'd be nothing left of me to destroy. How sweet. I had to set this man straight, impertinence or not. If he could hesitate even a moment before sending any more death-casts my way, that would be something—something small, but not nothing. I had to risk it. Maybe this powerful man could stop hating me.

"You're the last person I'd disrespect, Azwan."

"And why is that?"

I managed a smile. It was thin and tight and felt more than a little forced. "Anyone who's willing to wade into the muck, shimmy up a tree, stare down the Gek, and then run like Nihil himself is after him while having enough wits to cast spells the whole time gets my flat-out, whole-hearted respect."

I discovered something else important about S'ami: he had a deep, full-throated laugh that he put his whole body into. My smile became more heartfelt and burst into a grin. He'd never been anything but open about my being expendable. If he was restraining himself from snuffing out my short life, I had to accept it, at least until I figured out a way to wriggle out of the Temple's grip for good.

"And may I risk one more act of impertinence?" I asked. I had to know just one more thing, something that had nagged at me from the moment I'd awakened. Had my entire ordeal been in vain? "There is a soldier who was sick. A Prince. Valeo, his name was."

S'ami's face darkened. "I know the name, yes. You have some special concern about him?"

His frown didn't give me much hope. I swallowed hard and tried to ask, but all I could manage was a feeble "Did he make it?"

S'ami turned away and murmured, as if unwilling to face me to give me the bad news. "Your tonic saved many lives, but not his. Forget him. You are the one in need of saving now, and to do that, you must relinquish your doubts."

Dead, then. I choked back a sob. Valeo had tried so hard to save me. He'd been so brave, even after all the trouble he'd caused my family. I'd wanted so desperately for him to be alright.

He was the first man I'd ever had any real feelings about. Every other man in my life had been someone I'd known since birth, or they were strange sailors on the wharf, barely worth noticing except to smile at and admire from a distance. But Valeo had been in front of me, close enough for me to touch, and we'd stared down death together with the mash cat and again in the treetops. Wasn't that supposed to mean something?

S'ami kept talking about my doubts, but I turned to the wall, unable to think of anything but that last sight of Valeo in his cot, dying and delirious. He hadn't even had a shred of privacy as I had in this tiny cell. He'd obsessed over my golden eyes and warned me of my city burning—which turned out to be nothing at all, just a final fever dream before he slipped away.

"Hadara?" S'ami leaned over me. "You're crying."

Indeed, I had crunched a big swathe of blanket into a ball, clutched beneath my chin, and it was already damp from tears. My voice came out raspy and thin. "He's dead."

S'ami touched my shoulder, his tone softening. "There is much living yet to do, Hadara. You are young yet. You will find love someday—I promise."

Isn't that the advice all adults give to people my age? What was I supposed to do, forget Valeo? Yes, of course, I'll just put him out of mind like a pair of sandals I'd outgrown; how inconvenient to have to replace him. I seethed. How inconvenient that biting S'ami's hand off wasn't literally possible, since it's what I felt like doing. Its presence on my shoulder wasn't the least comforting. I had a sudden need for him to leave and to be alone.

I sobbed uncontrollably and squeezed my eyes to shut out anything but that final image of Valeo, clutching my hand, his strength slipping away like sand.

As if sensing my discomfort, S'ami withdrew with a backward glance and a last warning. "You'll tell me your doubts, Hadara. You'll have no choice. You've been forgiven your missteps so far, but you'll come to me of your own accord before you wander much further. Of that, I have *no* doubts."

What if I stumble onto some other truth than yours, I wanted to say.

But he was already gone.

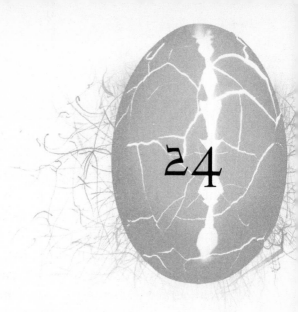

24

There's no stronger curse than that cast by a broken heart.

—*Meridian proverb*

I had failed him.

I had only one task, and I had failed. None of the stuff on the altar had ever mattered. Only the moonbloom tonic had, and I'd waited too long and done too little, and far too late.

I had failed him, and he was dead.

He was a prince, he was a soldier, he was brave; he never doubted himself or anything, ever. He was confident and strong and . . . and . . .

He was his own person.

He was independent and could come and go as he pleased, he knew what he was about, and he had radiated a certain authority, and not just with the muscles he could flex, though, yes, there was that, too.

Had he lived, he never would be told to stay away from the places he loved, to marry someone his father chose, to choose a career that kept him mostly at home, to hide his hair and much of his body. I had envied him his ability to do his job well, without apology, having grown up hearing Mami beg forgiveness for every sachet of herbs or drop of tincture she'd ever sold.

But even compared to other men, Valeo was alive in the world in a way I'd never seen. His gaze, his voice carried it, his stance, even when he stood in the rain, waiting half the day and into the night for me to do something so he could have an excuse to flex a little more of that power. My brain went around and around on that day, circling back to what he might've wanted, whether he was there by choice or under orders, and whether my grief was making too much of it. Instead, if I were being rational, I should see it as a symbol of our helplessness as the soldiers sacked a city that had always prayed for their protection. We were small and weak, and Valeo had been only the most visible reminder of how I had no power and never would.

So maybe Leba Mara was right in accusing me of self-pity. She'd warned me a few days ago against sitting in my boxy cell of a room, which had forced me out into the main part of the sick ward. Beyond its doors lay Ward Sapphire and its sprawling compound, but I didn't venture further than a bench along a far wall, watching all the people who would get up and walk out again in a way that Valeo never would. I don't know how many times I sighed, but I didn't wish to be seen crying. I didn't want to explain, and I didn't want to lie.

I was only a patient here and had no role in helping anyone. So I sat. And I watched. And I kept thinking to myself:

Why had I been spared?

So many had died. Valeo, the best of any of them, had died. Why had a lowly girl, granddaughter of a heretic, proved unkillable?

I didn't know how to answer that. Who could say why?

Nihil himself didn't know; it had been out of his control.

That was a dangerous thing to believe. But it wasn't belief—the Azwans had as much as confessed it. It must be true.

The Azwans, so casual in their hostility to each other, had let slip that Nihil cannot do anything he wishes.

And that, I realized at long last, was a very dangerous thing for me to know.

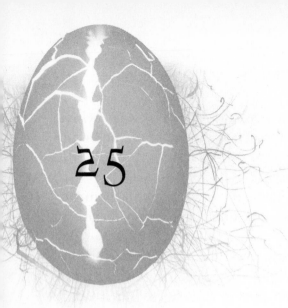

25

*Greet each day as if today you might gain entrance
to my Garden, and someday you may achieve it.
Pray to me this way in a public place set aside for
your exercise. Pray to me as if the work you do
was my special blessing to you, and it shall be so.*
—from *Oblations 6,* The Book of Unease

I managed to get myself to the dawn prayers the next day,
my limbs going through the Dance of Life only stiffly and
by rote. My lips couldn't quite form the words to the med-
itation, even as my limbs warmed up, the muscles slowly
uncoiling from too many days spent idle.

I stood far to the back of the crowd, where I could be
first inside the doors when prayers ended. My presence
must be an open secret, as no one took their eyes off S'ami
as he led the chanting and movements in the middle of the
Ward's central courtyard. I couldn't imagine no one had
seen me, even if Leba Mara had led me out a side door and
through an alley.

I wasn't being hidden, but no one had said I could go home, either, though I'd gotten word that my parents knew I was well, or at least outwardly alright. Or at least there was nothing visibly wrong with me. But I hadn't been allowed to send word to them. So I prayed to my flawed, imperfect god and kept my opinions to myself, and gulped greedily from the breezy, morning air. It was as if I hadn't properly breathed in days, or ever, and my lungs needed to learn how to do this whole inflating process, and if I stopped thinking about inhaling and exhaling all the time, I'd suffocate on the spot.

Finally, prayers ended, and I put my arms down from the final movements, my chest heaving. People milled around and past me, taking no notice. Maybe no one knew what I'd been through or what had happened on the altar. Maybe one day, everyone is told to evacuate the Ward, and the next day, they're back. And no one knows why.

So I let people elbow and bump past me, on their way to breakfast or work or home again, and smelled their sweat and breath and tried to remember what it was like to only think about gods and demons the way I was told to think about them.

"It is time."

I glanced up at the sound of S'ami's baritone voice, just steps away. He nodded at me. My lungs remembered their job, and I didn't faint or even wheeze. My heart didn't speed up, and my knees didn't shake.

Did the Temple no longer scare me?

"Good workday, Worthy Azwan," I said. It was something to say, at least.

I thought he would lead me away, maybe back to my tiny room in the sick ward, but he let the courtyard empty as he continued to regard me. He was in the bright whites of his dawn prayer vestments, not the purple robes he would likely wear after breakfast and a bath. He looked like anyone else, maybe a dock worker or sailor or cook, except for the iron gaze that never waivered or gave any ground.

When the last stragglers were too far away to overhear, S'ami cleared his throat.

"It is time," he said again.

"Azwan?"

"There are conditions."

There are likely always conditions, I thought. Whatever they were, I'd likely have no room to haggle. So I kept still.

"Your parents may know what you remember of your trip to the altar," he said, "as we don't encourage children to keep secrets from parents. But this is not something you discuss with anyone else. We have said little, and we plan to say nothing else. Neither will you."

"Then I'm going home?" A small hope budded inside me.

He nodded. "No one can think of a reason you shouldn't."

Hope blossomed into an entire bouquet. I clasped my hands and grinned at him. "Thank you, Azwan."

He ignored me.

"You will not brag about any favors the Temple bestows on you, or they will be swiftly revoked," he said. "Remember the lesson of Bardusre."

I'd no idea which of Nihil's wives she'd been, but likely Bardusre had come to a bad end. The lesson probably had something to do with remembering to act humble and grateful and utterly pliant. I'd probably fail at that sooner rather than later, but I could work at the not-bragging part. I might get the trick of it eventually. I nodded my assent.

Favors, he had said. There'd be favors?

"Good," S'ami said. "Then we are done here."

"When can I go home?"

And what kind of favors?

"When we send for you."

"And when . . ."

He cut me off.

"Good workday, Hadara," he said. "Be at peace."

Peace? What an unusual thing to say. I watched him go, puzzled.

It was only after he'd turned a corner that I realized I'd started holding my breath again.

He was right. I'd had plenty of quiet, but no peace.

I exhaled, slowly and deliberately, and headed back to my room.

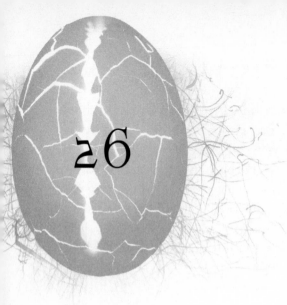

26

Blessed are those who give and those who keep.
—Nihil, from the Blessings of Keeping

The sun was barely up when the Azwans and a contingent of guards escorted me home. I tried to enjoy the thump-thumping of Feroxi boots on the wooden planks and watched their plumes advance in front of me. Up, down, march, march. I pretended it was a parade and I was a hero. I wasn't sure what I was any longer, and it wasn't as if I felt free to ask. Reyhim's head bobbed up and down as he plodded in front of me, and I pictured some of the neighborhood boys tossing it around for sport.

Meanwhile, S'ami had given me "an insignificant little gift," as he'd called it. This was like calling the fire in the swamp an insignificant little campfire. He'd given me a wholly breathtaking weave of spider-silk scarves trying to disguise itself as a dress. It covered everything it was supposed to, from elbows to mid-calf, with no skin showing, to be sure, but it clung in graceful ways I wasn't used to, as if I'd grown a second skin, only more supple, though it perhaps cinched a little too broadly over my embarrassing shortage of bosom.

Alright, I admit it; I couldn't help reveling in its dozen eye-catching shades of orange and red, as if a sunrise had draped itself over my long torso. As with everything that came from the Temple, there was likely some price I would have to pay. Or maybe I had already paid it. And maybe I was being paraded like this because the Temple already owned me.

I shunted these feelings aside. I'd earned this, hadn't I? I felt like a Tengalian princess, only without the ability to snap my fingers and have the guards drag the Azwans to some well-deserved doom. Instead, I basked in the late summer sun and a fresh breeze off the canals that carried the perfume of ripened berries. It eased the ache in my heart a little. Not many people were around to see me, though. I passed empty hearths and open doorways. Maybe everyone was off at work or their daily chores, and that explained the quiet.

As we got closer, however, I could hear a throng at my parents' hearth. We turned the corner to people milling up and down my street, maybe three hundred or so—it was hard to count. Houses and hearths sported cloth streamers dyed blazing crimson, the Temple's color, heralding a religious celebration. A red banner hung over my parents' doorway with my name painted in gold letters in a sweeping calligraphy. I'd be getting my Keeping Day celebration after all.

Reyhim nudged me. "Surprised?"

I put my hands to my burning cheeks and nodded.

S'ami fanned himself with a silk fan. "My idea."

Reyhim grunted his disapproval. "Nihil's idea."

"I suggested it to him," S'ami replied.

I pretended I didn't hear them.

It looked like everyone I'd ever met had turned out to welcome me home. There were many I didn't know. Some wore the deep blue robes of Ward Sapphire, others the jade uniform of the Customs House. I felt the honor deeply. I wanted my family to know I was alright—more than alright, and keeping my head aloft and my gaze steady around so many dignitaries was the least I could do for them.

Keeping Days are usually noisy events when a girl turns sixteen or a boy eighteen, but this was as big as an Equinox Feast. I was torn between elation and remorse. How could anyone have afforded this? Where, after all the ransacking, had they found the food and unbroken dishes?

I couldn't pretend I didn't love every last hurrah, and I couldn't blame my family for needing an excuse to celebrate. If it meant letting go of my dislike of the Temple, I wasn't sure I could do it, though. I tried to shake off my unease, but it clung deep within me, knotted around some key part of myself.

Everyone began cheering at first sight of me and I swallowed back a lump in my throat. The crowd parted around the guards, with boys climbing rooftops and dangling off tree limbs to shout down at us. I spotted Dina's younger brothers and other cousins, neighbors, schoolmates, and friends. I hoped the thatching didn't cave.

The guards halted in front of my parents' door before the flapping crimson banner, and I stopped, too. The men snapped to crisp attention, and the crowd hushed. Priests crowded around me, but all I wanted was to peer between them for a glimpse at my doorway.

Babba and Mami stood in front, holding each other, holding Amaniel and Rishi; there they were, everyone crying except Babba. That's all I wanted. The four of them, and hugs, and to run inside and tell them what happened. Oh, and to eat everything and dance my feet off.

And to forget.

My eyes met Mami's, and we both teared up at once. She gave a long, slow nod. And smiled.

Babba's chest stuck so far out I thought he might fall over. He was proud of me. Pious me! I should be snorting in disgust, but how could I? He had faced days of sorrow, thinking me dead. Everyone performed the appropriate genuflections as the Azwans brought me forward. The Azwans bowed low before my parents. Reyhim cleared his throat in his peculiar fashion. His rasp carried over the quieted throngs and even above the breeze, his tone formal and commanding: the voice of a man who could still bring a congregation to its knees.

"Are you Rimonil, son of Mansoril of Port Sapphire in Nihil's own nation of New Meridian, father of the woman Hadara?"

Babba's voice boomed. "I am."

I was a woman now. It was official.

Reyhim continued.

"And is this your wife, Lia, the mother of the woman Hadara?"

271

"She is."

"The Temple of Doubt has word of her coming of age. We claim her for service to Nihil, unless you wish to keep her. Do you keep her, Hadara who is your daughter?"

"I do."

"And is that the wish of your wife as well?"

"It is."

There was the briefest pause, scarcely half a moment, when I thought the ceremony would take a wrong turn, and I'd be marched away again.

Reyhim raised his arms overhead and lifted his voice to a hoarse shout.

"Then so be it," he said.

I almost collapsed with relief.

A cry of "So be it!" rang through the crowd. The guards didn't flinch. Reyhim smiled toward the crowds gathered far up and down the street and grew solemn again. "May she be a blessing to your house for all the days and nights she dwells herein."

Babba's eyes reddened, and his voice cracked. "So be it."

The Azwans stepped back, and I stumbled into my parents' arms. My mother sobbed; I snuffled and sniffled and leaked tears everywhere. Behind me, S'ami's ringing baritone crooned the Blessings of Keeping. I turned, and we bowed our heads to accept his prayer.

The unplanted seed is a hope
The uncut gem is a promise
The uncast spell is a wish
The unforged steel is a dream.
Comes now the parents who tended this seed,

who polished and conjured and forged this woman of their own flesh.

This grown child is their harvest,
their treasure, their magic, their strength.

Let us forgive them for keeping from Nihil what Nihil himself gave.

Nihil blesses those who give and those who keep.

So be it.

With a final cry of "So be it" from the crowd, the short ceremony was done, and my family had been officially absolved of not giving me over to the Temple to become a priestess or healer or Temple servant. Most families kept their newly adult children, but no one wanted to skip a celebration. That included mine, judging by the hordes they'd invited. I nestled in closer, between Babba and Mami until their arms pulled tight around my shoulders. Mami tucked a lock of hair that had escaped my scarf and smiled at me, her eyes glistening.

"Beautiful gown," she whispered. "I'm glad you knew to accept the Temple's tokens."

"I figured I'd earned it," I said.

Her smile was bittersweet. "I ought to laugh, but there's too much truth to what you've said. How sad to have to acquire such wisdom so young."

I choked back a reply. The crowd was cheering again, until Reyhim stopped them with a wave of his arm. When the crowd had hushed, he continued.

"This is, as you can see, a more sacred occasion than most. This glorious young woman has an additional blessing, composed by our gracious Master for her unique service to him."

Approving murmurs rippled through the crowd. I had no idea what was coming. What unique service had I done? I'd lived. That wasn't my doing, either.

The two Azwans held their arms outstretched, hands up in benediction. Reyhim called above the whispers of the crowd, "Hear us, Fey One, as we remove all doubts from your servant's name."

The men raised their hands and invoked Nihil's name and my own with it, linking my mortal self with his eternal life force, at least in words. This blessing was also short, and it was over promptly with a final "So be it," echoed by the throngs behind us. People sang good-luck songs and shouted congratulations. I'd been forgiven for whatever I'd done, or hadn't done—I wasn't sure. I wondered how many people knew that the Temple's tyranny wasn't over. The ceremony was an empty ritual to me. If I cried, it was with relief and love bound up with a lingering rage I couldn't seem to either pinpoint or set aside.

Unknown arms pulled me into the festivities. I sampled delicacies from brimming platters and air-kissed well-wishers. Almost despite myself, I found my head bobbing to riotous music and my whole self dragged into dizzying dances that weaved in and out of the crowds and around and 'round. Mami danced with me first, then Amaniel and Rishi, then girl cousins and aunties, while on the other side of the patio, the men hoisted Babba onto their shoulders and whirled him overhead. He spotted me in the crowd and laughed.

I returned his laugh because I was happy to see the worry lifted from him, worry that I'd caused. Inside, however, I ached. I would never be able to tell Babba why, or

Mami, either. I couldn't ever tell them that I'd fallen in love at a dazzling speed and had already lost him. I knew what they would say, the patronizing speech parents give you when they want to comfort you, and they forget you're no longer five.

Maybe I had only loved the idea of him, as in those old poems where the king marries a beautiful commoner, or the princess runs off with the gardener.

I sighed and looked for a way to make an exit, even a temporary one.

I spied the guards to one side of our property, close to the water's edge. For a moment, I thought one of them might be Valeo. By all three moons, every one of them suddenly looked like him, when they never had before.

Maybe it was the armor, or the haughty way they stood at ease, aloof and to the side, just as he had. Sadness welled up inside me as I thought of the man who'd been poisoned trying to protect me. I would never get a chance to thank him, and I'd have to remember my searing last sight of him, sick and feverish on his deathbed. He hadn't been as handsome as these rangy guards in their gleaming armor, eyeing the prettier girls and their swaying skirts, but then that had been what I'd liked about him.

I sighed. I had to force thoughts of the fallen Valeo from my mind. I grabbed a tray of water jugs and went over to the guards, making a big show of courtesy and smiles as they quenched their thirst and thanked me. One of the handsomer guards smiled down at me, a hulk with gray eyes that twinkled with flirty mischief beneath that big brow.

"I have a favor to ask, a small one," I said.

"Anything, so long as it's pious," he said.

"And even if it's not," said another. "He'd just wait until he's off duty."

I felt my ears grow hot. I was a clumsy flirt.

The first guard elbowed the other. "You're scaring her. Worthy Hadara, what may the Temple do for you?"

"I love the Fernai tongue. All those rolling r's. It's like music. Can you say a few words? Something nice. Please?"

"Something nice. Hmmm . . . everything in the mother tongue is nice. How about this: *You're as beautiful as a thistle rose and twice as tough. If the Azwans hadn't threatened to blast a hole through any guard who touched you, I'd be chasing you all the way back to my barracks.*"

I grew confused. I'd understood it. "I . . . I meant . . . was that in Fernai?"

He smirked. "Perhaps our tongue is too beautiful for the untrained ear. How about this: *I'd give my father's flock to see what's beneath that gown. At least climb another tree and give us a peek.*"

Only a quick, mental reflex kept my hand from immediately smacking his leering face. He mustn't know. Something in me said *he mustn't know.* I could understand him, far beyond even my usual knack for languages. What had S'ami said about signs of possession? I felt flustered, heat and shame mixing with a sudden panic. Languages. I could understand their Fernai as if I'd spoken it all my life.

The other men laughed, thinking I didn't know what they'd said. I forced a smile and hoped they couldn't detect gritted teeth beneath my lips. I'd understood every awful syllable. That was worrisome. I managed to thank him without puking on his shiny armor.

"You want a translation?" he said, his face neutral.

Another guard sneered and muttered in Fernai: "Can't wait to hear this."

The gray-eyed guard said only this in the common tongue: "You're a very pretty woman, and I wish you a Joyous Keeping Day."

Good thing I was being too polite to spit at him.

I did a curtsy-bow without dropping anything off the water tray. I nearly forgot the reason I'd sought them out. They made me so angry, I wasn't sure I wanted to raise the subject of Valeo. I wanted to find someplace quiet to fret, but I owed him this, and that kept me rooted in front of these coarse, unkind men.

"Your prince was the bravest man I've ever met, and I'm so sorry he was stricken," I said with unexpected emphasis, immediately regretting it. I didn't sound mournful—just silly and shallow. But I couldn't bring myself to say the word *dead*. "I regret any role I may have played in bringing him to harm."

There. Nice and apologetic and humble. Amaniel would be proud.

A shadow crossed the man's face. "Harm. Yes. There has been much harm. But I should thank you for such humility. We'd wondered if it had occurred to you what we've all sacrificed here. Many good men died to free this island. But you are among the worthy now, and we must console ourselves by bearing witness to your blessings, which Nihil has found fit to bestow."

His formal manner pricked like pins under my skin. There was real pain beneath those overly polite words, whatever the intended insult. I knew better than to think he'd ever apologize for what the Guards had been ordered to do to us. His unchaste, rude words still stung in my ears, and my voice came out hoarse and sputtering. *He mustn't know.*

"I would, thank you," I said. "I know I am unworthy of such kindness."

Behind me, the music grew louder and more frantic; the bobbing rows of dancers swirled into a mass of noise and color.

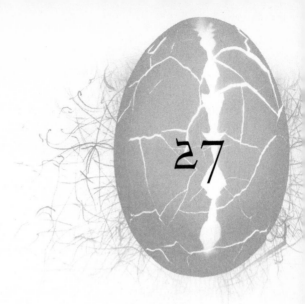

27

We must have faith in the power of the stars that guide us, for they are the birthplace of our lord and keeper, and their movements tell us much about our position here on Kuldor.

—from the Preface of
Anatomy of the Heavens

The other dancers swept me along, under and over and through others' arms. I stumbled over my own ankles a few times, letting the girls dancing next to me yank me back up. A few times, I took my immediate neighbors on the dance chain down with me. Everyone laughed, thinking I was giddy or tipsy or entirely too light-headed. I didn't say otherwise.

I could understand Fernai. That didn't sound right. I felt fine. And I was definitely myself. Who else could I be? I searched the high-stepping, swirling crowds for a familiar flash of deep amethyst. I shouldn't trust him. I knew that. The dress was nice—alright, more like striking and gorgeous. And we'd developed an odd almost-alliance, S'ami and I, though it was lopsided in his favor by a huge degree. He'd said I'd come to him if I had doubts. Did this qualify?

He'd kill me quickly, without apology. Then again, maybe he couldn't kill me. Hadn't he already tried? His strongest spell hadn't worked. I was unkillable. Maybe that and my sudden talent for language were linked to my time on the altar. I pulled S'ami away from my old uncle bending his ear about tithes, after lots of genuflecting for one and hugs for the other.

"Why aren't you enjoying your celebrations?" S'ami said. "You've earned them."

"Say something in Tengali."

"Any reason why?"

"I'm begging you."

S'ami's stare told me that he'd registered my panic. "Alright," he said, forming his words slowly. *If you can understand this, you fear you're possessed. Am I right?*

I fought to keep from shaking. I translated what he'd said, word for word. "But I'm not, right?" I glanced around, suddenly fearful of who might've heard. My voice dropped to a whisper, and I told him about the guards. "You said if I knew who I was, then it couldn't be that, that . . ."

"Do you know who you are?" S'ami's kept his voice low.

"Yes. Of course."

"Then go enjoy your Keeping Day."

"Is that it?"

"Say nothing to anyone else."

Before I could protest, he gently pushed me toward a circle of dancers, and I was dragged away by a schoolmate who used to snicker behind my back. I hoped I wasn't becoming popular among the pious set, or I'd go right back to that altar and fling myself on it. I glanced over my shoulder to see S'ami staring after me, brooding.

I danced long into the night, after the lanterns burned low and the platters were emptied, refilled, and emptied again, the wine jugs drained of all but a few drops, and the last old uncles and doting aunties teetered away tipsily after a few goodnight kisses. A hired crew cleaned up, and neighbors trickled back to their homes.

Babba waved the last stragglers off while swaying on unsteady legs. His sash sported odd food stains, and his broad skullcap tipped to one side of his head. He swirled the remnants of a wine cup and grinned at me.

"Blossom." He hugged me a bit more firmly than usual. "Got sumpin to show ya."

"Babba, you're drunk." It was weirdly out of character for him to drink too much. He was a completely different person, giddy and excited, a boyish grin bursting from his careworn face.

"By Nihil's wives, I am. Deserve it, too. C'mere."

His swaying made me laugh, the first real chuckle in many days. I followed him inside the house, though I walked in a decidedly straighter line. A low table stood where my sleeping pallet had been. It was covered with scrolls all tied with crimson ribbons. Babba hugged me again. "Your courting notes, blossom. Every bachelor in town is suddenly being very nice to me."

I shook my head in disbelief. Just a few six-days had turned me from the school laughingstock into some sort of festival prize. Did each of these men think me stupid? Or just shallow? If they wanted to share in the Temple's blessings, they could find their own altars to almost die on. Parasites, all of them.

Besides, despite wanting to join the mysterious ranks of womanhood, it felt too soon to think about a husband. I'd only just turned sixteen. "There must be dozens," was all I could manage to say.

"Well, you are the Lord Portreeve's daughter."

My jaw dropped. "When did that happen?"

"You've always been my daughter." The mirth on Babba's face made me want to poke him. I gave him another hug instead.

"You'd better tell me," I said. "When did the Merchants Guild pick you?"

"Oh, well, the old Azwan let it slip all over town that you were alive and sanctified and such. Had done Nihil some big service."

"So you owe it to the Temple."

"Yes, but then I owe a lot to the Temple." His face went serious. "I imagine I'll be owing them the rest of my life."

Which is exactly what Reyhim wants, I thought.

Babba tugged off his cap. Jet curls cascaded over his forehead, making him seem more boyish than lordly. He was likely one of the younger Portreeves ever appointed; I could remember only pompous grayhairs in the post. It would fall to Babba to oversee all the commerce in the city, from market stalls to mighty ships, and enforce its ordinances: the chief constable would answer to him, as would the tax and tariff collectors, and pretty much everyone but the magistrate. He was lord and protector of Port Sapphire.

But he'd returned to being the serious, stern father when he took my hand.

"I haven't heard your whole story, blossom. I want to know why we are suddenly in the Temple's good graces. Was it really Nihil himself who spared you?"

My need to unburden was a pang in my side. I began the long story, as S'ami had said I should do, hashing out what I remembered of the altar and what I didn't, but leaving out the part about understanding foreign tongues. I asked Babba what I should feel about the Temple since my trials. I wanted to know how deeply into the Temple's quicksand he'd sunk, though I couldn't say it in those words. It came out instead as a plea. "Babba, the Temple, their teachings. I just can't anymore. I feel like such a hypocrite. What am I supposed to feel?"

By way of an answer, Babba gave me a squeeze. "We're meant to feel doubt, as ever. Doubt like a damnable knife wound, like the stabbing my predecessor got."

"But I went through so much."

"And we owe them so much."

"Don't they owe us? Didn't Reyhim say so?"

"Do they?" Babba searched my face. "Do they ever?"

I couldn't answer that. My last semblance of dignity was crumbling. I'd kept it together all day, telling myself I'd bought us peace, that what had happened would be a benefit, a credit to my family, maybe my whole nation.

And here Babba was saying it would all go on, just as before, living day to day, waiting for the next banging at the door.

"I don't understand how even this could be another failure on my part," I said. "When I tried so hard."

Babba sighed and rubbed his temples. "You mustn't think that. I talked to one of the Azwans myself," he said. "He said flattering things about you."

"Which one?"

"The purple one."

I had to chuckle at that. "Babba, you're very drunk. Time for bed, I think."

"Aah, see, you sound like your mother." He grew thoughtful. "You know, there was no one to keep her when she was your age, and the Ward didn't want her. Isn't that the paradox? We want and don't want the Temple to see us. Which is worse? Ah, but, this is the wine talking. She's very happy for you."

"Where is she?" I'd barely seen Mami all day. She'd been busier than I'd been, if that were possible.

He shrugged. "Out back with Leba Mara, working out the terms of your apprenticeship."

"Apprent . . . I'm to be a healer?"

"Seems I don't get to keep you after all." He returned to his happy drunk look, and double-triple-moonlight beams of joy and pride radiated from him. "An apprentice healer! That's my Dara."

Me? A healer? My first thought: was I good enough for this? Healers were . . . well, they were extraordinary. Everyone loved them. They were allowed to get grubby and bloody—it was expected. And still they had more honor and accolades than anybody but priests.

Plus, they knew things. What kind of things? I don't know, but surely it wasn't which of Nihil's wives plucked her lute left-handed, or whatever useless trivia school had taught. I would know what healers knew, and no one would laugh or roll their eyes.

I would know what happened to Valeo, and there would be no more like him, if I could help it. I owed him that, too, didn't I?

Babba squeezed my mute, shocked self in a giant hug again and rocked me all around, until he had to stop himself from spinning, still grinning even through his wooziness. He cupped my chin in one hand.

"You're happy, aren't you?" he asked. "This is a big honor, Hadara—think of all you can do, and you know they don't take many . . ."

I nodded dumbly, my eyes round as wine cups. Leba Mara must've been impressed with me that night at the sick ward. I had done something worthwhile, something helpful, and that meant more to me than any party. But still. The Temple. The Ward! "I don't know how I feel."

"It's done. Told the purple one I was alright with it. More than alright. You'll come home at night to stay with us. It's a good compromise."

"When did he ask?" I'd stay at home? What a relief not to live under the Ward's roof.

"Just before he left. Told, by the way, not asked." He shook his head. "If only this wasn't the Temple asking. Ah, but, all the Temple gives us is both wondrous and terrifying. Why can we never have the first and not the latter?"

His meaning was lost on me, as all I heard was that the Azwans had wanted me to keep me after all. Leba Mara was doing as she was told. So much for impressing her.

Probably all those hints Reyhim dropped about Babba to the Merchants Guild came with a price, one that either of the Azwans could collect at any time.

I felt betrayed, but I shouldn't have been surprised. Like my mother, I balanced on a knife's edge when it came to the Temple. I loved the wild, but I was a kind person; I was outspoken, but did as I was told. I had a thick skull for theology, but I wanted to do what was right. What had I done? I'd trusted S'ami. He must've known what he was doing when he sent me dancing away. He wasn't done with me. As a healer, the rest of my life would be played out under the Temple's gaze.

Yet how could I ignore the fatherly pride that brimmed over in Babba, the sheer giddiness?

That decided it. I'd do whatever needed doing. I'd be the best pupil Leba Mara could ask for, even if it hadn't been her idea.

Yes.

It had the ring of truth. Hadn't I vowed back in the swamps with Mami that day that I'd never withhold my talent from anyone? Here was a chance to make good on it. I straightened my shoulders. Everything would be alright.

"We did it," Babba said. He threw his arms wide and his head back. "We survived the whole damn lot. They threw everything they could at us, Dara, and we're all here. All together."

He plunked himself down on the table, squashing a half dozen of the courting notes, and rested his elbows on his knees. "Ought to be a man gets judged by how well he looks out for his family. And Nihil blast me to the Soul's Forge and back if I didn't think we were falling apart there. Didn't know from one day to the next. You. Your mother. Amaniel and Rishi with that stuff the soldiers took.

"Worry a man onto an early pyre. Fetch me a drink, blossom. The cup's sad when it's empty." He swirled it for emphasis.

I gingerly sat down next to him, being more careful of the fancy scrolls and their cheery ribbons. "You've had enough, Babba."

That was true on so many levels, I thought.

"You're going to take the job, of course."

I smiled and spoke from the deepest part of my soul, though I wasn't sure if Babba would notice my intensity as I took one of his hands in mine. "Of course. I won't bring you any more shame, any more worry. I swear it. You're done worrying on my behalf."

I leaned over and kissed his temple, and he wrapped an arm around me and looked me straight in the eye. His gaze was suddenly serious and quite sober.

"I've never been anything but proud of you, you know?"

My eyes welled up again. "I can't see why. It's Amaniel . . ."

He shook his head and quietly shushed me. "I have three daughters, and only one is going to be a healer, yes? And only one deserves it."

"But I worry . . ."

". . . about being the best healer our little island's ever seen." He tweaked my chin between thumb and forefinger. "And that's probably one of the last orders I can give you, until I arrange a marriage for you."

I shook my head. "I told you, I'm not ready for that."

Babba looked down at the squashed pile of scrolls. "Seems others disagree."

"Oh, Babba, don't you think all these men are being a bit mercenary?"

He shrugged. "Many men feel that way about the women who marry them, that it's all about the man's money and status. You're lucky to have it the other way around."

I didn't feel lucky. I felt exhausted.

But sleep wasn't going to come. Everyone else eventually filed off to bed, with so many more hugs and squeezes, I didn't think my rib cage would ever recover. Long after Babba's snoring drifted from my parents' sleep loft, I crept outside to the hearth, wrapping a thin blanket around me.

There was one more language I had to see if I knew.

I scouted around the hearth, hoping Bugsy was there and not hiding beneath the house again. But she was curled up in a still-warm clay oven and woke instantly when I tapped on its side. There was no light but the moons, but the Gek have enviable night vision, and I knew she could see my fingers as they flew in greeting.

She sniffed me and croaked. "You smell different," she said, or at least that's how my mind heard it.

Well, that answered my question. The Gek's croaks were a language, and it was one I could understand. I told her as much.

She perked up at that and crept out of the oven then scampered over to a clear area and gazed at the stars. I sat on my haunches beside her and just watched, waiting for her to say something else. Finally, she pointed.

"That was you," she said. "That empty spot there, between those two larger stars."

I tried to follow her finger, but there were thousands of spots it could be. And what did she mean, that was me? She said it with such certainty, as if it were something she'd witnessed.

"When the star fell down to us, I asked if that meant the sky was missing one," Bugsy said. "My mother and I climbed all the way to the top of the tallest tree one night to search for a hole between the stars. She said she couldn't be sure that had been you, that sometimes stars twinkle and fade and then come back. But it didn't come back, so I think that is where you were born."

I searched her face before signaling back to her. "I was born here, Bugsy. My own mother will swear to it."

I couldn't get her to look at my hands. She was deaf to me, her eyes trained on the sky. "You are the star. You will unmake what the Nothing Man has ruined."

I shook my head, but how could I translate what I was thinking and feeling into clumsy hand signals? I didn't want to unmake. I wanted to do—to heal and help and comfort. Unmaking sounded dangerous and wild, and taking on Nihil—for who else could she mean—didn't sound wise. My father had only just set aside his anger and fear long enough to say he was proud of me. My mother had at last found the right balance between avoiding and obeying the Temple. I was the key to my family's safety and even their honor, as odd and unexpected as that seemed.

And I had returned home with some new power I couldn't explain. After thinking and fretting about it all night, I realized I'd been glad to know what the soldiers were saying, all the more so because of their crudeness. I was too fascinated to be afraid of hearing people's languages, whether they wanted to be understood or not. Was that an ugly thing to admit? I wasn't sure. Bugsy believed my soul held a speck of a star, and S'ami kept examining me for some remnant of a demon. Maybe I was something of both, and maybe we are all part of some great constellation, a mix of night and fire, of inexplicable darkness and unruly light.

I tilted my head back as far as it would go, searching again for the empty space that Bugsy insisted was there. Finally, after much more pointing and directing, I thought I'd found it.

Bugsy's gap rested deep within the Wisdom Knot, with its intricate, swirling layers of stars within bands of stars, tangled and twisted, bright with possibility. The Wisdom Knot, reminder of lessons learned, guide to all who seek to repair what they've ruined, a beacon to light the way out of despair.

The Gek kept her eyes on what she insisted was missing, and I kept mine on everything else, and we both stared up at the brilliant night sky for a long, long time.

THE TEMPLE OF DOUBT

PRONUNCIATION

KEY

Amaniel	ah-MAN-yell
Hadara	Ha-DA-rah
Lia	LEE-ah
Nihil	NIH-hill
Reyhim	ray-HEEM
Rimonil	ree-moe-NEEL
Rishiel	RIH-shee-ell
S'ami	SAH-mee
Valeo	vah-LAY-oh

ACKNOWLEDGMENTS

An influenza bug in late 1999 kept me bedridden for a week, long enough to work out the premise and most of the plot for what would become this series. Thanks, germs! In some alternate universe where viruses are sentient, there is a DNA strand that is shrugging right now.

My patient, long-suffering husband, Brett, has lived with the entire population of Kuldor for fifteen years and counting, and still puts up with them—and me. He is my hero, and I'm his unexpected plot twist.

My two children have shared me with a bunch of imaginary people their entire lives and have almost forgiven me for not including any dragons in this story, or at least a kitten.

The incomparable Bruce McAllister coached, coaxed, and cajoled me into being a better writer and saner person.

No matter how many incarnations Nihil & Company went through, my writing group patiently helped me separate wheat from chaff. Big, weepy hugs go to Tanita Davis, Sarah Jamila Stevenson, Sara Lewis Holmes, Kelly Herold, Jennifer March Soloway, Yat-Yee Chong, and several other members who've given me sage advice and a virtual shoulder to cry on.

My agent, Regina Brooks, plucked me from obscurity and helped turn my raw manuscript into something polished and saleable. Her infectious enthusiasm for this book and her army of awesome staffers helped assuage my own temple of doubts.

My editor at Skyhorse, Nicole Frail, took a chance when so many others would not, and the English language has not enough words with which to thank her. Also to Rain Saukus, for his work on the cover art; Adrienne Szpyrka, for her assistance on first and last read-throughs; and everyone else at the Sky Pony Press imprint.

My four brothers and their wives are the best people I know, and they're all still speaking to me, which is kind of a nice surprise. In particular, Howard and Melanie Schloss gave needed support way back when, for which I'm still indebted.

Somewhere out there is Pam Noles, who told me my first draft sucked and was very explicit about why. I'm sorry, Pam, wherever you are. If this version is any better, it's because I listened.

COMING SPRING 2016 . . .

THE

WELL

of

PRAYERS

Book II of
The Temple of Doubt series

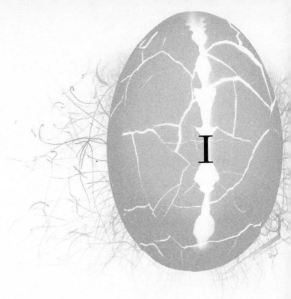

*Your soul must come to me, clean and unblem-
ished, purged by fire of sin and fleshly weakness.
From the fire shall your soul be released, and your
ashes scattered that your sins do not stick to one
place and curse it.*
    —From *Oblations 3,* The Book of Unease

It was my task to clean up after the drunks, sobered by
having their heads split open, who huddled in corners,
puking, looking unsure how they'd gotten there. A mop
became my best friend as I swabbed away piss and blood
and worse things. The gore wasn't much different than the
muck and mires I'd once waded through, and a mop han-
dle was lighter than an herb basket. I threw myself into my
job, the more mindless the better, happy for any distraction.

It'd been a fortnight since I'd begun my apprenticeship
as a healer for Ward Sapphire, reporting each morning to
the main room of the sick ward, which consisted of two
large rooms, one lined with benches for people who could

be healed immediately and one with cots for those who couldn't. By breakfast, the rows had already filled with the woozy and the wounded. They looked more fidgety and anxious than usual that morning, with everyone glancing around suspiciously, even narrowing their gaze at others, as if they'd each appointed themselves magistrate over others' misfortunes, and were sitting in judgment over every clot or bruise.

Today had begun as always: bandages needed rolling, bedpans needed cleaning. There were sheets to lug to the laundry and rows of cots to make up, with blanket corners folded and tucked. A healer would inspect my work, rip out the neat little "y" at the bed corners, and make me start over. But there was a new tension in the air, a terseness with the way healers snapped orders, even at patients.

Healer Mistress Leba Mara, a big woman with a voice to match, worked the line herself, her sturdy frame squeezing between the rows, using magical incantations to heal cracked ribs and the shallower stab wounds. I hated to watch the spellcasting: it created a jarring shock of electricity that fizzed in the air that only I could see and a metallic taste that only I could sense. It was one of many secrets I kept, and one more reason I should've kept my head down and bent on minor tasks. But I never could. I was always looking up and butting in. I didn't aspire to be an orderly, after all. I wanted to do what Leba Mara and the other healers did—but without all the irritating magic.

All I had to do was figure out a way.

Leba Mara did triage as she went, sending the severely injured inside to a cot, with me following along to sop up any trail of blood. Orderlies carried them to and fro on stretchers that never looked empty. I hustled from one room to the next, darting around busy people, my hands trembling only partly from fatigue.

There had to be a way. All this magic—it belonged to Nihil, and it should've stayed with him.

"You should do me first," a shopkeeper shouted out, waving his swollen and obviously broken wrist. "I'm the only one who's legitimate."

He cradled the injured wrist in his good hand as Leba Mara gave him a disapproving up-down glance.

"Well, it's true," he persisted, his haughty air crumbling into a working class accent. "I just got mine's with a fall. Tripped over my own clumsy feet, is all. These others . . . huh. Guards had to drag 'em out of doorways and knock 'em sober. They're pyre fuel for sure."

I had to wedge myself between a suddenly very awake and angry drunk and the shopkeeper. I got a face full of stale, boozy breath and my smock became dotted with blood as the man wobbled into me. I propped him back up, but he swayed like a buoy at high tide, making me dizzy, too. This too was part of my job.

"Tripped and fell, by Nihil's scrawny buttocks, you did," the drunk man said, waving his fists. "The guards was settling accounts with you again, wasn't they?"

Leba Mara cut in with a harsh, "Gentlemen!"

"Don't know what you're saying, you souse," said the shopkeeper. "Sober up and shut up."

But the drunk wasn't letting up and shouted past my shoulder at the other man. "Tipping your scales again? We'll see who ends up in an ash heap."

An orderly and I ended up pinning the drunk's arms to his side and walking him back to a bench while Leba Mara held a meaty hand over the shopkeeper's mouth.

"You've both said enough," she said. "Nobody's going to the pyre today. Seal those lips or I'll sew them up."

She looked like she could do it, too—she was bigger than both men combined, and most of that heft was muscle. Add to that her infamous Glare of Doom and both men settled into a terse truce.

"Worse than usual," muttered the orderly who'd helped me, a stocky man named Til. "This place is getting crazy."

I shook my head but didn't argue. To my mind, all the crazy was being marched right out of us. Port Sapphire was a busy way station between continents, and we'd been a prosperous port until the Temple of Doubt sent us two Azwans and four hundred guards to hunt down a demon. They'd stuck around longer than anyone had wanted. Far longer. The throngs, the shouting, the hustle and bustle and daily messiness of living in the middle of the map had steadily seeped away last summer, replaced by a wary silence, empty canals, and orderly streets.

Somehow, the Temple had gotten sixty thousand stubborn, willful, wayward people to behave themselves and suddenly find religion. How awful. All my favorite shops closed early, and even when open, people were too polite, too restrained. No one argued or haggled anymore, though no one could remember anyone banning it, either. It's like we all knew we'd been naughty children, filing obediently, heads down, onto ferries instead of paddling ourselves home every which way. No one bothered telling us what, exactly, we'd done, and we were all trying to guess what good behavior looked like after so many years of getting it wrong.

The gloom added to my own sadness, the storm cloud that had gathered over my heart that wouldn't stop raining self-pity. If I didn't have that mop to distract me, I'd be wallowing in grief over, ironically enough, one of the very guards everyone feared and hated and yet couldn't figure out how they'd ever gotten along without. Valeo, his name had been. He had died, and I had my duties to help me forget.

"What's all this talk of the pyres?" I whispered to Til.

"Dunno," Til said. "They're all jabbering about it this morning."

"Well, let's go see," I said.

He shrugged. "Should tell a healer, I suppose."

The healer we asked insisted on coming with us, and said he knew a way onto our roof. It involved me hitching up my skirt and clambering up the narrowest flight of steps I'd ever seen, only to find myself sitting precariously on the roof's terra-cotta tiles. I had to dig my sandals into a groove to keep myself from sliding down, but I loved the feeling I was doing something vaguely forbidden, even though there were already several other people around. We all squeezed shoulder to shoulder and peered northward, where smoke drifted lazily out to sea.

The funeral pyres usually burned far north of Port Sapphire on a stretch of solid ground too far away to leach any of the smoke or stench into the city. Pyres were a normal thing: all of us could expect to be burned after we died so our souls could be freed from our bodies and fly to the Eternal Tree if we were found worthy of such redemption. At least, if you believed all that, which I didn't.

I followed everyone's stare to the place where thick, gray plumes lifted above the line of thatched rooftops. The smoke looked thicker and more robust than usual. The last time there'd been that much smoke had been when Ward Sapphire held funerals for all the fallen guards. They'd battled the fierce Gek in the swamps, and Valeo had been one of the men felled by poison darts. Measely, lousy, tiny little darts.

And I'd never forgive myself for it.

I'd been moping about his death for three six-days, ever since I'd heard the news from one of the Azwans. I'd stared at the horizon a few times, wondering which puff of smoke would contain the last cinders of his bronzed skin or stately frame, the ropes of muscle or the hard angles of his scarred and rugged face.

But where were all these new bodies coming from? I hadn't remembered any sort of plague, and while the guards were gleefully breaking open heads, no one had told me of any sudden killing spree.

"This is just since this morning?" I asked.

The people around me shrugged. No one said anything, so I kept asking questions. Who are they burning? Who died? What does anyone know?

I received only uncomfortable silence, a few coughs and cleared throats and faraway looks until a familiar woman's voice bellowed from below us.

"Well, blast you all to the Soul's Forge," shouted Leba Mara. "Is my entire staff taking a sabbath? What's going on up there?"

One of the healers shouted down to her about the billowing smoke, prompting her to crane her neck as she struggled to make out the distant plumes. All she did was shake a fist at us.

"Beat on my doubting behind, then," she said. "Get down here, all of you."

We clambered down, most looking more defiant than chastened. The healer who'd escorted me there folded his arms across his chest and huffed at the Healer Mistress.

"If you know what this is about, we sure wouldn't mind the explanation," he said. "A lot of scared folks on those benches today."

"Yes, but not many on the roof, is there?" she snapped right back at him. "While you're talking, people are hurting."

The healer held his ground. "Ah, right, then we'll just watch them all hang, one by one, for a bunch of doodads and whatsits the Azwans decided weren't worthy enough. That's what this is, isn't it?"

"Then pray they don't find anything of yours in that pile. I hear it's all sitting in a warehouse right outside the Customs House, anyway. Right where a certain Lord Portreeve might see it."

She was talking about my father. The small group looked at me. My jaw flapped open and closed. No sound came out.

"Me?"

My voice squeaked.

"A big warehouse holding all our little heretical items," Leba Mara said. "Practically out your babba's back door, stuffed to the rafters with all our contraband."

Heretical items? Contraband? I caught my breath, unwilling to believe what I was hearing. Every time I thought the worst was over, the Temple returned with something else.

When they'd first arrived, the Temple Guards had raided our homes and seized anything with even the faintest taint of sacrilege to it. Even my two younger sisters had had items taken: a scrap of needlework and an old doll. And here we'd thought everyone would be safe and fine and that the Azwans were on their way back to the faraway Temple compound now that the demon business was all over. Apparently, the many tokens of our doubtfulness were keeping them busy.

It was as though Leba Mara heard my thoughts and picked up the thread of my anxiety, weaving it into something fiercer. She scanned the horizon for the smoke and shook her head.

"Of all the unambiguous nonsense," Leba Mara fumed. "I'd have just burned those little whatnots, not the people who made them. And how do they know what belongs to whom? By all Nihil's incarnations, the Temple folk aren't like our local priests. Can't leave a single doubting soul alone, can they?"

The other healer scratched his chin. "So, you're no wiser about this than the rest of us."

"Wiser? I'm wise enough to keep myself to the certain path," Leba Mara chuffed. "We're to doubt our merits and be sure of Nihil's. If there's more reasons you want, you'll find them on the benches inside. Off, now, and do what the worthy priests pay you for."

The other healer sighed, and it was riddled with defeat. He held a hand to his heart. "Nihil's ambiguities are the best salves."

"That's more like it," Leba Mara said, patting her own chest.

I bit back any response I might've wanted to give. My days of defiance were also over. I might not believe a word of it, but I kept that to myself. I just wanted to heal people, that's it, especially if it could be done without magic. And if I had to do that under the protection of the hated Temple, well, so be it, then. There was nothing I could do about any of this anyway—just one person, a girl at that, and a lowly apprentice. I'd rid myself of anyone's expectations of me but my own.

We filed back inside, or at least everyone else did, but Leba Mara waved me over.

I thought she meant to ask me more about my father and whatever connection he'd have to the sudden increase in pyre smoke. Instead, she adjusted the blue uniform scarf that wrapped my waist-length curls in a high pile atop my head. A few wayward strands had flown loose atop the roof.

A guard stationed by the doorway kept his eyes on my head wrap, despite people coming and going around us, as though he'd zeroed in on an archery target, taking careful aim. Like his comrades, he was a good two or three heads taller than human men and stared down his long nose in a way that could be both condescending and cruel.

I fumbled to fasten my scarf even with Leba Mara's help, my breathing coming rapidly. My fingers couldn't seem to make the knot, and I finally gave up and let Leba Mara fix it. It wasn't perfect, but I had no mirror and however it looked would have to do. The guard gave a short nod at Leba Mara and turned his attention to the flow of wounded and sickly through our doors.

"You're lucky," she said, her voice a whisper. "They've been cutting women's hair off right on the spot, whipping out daggers at the first stray lock. You can't even let a flirty curl or two show."

"Yes, and now the pyres," I said, shuddering. "What is going on? I'm sure my father doesn't know."

If he did, would he have said anything to me? I wondered.

"I'm just as sure he does," she said. "Even if he knows no more than I do, it's still plenty. And he has pull that even I don't have."

"He's only a civilian though," I said, which drew a sharp scowl from Leba Mara. For all her brashness, she didn't tolerate a sharp tongue from subordinates. "With all due respect, Healer Mistress. He is secular. Anything he says to the Azwans wouldn't be the same as coming from a priest or, surely, a healer?"

"Ah, but his eldest daughter is the Temple of Doubt's new favorite, no? Surely, there's something to be made of that, especially if that daughter should ask her father to intervene on our poor little city's behalf? Maybe ask them to spare a few of us, or find out when they intend to return to our Great Numen's side, where I'm sure our Kindly Master has more need of them?"

These were serious hints she was dropping. I'm lousy with hints. Usually, I need someone to beam me across the head with whatever they want, but she was making her message as obvious as she could without embroidering it onto my smock.

I hesitated. Babba hadn't mentioned my almost-sacrifice since my Keeping Day, as if there were some sort of taboo against it. It also felt wrong to use my father's new position to wheedle him into helping. He'd been made Lord Portreeve, head of the civil government, a position the Azwans had wanted him to have as a sort of repayment.

And, yes, the Temple owed us a lot. More than a lot. Reyhim, the Azwan of Ambiguity, had said as much the night he took me to the altar to be sacrificed, which hadn't worked out the way anyone had expected. But if anyone could make anything happen in the secular world outside of the Temple's sphere of influence, it would be Babba. The warehouses were all in the commercial district, so they would fall under Babba's jurisdiction, right?

At least, that seemed to be where Leba Mara was headed with this. Maybe she was right. I might be helpless, but Babba would know what to do. I had absolute faith in my father's ability to make it happen. Even so, it didn't pay to over-promise.

"I'll try," I said, with as much unconcern as I could fake. "I can't promise my father has any more pull than anyone here."

"It'll have to do, then."

We went inside after that, under the careful eye of the guard, who gave me a disapproving once-over as we passed.